THE SUGAR HOUSE

Antonia White

With an Introduction by
Carmen Callil

Virago

To Susan

VIRAGO

Published by Virago Press Limited 1979
Reprinted 1981, 1982, 1985, 1987, 1991, 1993, 1998, 2006

First published by Eyre & Spottiswoode 1952

Copyright © The Literary Executors of Antonia White 1952
Introduction Copyright © Carmen Callil 1979

A CIP catalogue record for this book
is available from the British Library

ISBN-13: 978-1-84408-379-4
ISBN-10: 1-84408-379-9

Typeset in Goudy by M Rules
Printed and bound in Great Britain by
Clays Ltd, St Ives plc

Virago Press
An imprint of
Little, Brown Book Group
Brettenham House
Lancaster Place
London WC2E 7EN

A member of the Hachette Livre Group of Companies

www.virago.co.uk

INTRODUCTION

It is unusual for the publisher of a book to provide its preface. Antonia White wanted to write a new introduction to the three books – *The Lost Traveller*, *The Sugar House* and *Beyond the Glass* – which complete the story she began in her famous novel *Frost in May*. Now eighty years of age, and a novelist whose small output reflects the virulent writer's block which has constantly interrupted her writing life, she preferred to talk to me. For though separated by age, country of birth and nationality, we share a Catholic upbringing which has been a dominant influence on both our lives. What follows is based on a long conversation I had with Antonia White in December 1978, and on the many times we've talked since Virago first republished *Frost in May* earlier that year.

'Personal novels,' wrote Elizabeth Bowen in a review of Antonia White's work, 'those which are obviously based on life, have their own advantages and hazards. But we have one "personal" novelist who has brought it off infallibly.' Antonia White turned fact into fiction in a quartet of novels based on her life from the ages of nine to twenty-three. 'My life is the raw material for the novels, but writing an autobiography and writing fiction are very different things.' This transformation of real life into an imagined work of art is perhaps her greatest skill as a novelist.

Antonia White was the only child of Cecil Botting, Senior Classics Master at St Paul's School, who became a Catholic at the age of thirty-five taking with him into the Church his wife and seven-year-old daughter, fictionalised as 'Nanda' in *Frost in May*. This novel is a brilliant portrait of Nanda's experiences in the enclosed world of a Catholic convent. First published in 1933, it was immediately recognised as a classic. Antonia White wrote what was to become the first two chapters of *Frost in May* when she was only sixteen, completing it sixteen years later, in 1931. At the time she was married to Tom Hopkinson, writer, journalist and later editor of *Picture Post*.

'I'd written one or two short stories, but really I wrote nothing until my father's death in 1929. I'd worked in advertising all those years, as a copywriter, and I'd done articles for women's pages and all sorts of women's magazines, but I couldn't bring myself to write anything serious until after my father died. At the time I was doing a penitential stint in Harrods' Advertising Department . . . I'd been sacked from Crawfords in 1930 for not taking a passionate enough interest in advertising. One day I was looking through my desk and I came across this bundle of manuscript. Out of curiosity I began to read it and some of the things in it made me laugh. Tom asked me to read it to him, which I did, and then he said "You must finish it." Anyway Tom had appendicitis and we were very hard up, so I was working full time. But Tom insisted I finish a chapter every Saturday night. Somehow or other I managed to do it, and then Tom thought I should send it to the publisher – Cobden Sanderson – who'd liked my short stories. They wrote back saying it was too slight to be of interest to anyone. Several other people turned it down and then a woman I knew told me that Desmond Harmsworth had won some money in the Irish sweep and didn't know what to do with it . . . so he started a publishing business and in fact I think *Frost in May* was the only thing he ever published . . . it got wonderful reviews.'

Between 1933 and 1950 Antonia White wrote no more

novels. She was divorced from Tom Hopkinson in 1938, worked in advertising, for newspapers, as a freelance journalist and then came the war. Throughout this period she suffered further attacks of the mental illness she first experienced in 1922. This madness Antonia White refers to as 'The Beast' – Henry James' 'Beast in the Jungle'. Its recurrence and a long period of psychoanalysis interrupted these years.

'I'd always wanted to write another novel, having done one, but then you see the 1930s were a very difficult time for me because I started going off my head again. After the war and the political work I did I was terribly hard up. Then Enid Starkey, whom I'd met during the war, suggested to Hamish Hamilton that I should have a shot at translating and they liked what I did. After that I got a number of commissions and I was doing two or three a year but I was completely jammed up on anything of my own, though I kept on trying to write in spite of it. I always wanted to write another novel, and I wanted this time to do something more ambitious, what I thought would be a "proper" novel, not seen only through the eyes of one person as it is in *Frost in May*, but through the eyes of the father, the mother and even those old great-aunts in the country. Then suddenly I could write again. The first one *The Lost Traveller* took the longest to write. I don't know how many years it took me, but I was amazed how I then managed to write the other two [*The Sugar House* and *Beyond the Glass*]. They came incredibly quickly.'

In 1950, seventeen years after the publication of *Frost in May*, *The Lost Traveller* was published. In it Antonia White changed the name of her heroine Nanda Grey to Clara Batchelor. 'Of course Clara is a continuation of Nanda. Nanda became Clara because my father had a great passion for Meredith and a particular passion for Clara Middleton (heroine of *The Egoist*). Everything that happened to Clara in *The Lost Traveller* is the sort of thing that happened to me, though many things are changed, many invented. I wanted *The Lost Traveller* to be a *real* novel – *Frost in May* was so much my own life. So I changed her name . . .' In every other respect this novel begins where *Frost in May* ends. It is a vivid account of adolescence, of the mutual relationships of father, mother and daughter as Clara grows to maturity and comes to grips with the adult world.

'When I finished *The Lost Traveller* I thought of it as just being one book, and then suddenly I felt I wanted to write another one about my first marriage. That was *The Sugar House*, which I think is much the best of the three. In it I see Clara's relationship with Archie (her husband) entirely through the eyes of one person, as in *Frost in May* – I think that suited me much better.'

The Sugar House was published in 1952 and takes Clara through her first love affair, work as an actress and a doomed first marriage. Unsentimental, often amusing, it is unusual for its moving description of a love between a man and a woman which is not sexual but which is nevertheless immensely strong.

Two years later Antonia White completed the story of Clara's young life in *Beyond the Glass*.

Carmen Callil, Virago, London, 1979

Antonia White died on 10th April, 1980

PART I

1

The train call for the Number One Company of A *Clerical Error* was for nine o'clock. At half-past eight Clara Batchelor had already been sitting for a considerable time in the Refreshment Room at King's Cross spinning out cups of tea and trying not to turn her head hopefully every time the door swung open. Stephen Tye had promised, if he could possibly manage it, to come and see her off. He would be off on his own first tour next week, and, having failed to get into the same company, it might be months before she saw him again.

'I shall make inconceivable efforts to break away,' he had said at lunchtime as, perched on stools in a crowded bar, they gulped beer and sandwiches in the brief space between his two rehearsals. 'I'd cut the whole thing if this chap who wants me to have a drink hadn't some sort of pull with the management. You *do* understand, dear girl?'

Naturally, Clara had understood. For several months the main object of her life had been to understand, comfort and amuse Stephen Tye. This excuse was, at any rate, reasonable. For three weeks the two of them had been no longer acting students but professionals. And, of all the new batch who in that summer of 1920 had begun to haunt agents' offices, Stephen could least afford to miss any chance. He was thirty, far older than the other

7

ex-officers who had used their gratuities to train at the Garrick School of Drama. Though his age gave him great prestige in Clara's eyes, he himself was sensitive and occasionally morose about it. He was fond of exaggerating Clara's youth and treating her as if she were a schoolgirl instead of just turned twenty-one. Whenever she tried to claim any experience of life he would say inaccurately: 'You were in the nursery when I was mouldering in a Flanders dug-out.'

Since Clara was in love with Stephen Tye, she found it wiser not to argue with him. Above all, she tried never to make a fuss however much he teased her, patronised her, missed appointments, or turned up late in various stages of drink; wildly gay, pugnacious or suicidal. It was the war that had made Stephen drink, and, though she hated to see him drunk, she took it as a sign that he was more sensitive than other people and felt a respectful pity. She knew that Celia, the wife some years older than himself, who had died in the 'flu epidemic of 1918 had been in the habit of making fusses. Clara was sure that the faint hope of Stephen's asking her to marry him depended on her being as unlike Celia as possible.

As she sat forlornly, trying not to watch the buffet clock and see how few minutes she would be able to snatch with him, she almost hoped he would not come. Try as she would, she could not help feeling hurt. How terrible if, from sheer tension, she were to make a fuss at the last moment. Better to lose her farewell kiss (he had, after all, kissed her very sweetly in the bar at lunchtime) than spend the long night journey to York tormenting herself for having said the wrong word or used the wrong voice or look.

Already, at distant tables, she could see some of the members of the *Clerical Error* company. There were the two elderly ones, Merton Mordish who played the heavy comic and Millicent Cooke who played the spinster aunt, deep in conversation. No one could have mistaken Merton Mordish, with his mane of grey hair, his wide hat and his caped ulster, for anything but an old actor. Even the way he slammed down his tankard and threw back his head as he drank suggested 'business'. Millicent Cooke, whom the whole company instinctively addressed as Miss Cooke, looked more than ever like a real spinster aunt as, wearing a raffia-trimmed hat and a suit obviously knitted by herself, she sipped her tea with her prim unpainted mouth. At another table, alone, sat Maidie Spencer who played the bigger of the two girls' parts and who was to be Clara's room-mate. Under a black velvet hat with a stiffened lace brim, Maidie's wide blue eyes were scanning the room as if in search of someone. Terrified that she should see her and come over, Clara bent down and pulled out of her suitcase the Herrick that had been Stephen's parting gift and propping it open against the tea-pot, she kept her face well hidden and hoped that her new hat and coat would act as a disguise.

Her anxiety now became acute. She dared not raise her head to look towards the door for fear of catching Maidie's eye. Yet, if Stephen were to come in, he would not know her new clothes either. He might waste some of those ebbing minutes searching for her. He might even give up and go away.

Without raising her head she managed to glance sideways into the steamy mirror behind the counter. Each time the swing-door was pushed open she could see the face of the newcomer dimly reflected. But it was never the narrow high-nosed face of Stephen; that face so easy to pick out at a distance because of its bleached pallor and hair so fair that it looked almost white. Her own reflection, at that odd angle, looked like a stranger's. She could see little but her anxious eyes and two tufts of fair curls pulled forward on either cheek under the small unfamiliar hat. Her cheeks were still pink enough to need no rouge and her hair, though darker than in her teens, still bright enough for enemies to accuse her of peroxide. Stephen was fond of studying their two reflections in bar mirrors. 'The sun and moon,' he had said once: another time, when he was feeling morose, 'the milkmaid and the ageing Pierrot'.

She stared into the mirror, as if by sheer force of will she could conjure the beloved face into it like a girl on All Hallow E'en. Her first sight of Stephen had in fact been almost like an apparition. She had gone one evening into the rehearsal-room at the Garrick, believing it to be empty as it was almost dark. Just as she was about to switch on the light she saw a man's face reflected in one end of the long ballet practice mirror which took up the whole of one wall. She stood, frightened yet fascinated, half convinced she was seeing a ghost, for she could not make out anyone in the room itself. The narrow white face under the thin crest of hair almost as pale in the dimness, appeared to be suspended in the air. Then two long hands appeared, gesticulating, and she realised that the man in the mirror was wearing a black doublet and hose which, in the dusk, made his body almost invisible. She watched for a minute or two while the face and hands performed over and over again the same series of movements with very slight variations. By now she had realised that the reflection must have an original but that the real person was screened from her by a curtain. But already she had felt so strangely drawn to the face in the mirror that when, a few days later, she recognised it in the students' canteen, she was already half in love with Stephen Tye.

It was not till some time after they had become an acknowledged and almost inseparable pair that she had asked him what he had been doing at that moment.

'Rehearsing Biron. *Love's Labour's Lost*. I'm not worried about my voice. I can get most of the effects I want with that. But I need a lot of practice for gesture and facial expression. I must have looked slightly insane, mopping and mowing at my own reflection. I keep it up for an hour sometimes till I get what I want.'

'But you get what you want in the end?' she had asked earnestly.

He had laughed the musical, slightly ironic laugh she was to come to know so well.

'As a stage character, yes, on the whole. In private life, by no means invariably.'

Much later she had ventured to ask him when he had first noticed her. He considered, with his head on one side and one pale eyebrow cocked.

'Let me see now. Such a momentous occasion should not call for a great effort of memory. But 'pon my soul it does. I think you must just gradually have impinged upon my consciousness till I was aware of a certain hiatus when you weren't about.'

Looking at the buffet clock and seeing how little hope she had left, she sighed. Already, absent from him only a few hours, she was conscious, not of a 'certain hiatus' but an enormous void. She wondered how she could possibly endure weeks, possibly months of separation.

Suddenly a large lace-brimmed hat blocked her view of the mirror and two large, angry blue eyes flashed accusingly at her.

'There you are, you silly Wurzit,' exclaimed Maidie Spencer. 'What the hell are you doing, sitting there as pop-eyed as a ventriloquist's dummy?'

'I . . . I was waiting for someone,' Clara stammered.

'Well, he's left you in the lurch, old dear. And you'll get left in the lurch if you don't stir your stumps. Our train's been in five minutes. Everyone but you is aboard and Lister's fuming. I signed on in this show as leading ingénue not as a bloody nursemaid.'

2

Clara sat crushed between two other members of the company in the middle of the seat of their reserved compartment. The lights were dimmed and she was the only one left awake. A heavy head lolled on each of her shoulders so that she could hardly move her own. Occasionally she dozed for a few moments only to be woken up by a crick in her neck or cramp in her legs. Though it was an August night and the carriage was stuffy, her feet were so cold that she wished that, like the others, she had brought a rug or a shawl or even a newspaper to wrap them in. They had chattered and played nap till midnight; then one by one, heads had sagged, eyes shut and mouths opened till the smoky air was filled with uneasy sighs and snores.

Maidie had cursed her soundly for making them too late to snatch corner seats. She had taken the cursing meekly, realising that it would be rash to quarrel on the first night with someone with whom she would have to share a room for months.

Clara, who had never shared a room with anyone, was by no means sure that she wanted to share one with Maidie Spencer. At one moment Maidie would be so refined that Clara felt she could never live up to such respectability; the next she would swear like a coster. Sometimes she behaved like a convent girl carefully guarding her modesty at a wild party; at others her great blue eyes would glitter knowingly as she egged on the men to outdo each other in dirty stories and found a double meaning in the most innocent remarks.

In three weeks of rehearsing that aged farce *A Clerical Error*, Clara had seen the theatre from an angle very different from that of the Garrick School of Drama. Never at student rehearsals had a producer addressed Clara as 'You bloody little cow' or shouted '*Walk* to that chair, damn you. Don't teeter as if you thought your drawers were coming down.' There had been moments when she had felt like walking out and never coming back. It was not as if she had always set her heart on being an actress. She had gone to the Garrick just as she had gone, at seventeen, to be governess to the Cressetts simply because someone else had suggested it and she had been anxious for a change. Her father had been strongly against it as, at the time, he had been against the other plan. Both times her mother had backed her up. In the end he had become reluctantly reconciled to the idea. As she had paid her own fees by writing slick short stories and advertisements, an aptitude she had discovered during a penitential year of war-work in a Government office, he could make no practical objection. Later, when he had come to some of the Garrick student shows and discovered that two of the actors on the staff had been at Cambridge with him, he had gone so far as to admit that the profession appeared to be becoming almost respectable.

As she studied the unconscious faces of the people who were to be her only companions for months, she realised that his worst fears would have been confirmed. The grey-haired Miss Cooke, sleeping composedly in her corner with a rosary twisted round one hand and a book on landscape gardening on her lap, was the only one to whom she would have dared introduce him. James Munroe, the elderly-looking young man with the frightened expression who never swore and never gave her beery kisses in the wings might have passed muster till he opened his mouth and piped 'Pleased to make your acquaintance. I'm shore.' But what would Claude Batchelor think of Brett Wilding, the rather more than middle-aged lead with his dyed hair so ingeniously pasted over the top of his head to hide the bald patch, his stock, his pointed shoes and his absent way of squeezing Maidie and herself every time he caught one of them alone? Lister, the stage-manager, looked like a racing tout and swore like a sergeant; Sam Brilliant, the A.S.M., was pure Commercial Road. She glanced down at the heads, one sleek and dark, the other fair and wavy, of Peter Belsize and Trevor Eton, leaning so heavily against her shoulders. She rather liked this preposterous pair, partly because they never tried to make love to her, partly because they had been kind and covered her mistakes in the first alarming days of rehearsal. Nevertheless their behaviour puzzled her as much as their strange, synthetic accents; a compound of cockney and stage public school spoken in a high-pitched lilt. They called each other: 'Peter dear' and 'Trevor dear' and criticised each other's clothes in minute detail. During the first part of their journey, they had sat side by side manicuring each other's nails. Then, as they grew sleepy they had asked Clara to sit between them. 'We'll protect your virtue, dear. You don't mind if we use you as a pillow?'

Peter had said, rather unexpectedly: 'Like Alice with a queen on each shoulder,' and Trevor had giggled. 'Naughty, naughty.' Maidie had giggled too and then had asked, 'Who's Alice when she's at home? A fairy?' Whereupon they had all three giggled again and Clara had thought it diplomatic to giggle too. There were many occasions in the *Clerical Error* company when Clara was extremely vague as to what the joke, if any, might be. She found it safest to take her cues for laughter from Maidie so as not to risk being thought stand-offish.

As the train wheels turned in her weary head and the sparks flew past the window crowded with dim, sprawling reflections, she seemed to be embarking on a dream rather than a new life. The sense of isolation she always felt on railway journeys was emphasised by her being the only person awake. Already

Stephen seemed remote, almost unreal. Her mind slipped back to other journeys; to a particular journey with her parents to Paget's Fold, the cottage where they always spent the summer holidays. She had been fifteen then . . . a child as it seemed to her from the huge distance of six years. War had been declared while they were down there, but that was not her most vivid memory of that August. She remembered a hot day alone on the downs and a sudden, intense desire to find a companion, a lover with whom she could share her most absurd and secret thoughts. No one had appeared but a horrible, red-faced man as old as her own father who had leered at her and called her 'Missy'. Her thoughts grew scrappier and scrappier till, cold and cramped as she was, she fell into a doze. Only a second later, it seemed, she was awakened by a smart kick on her ankle.

'Rise and shine, old dear,' said Maidie's voice. 'We're nearly there.'

Clara blinked at her with aching eyes. 'It's on—only about two, isn't it?' she yawned miserably.

'It's four a.m. and raining like hell,' said Maidie briskly. She looked incredibly fresh as, with a hatpin between her white teeth, she powdered her nose and tidied her hair. Having tied a scarf over it before she went to sleep, the smooth plaited shells needed only a pat before she skewered on the lace-brimmed hat at a smart angle. In a few seconds she was gloved, shod, buttoned and preened till she was as neat as a doll just unwrapped from tissue paper. Struggling to her feet, Clara caught sight of herself in the mirror. Her face was pale and sticky; there was a smear of soot on her nose; her hair hung in limp tangles under the crushed hat that had slipped over one ear. For the first time she was glad that Stephen was not in the same company. There was nothing of the milkmaid or the pink-tipped daisy about that reflection. Before she could attempt any repairs, she was pushed from the mirror by Peter Belsize.

'My dear, I look like the morning after the night before. Trev, you don't know how lucky you are not having to shave twice a day.' He felt his blue chin anxiously. 'I'm *positive* I've got a spot coming.'

Clara, who had never seen men wake from uncomfortable sleep at dawn, was relieved to see that they looked worse than she did. The older ones, with their faces sagging in pouches, seemed to have aged overnight; even Peter and Trevor had jaundiced eyes and a leaden tinge. The train drew into the station; the yawning actors huddled into their coats and began to pull down their suitcases. Clara half expected one of the men to help her with hers but none of them offered a hand. It was Maidie who helped Miss Cooke with her heavy old-fashioned bags.

At last the whole company stood yawning and shivering on York platform. In the murk under the sooty roof on which the rain drummed steadily, it was hard to realise that it was half-past four on a summer morning. Everyone was longing for a cup of tea, but no buffet was open at that hour.

Dismissed with a call for half-past two on the stage, the actors scattered in twos and threes. Clara, lugging two leather suitcases, found it hard to keep up with Maidie who carried only an oil-cloth hold-all and an umbrella. The rain poured steadily on Clara's unprotected hat and hair and sent cold trickles down her neck. After what seemed to her miles of wet grey streets, she panted:

'Is it much further? Perhaps we could get a taxi.'

'Taxi,' snorted Maidie. 'If my screw won't run to taxis, yours certainly won't. Unless you've got private means, Lady Clara Vere de Vere.'

Clara was silent. She had four pounds in her bag; all that was left of her last cheque for a set of face-cream advertisements. Apart from that she had only her salary of three pounds a week. Out of that she would have to pay ten per cent to her agent and all her expenses except railway fares. Expenses included not only food and lodgings but the shoes and stockings she wore on the stage, make-up and tips to the theatre staff.

'Five bob every bloody week to the dresser,' Maidie had

warned her. 'A bob to the callboy. And if you're wise, you'll slip the baggage man half a crown now and then. Otherwise you may find your heavy stuff getting left behind.'

Clara became so absorbed in alarming mental calculations that she almost forgot the rain and the ache in her arms. Blind to the beauties of York she staggered along with her heavy cases till at last Maidie stopped in front of a shabby house in a back street.

The bell was answered at last by a woman who seemed surprised to see them and kept repeating:

'Ah tell you, ah never got postcard. Ah'm full up back and froont.'

To Clara's surprise, Maidie merely said, in her most refined voice: 'Sorry to have troubled you, Mrs Canning. There must be some mistake.'

Not till they were halfway down the street did Maidie begin to curse volubly.

'Old bitch bloody well had got it an' all. But you daren't get on the wrong side of landladies. Never know when you might play their town again. The girl who gave me this ad said Canning's place was clean. More than you can say for some of them.'

She stood in the rain, consulting a map, while Clara, thankful to drop her luggage for a moment, admired her competence.

'The boys gave me a couple of ads. We'll try those. Where the hell are we? Micklegate . . . Blossom Street . . . at least we don't have to cross that bloody river again.'

Even Maidie's spirit began to flag when Park Street and South Parade turned out also to be full up. A *Chu Chin Chow* company which was playing at the other theatre had arrived the night before and snapped up all the good lodgings. Her pink mouth was drooping and her doll's face looked washed out under the black lace brim which was losing its crispness in the damp.

'Nothing for it, Vere. We'll just have to ask wherever we see a card.'

They tramped on in silence. Maidie's patent shoes were splashed with mud. Occasionally she stumbled from tiredness and swore, but without conviction, as her ankles twisted on her high heels. The first house that displayed an 'Apartments' card between its lace curtains was also full up. The landlady of the second, though they begged and pleaded, was resolved that never again would she take in actresses.

'I'm fed oop with you professionals,' she said, crossing her arms and eyeing them with implacable disapproval. 'Smoking in bed an' all and wanting hot water all hours of the night for what purpose I don't know.'

As they started off again, Clara began to get a kind of moral second wind. The fact that Maidie, who was always extremely tart about people who did not use their handkerchiefs, was sniffing, could only mean that she was on the verge of tears. This unexpected weakness made Clara feel protective.

'Look here, Maidie,' she said. 'I've got four pounds in my bag. Let's go to a hotel . . . just for today. I mean . . . on me of course.'

Maidie said quite meekly, 'Decent of you, Vere. But never say die, as the monkey said.'

Suddenly she stopped. 'Nothing for it old dear. We'd better pray to St Joseph.'

Clara was startled.

'Why . . . are *you* a Catholic then?'

'I should bloody well think I am,' said Maidie indignantly.

'I'm sorry . . . I didn't know.'

'All the women in the company are R.C. thank God.'

'How did you know I was?'

'Don't ask silly questions. Get busy with St Joseph,' ordered Maidie. She stood still, shut her eyes tight, and Clara saw her pink lips move. She was so fascinated by the sight that her own prayer was so vague as to be negligible.

'Come on,' said Maidie, snapping her eyes open again. 'He'll find us something. Never failed me yet. I warn you it won't be the Ritz. Hasn't got modern ideas, the dear old Wurzit. But it'll be something.'

Sure enough, the very next landlady, who looked a good-natured slattern, could take them in. By now Clara was so exhausted that she would have been grateful for a heap of straw. She could have wept on the landlady's slack bosom as she heard Maidie say they would like to go to bed at once please as they had to rehearse in the afternoon.

'You'll 'ave to wait a bit, dears,' said the landlady. 'The beds isn't made yet. The two other young ladies only went off by the early train. Sit down and make yourselves at 'ome and Florrie'll make you a nice cup of tea.'

The strong leaf-speckled tea sweetened with condensed milk tasted better than anything Clara had ever drunk. Her aching head cleared; she began to take in her surroundings and even to feel a thrill of adventure. For the first time in her life, her parents would not even know her address and this gave her a delicious sense of freedom. The dingy surroundings were to become so familiar that, after a few weeks on tour, Clara had the impression that, though towns changed, landladies sitting-rooms remained the same. There were always round tables with red or green serge cloths, aspidistras, photographs of seaside towns in plush frames and, in lucky weeks, a tinny, yellow-keyed piano.

Maidie was in bloom again after her tea. Even her lace hat seemed to have revived like a watered flower. She wandered about the room making unflattering comments on the photos of the landlady's relatives and running a critical finger over the tops of furniture.

'You could write your name in the dust, and her lace curtains are filthy,' she said. 'Pity she's not a Yorkshire woman; they're ever so clean and they give you butter, not marge. Not used to this kind of thing, are you, Vere?'

'Oh well – it's rather what I expected.'

'I don't know what *my* mother would say if she saw some of the places we have to live in.'

Maidie sat down again after having dusted the chair with her handkerchief.

'We have some really beautiful furniture at home,' she went

on in her most genteel voice. 'Antique. My mother always dusts it herself. She says you simply can't trust maids nowadays. She's ever so particular. And I take after her. That's why I wanted to room with someone refined. My mother would have kittens if she knew what common girls there *are* in the profession.'

'Did she mind your going on the stage?' Clara ventured.

'She'd ever so much rather I'd been a music teacher. But Mr Finkelmann – he's a great friend of the family – persuaded her that I ought to train for ballet. I sing too – mezzo-soprano. I was on the road for two years in *The Maid of the Mountains* playing the *soubrette*.'

'Is musical comedy what you like doing most?'

'I'd prefer opera. Think dear . . . I might have been billed as the only Mimi with genuine T.B. Had to put in six months in a san. Only a spot. I'm all right now. But I'm not allowed to dance for a year.'

'You're awfully young. You'll soon get back.'

'Twenty-three,' said Maidie. 'No chicken for a dancer. Specially when you're out of practice. I've been on the stage since I was fifteen.'

Clara sighed.

'I envy you. I wish I could do one thing and do it really well.'

'You're ever so brainy though, aren't you? The boys told me you have things printed in the papers. True? Or s'only a rumour?'

'Only advertisements and rather silly short stories.'

'They pay you for them?'

'Why, of course.'

'Then they must be quite snappy. Honestly, Vere, I can't make you out.'

'What's so puzzling?'

'If you can make good money just sitting on your fanny writing whatever comes into your head, why on earth did you go on the stage?'

Clara mumbled something about experience. Maidie took her up sharply.

'Some people might call it taking the bread out of other girls' mouths.'

'Hang it all. I took a training course. *And* paid for it.'

'You'd have learnt more playing the hind legs of a donkey.'

'No doubt,' said Clara, yawning.

Maidie snapped: '*If* you're going to yawn in my face, you might at least say "Pardon". Not to mention putting your hand in front of your mouth. I *thought* you'd been decently brought up.'

Luckily the landlady arrived before they both lost their tempers. The prospect of a few hours' sleep was so delicious to their edgy nerves, that Maidie even squeezed Clara's arm as they went upstairs.

They were shown into a dismal bedroom. Clara was relieved to find that, at least, there were two beds. She was careful to offer Maidie first choice. The sheets looked suspiciously grey and the mattress sagged like a hammock but at least it was something on which to lie down and sleep. Clara hastily pulled off her clothes, instinctively remembering the convent technique of 'undressing with Christian modesty' and plunged into bed. Through her half-closed eyes she could see Maidie's pink mouth pursed in disapproval as she surveyed the clothes flung in an untidy heap on a chair. Maidie shook out her skirt, brushed her coat and carefully folded each of her garments before she put on a virginal nightdress of white lawn threaded with blue ribbons.

'I didn't think *you'd* be so untidy, Clara,' she said reproachfully. 'Still, I'll forgive you this once. You look bloody tired, poor kid. Got that fed-up, blank and far from home feeling?'

'Mmm,' murmured Clara, conscious of nothing but overwhelming drowsiness.

'Nighty night and sweet dreams.'

Maidie was half in bed when suddenly she leapt out again and fell on her knees.

'Oh damn,' she exclaimed. 'Forgot to say my night prayers. S'pose they count when you go to bed in the morning?'

Clara opened her eyes guiltily, trying to pull herself out of the exquisite gulf of sleep, to do the same. She kept them open just long enough to see Maidie with her long gold plait and her long white nightgown, her eyes closed in an expression of such spotless piety that she looked exactly like Little Eva before her lids dropped like plummets and she remembered nothing more.

Not long afterwards she awoke with the certainty that someone was sticking pins into her. She sat up, ungluing her eyes with difficulty, to feel new and sharper jabs.

'Maidie!'

'What the hell's the matter with *you*?'

'I think I'm being *bitten*.'

In a moment Maidie was out of bed and pulling back Clara's sheets.

'If it's bugs,' she said authoritatively, 'we move. If it's only fleas, wet soap will fix them.'

Luckily it was fleas. Maidie handsomely stood by, directing Clara's unskilled manoeuvres with a damp cake of soap.

'Live and learn, as the monkey said,' she observed as she returned to her own bed. 'You said you wanted a spot of experience, didn't you?'

3

The first night of playing in a real theatre to a real audience had an almost miraculous effect on Clara's spirits. From the moment she found a telegram from Stephen stuck in the cracked mirror of the dressing-room, the blight that had settled on her since she had left London, lifted. Even the most seasoned actor is excited on an opening night, even if it is only the opening night of a tour. Clara felt a passion of gratitude to Stephen for his telegram, not only because it contained the magic word 'love' and a hope that their companies might coincide some week, but because it made her feel like a real actress. Everyone in the company had telegrams; Maidie, half a dozen, and the lead so many that Merton Mordish swore that he must have sent them himself.

'Pathetic,' he said, as he came into the girls' dressing-room and presented them with a bottle of Guinness with a gesture which converted it into champagne. 'He's signed them Matheson Lang, and Godfrey Tearle and Gladys Cooper and the Lord knows who. Poor old Brett.' When the callboy banged on the door, shouting 'Overture and Beginners, please,' letting in the faint sound of an orchestra playing 'Take a pair of Sparkling Eyes', Clara began to shiver with delicious apprehension. She shivered so much that she dropped blobs of eyeblack on her newly made-up face and had to begin all over again. When, after what seemed only a few seconds, the callboy knocked again and yelled 'Curtain Up' excitement gave place to panic. She would never be made-up in time for her entrance.

As she fumbled frantically with hare's foot and wet white she made an appalling discovery.

'Maidie,' she cried. 'I can't go on.'

Maidie clapped her hand over Clara's mouth.

'Don't shout. Curtain's up. They'll hear you in front.'

Clara muttered: 'Maidie . . . I've forgotten all my lines.'

Maidie removed her hand from Clara's mouth and deftly rearranged her hair.

'Then make 'em up as you go along.'

'But . . .'

'You'll be O.K. once you're on. It's only stage-fright. Everyone gets it.'

'I've never felt like this before,' said Clara in a hoarse whisper. She was now convinced that her voice had gone as well as her memory.

'Well, you've never played to a real house, have you? Cheer up, kid. We're on together most of the show. I'll pull you through. You look a picture and that's all *they* care about.'

Somehow she found herself standing in the wings at the right moment, though with an agonised conviction that the words she could hear being spoken on the stage bore no relation to the play they had been rehearsing. Her knees were trembling so much that when her cue came Lister had to push her on. However, the moment she found herself on the stage, her legs carried her to the right place and she heard herself say her entrance line in a clear, composed voice.

For the rest of the evening she thoroughly enjoyed herself. The stale, creaking old farce suddenly came to life. Even its dreary jokes seemed witty when they were greeted with a roar of laughter from the tiers of pale masks in the darkness behind the glare of the floats. The first time one of her own lines was interrupted by one of those roars she was panic-stricken. Soon she began to sense when the laugh would come and pause for it.

Her scenes with Maidie went better than she had ever imagined possible. She knew she was not doing too badly from the fact that Maidie risked one or two unrehearsed pieces of 'business' and she found herself playing up to them. At the end, Lister thrust the two of them on for a curtain call of their own and the claps and appreciative whistles, though Clara knew she had only a small share in them, were the most intoxicating sounds she had ever heard. Almost more intoxicating were Lister's slap on the back in the wings and Maidie's, 'Not half bad for a beginner, Vere. You might make an actress yet.'

During the next few weeks, Clara became accustomed to a diet of sausages, strong tea and grilled herrings, to having a perpetual smear of blue on her eyelids and to never feeling properly washed or groomed. She could not acquire Maidie's technique of 'living in a suitcase' yet always appearing perfectly neat and fresh. Her own were overloaded with second-hand books she could not resist buying and which crushed her clothes and seduced her from ironing them. She became used to sitting up all night in trains and playing nap at dawn in station waiting-rooms. She even became used to seeing her own name in print coupled with such phrases as 'sprightly performance', 'promising newcomer' and 'vivacious freshness' in the Tuesday editions of provincial papers. At first she was interested in each new town and would explore its streets and even take a bus into the country outside. But soon, like the others, she no longer bothered to find out more than the shortest way from that week's digs to that week's theatre. Except for the long letters she wrote to Stephen and which he quite frequently answered and the postcards she occasionally scribbled to her parents in return for their faithful weekly budgets she was quite cut off from the outer world. Maidie curbed her natural extravagance so successfully that she just managed to make both ends meet on her salary. Only once or twice did she reluctantly force herself to dash off a few pieces of copy to mollify the advertising agents with whom she dared not break completely in case she suddenly found herself out of work.

A company on tour is not unlike a boarding-school. There were times when its changing feuds and friendships reminded Clara absurdly of Mount Hilary. She thought ironically how horrified the nuns would be that she should find any connection between this slipshod existence and the ordered, spotless life of the convent. Yet here, as there, she found herself both accepted and a little apart. She was beginning to wonder if there were any place where she did perfectly fit in; any life to which she could wholly commit herself. Ever since her childhood, she had believed that, just round the corner, her real life was waiting for her. Perhaps, after all, there was nothing. Nothing . . . or possibly something so frightening that she would dash blindly up any path to avoid it.

Friendships struck up in Huddersfield would dissolve acrimoniously in Nottingham; people who had cut each other dead in Leeds would be found rooming together in Liverpool. Apart from herself and Maidie, who, though they quarrelled, never quite split up, only one pair remained inseparable. Occasionally Trevor would complain that Peter had been 'really rather beastly, dear', or Peter would sulk because Trevor had snatched a corner seat twice running on night journeys, but they were usually a most peaceable couple. They made a kind of protective alliance with Clara and Maidie. Though they would not, of course, give up a corner to either girl, they would hold seats for them against other claimants and sometimes offer them the dregs of their Thermos flask. Clara had found them puzzling at first but she came to accept them as she accepted Maidie's extraordinary switches from primness to bawdiness and her own nickname of 'Vere'.

She soon discovered that Trevor looked up to Peter with almost worshipping awe. Peter knew just enough French to decipher Le Jardin des Supplices with great labour and translate it in whispers to Trevor on train journeys. He was also expert at embroidering. Sometimes, on Sunday mornings, the four would meet at each other's digs. If it was a piano week, Maidie would sing, while Trevor admiringly watched Peter stitching sprays of almond blossom on a cushion cover. 'Why not pansies, dear?' Maidie had asked once and Peter had giggled, 'Too obvious, darling.' Maidie had an unexpectedly pure small soprano. When she was not in the mood for indecent songs, she would sing 'my classical pieces', 'Caro mio' or excerpts from *Aida* and *Butterfly*. When she sang these she would sit bolt upright, like a schoolgirl practising before her mistress, breathing very conscientiously, and wearing her most refined expression, occasionally breaking off to snap: 'For God's sake, turn over, Vere' or 'Damn that bloody Wurzit of a chord.'

Those Sunday mornings in dingy furnished parlours had a character of their own. Sunday, if they were not travelling, was the only day they had to themselves; there was a sense of peace, even of luxury, in being for once out of harness. They reminded Clara again oddly of the Sundays at her convent school though they had little in common beyond the fact that she and Maidie and Miss Cooke went to early Mass. She was not surprised to find that Miss Cooke went to Mass nearly every day but she was amazed at the devoutness of Maidie. Often when Clara herself could not face the thought of getting up before breakfast after a late journey, Maidie would walk a mile or more fasting to go to Communion. Clara felt that Maidie had a right to reproach her, as she often did, for slackness. During the last few years, and particularly since she had known Stephen Tye, her religion had become a habit rather than a preoccupation. Stephen was fond of saying: 'How lucky you are to be able to believe in something. I have no refuge of that kind,' or 'Poor Celia should have been a Catholic. Women need religion.' Such remarks made her feel that there was an unfair advantage, almost a kind of mental cheating in being a Catholic.

Though she and Maidie frequently exasperated each other, they never quite came to the point of splitting up. Clara, bookish, untidy and accustomed to privacy, would have found it a severe strain to share a bedroom even with someone of her own type. Maidie was as horrified by Clara's disorderliness as Clara was alternately shamed and irritated by Maidie's almost pathological neatness. She could keep up neither with Maidie's heights of refinement nor her moods of rollicking relaxation. Maidie, whose prim rosebud mouth could produce the most startling language Clara had yet heard, was deeply shocked when Clara once exclaimed 'Mon Dieu'. 'God, Vere,' she had said. 'You shouldn't say that. It's not just unladylike, it's blasphemous.' She was almost as shocked because Clara sent her underclothes to the laundry instead of, like herself, washing them in a basin at their digs. 'I'm surprised at you, Vere. Why, you went to a convent, didn't you? For all you know, there may be *men* working in laundries.' Sometimes the two quarrelled bitterly and continued to share bed, board, and theatre dressing-room in silence broken only by: 'May I trouble you for the sugar, Miss Batchelor,' or 'I *believe* that's my number five, Miss Spencer.'

If it had not been for their both being Catholics, their feuds might have been permanent. But, inconsistent though they both were, it was impossible for them to kneel side by side at Communion and return to their lodgings to glare in icy silence at each other across the breakfast table. Sundays, for this reason, were usually an oasis of peace before the next quarrel began to brew.

4

One particular Sunday morning – it was in Nuneaton – Clara and Maidie went round to Peter and Trevor's digs. It was a warm morning in late October; a strong smell of tanneries came in through the open window. Maidie was sitting at the yellow-keyed piano playing and singing; Trevor was manicuring his nails and Peter, as usual, stitching his cushion cover. The photographs on the piano jangled every time Maidie struck a powerful chord; at intervals a cracked bell sounded from the neighbouring chapel. Clara listened idly to the old musical comedy songs, watching Peter's needle moving expertly in and out.

Maidie broke off in the middle of 'Florrie was a Flapper' which she was singing with great verve and said primly:

'I don't think I ought to sing that on Sunday. Let's have something classical.'

Sitting very upright, with the sun glinting on her coiled golden plaits, she began in her unexpectedly pure, violin-like voice:

> 'One fine day you'll notice
> A ship . . . a ship arriving . . .'

Inevitably, Clara's thoughts flew to Stephen. Her situation was becoming very like Butterfly's. Week by week she went on hoping that his company would catch up with hers; sometimes they missed each other only by a day. In Liverpool there had been a chance that he would get over from Chester for the Sunday but a telegram had cancelled their meeting. Lately she had begun to wonder whether he would come at all.

Maidie sang without passion, like a conscientious schoolgirl, yet the very impersonality of her choirboy voice made the song more poignant. All the yearning of all women waiting for their lovers to return seemed to rise and fall like a fountain jet in the ugly parlour crowded with plush and bamboo, among the smells of cabbage water and tanning, the scratching of Trevor's nail file and the tinny clang of the chapel bell. All at once, Clara forgot Stephen and was carried into that other realm where everything had a significance beyond itself. She thought 'This moment is like no other. Only *now* will all these things come together in this particular way . . . this music, these smells, these sounds, these people.' At the same time she felt not that violent yet vague urge to write which usually turned to impotence after a few pages, but something calmer and more concrete. Certain loose threads which had been floating in her mind for weeks spun themselves together; she saw the rough shape of a story quite unlike the slick mechanical ones she constructed for *London Mail*.

Maidie banged down the piano lid; the pink glass lustres on the mantelpiece shuddered and tinkled. Peter pricked his finger and swore.

'Nothing like a spot of classical music,' she said. 'My soul feels better already. Think I'll even go to twelve o'clock Mass and hear a sermon. Coming, Vere? We've just time.'

'N—no,' stammered Clara. 'I'll go back to our digs. Something important I've remembered I must do.'

'Can't be more important than going to Mass.'

'I *have* been once.'

'I should bloody well hope so.'

'Tst. Tst. Girls, girls,' said Trevor.

30

'Shall *we* go with Maidie?' asked Peter. 'Anything for a new sensation. I adore incense and candles.'

'There won't be any. It's a Low Mass.'

'Oh, we can't abide anything low,' he giggled. 'I'll stay here and let Trev do my nails.'

For the rest of the day, Maidie had one of her fits of exceptional piety while Clara stayed in their stuffy bedroom writing hour after hour with a sustained concentration that amazed her. Her attempts to write anything serious usually petered out in impotent misery after a few paragraphs. Today she was too absorbed to tell herself as usual that she could never hope to be anything but a hack with a certain trite facility. By seven when Maidie returned, announcing that she had been to the Rosary, Benediction and Holy Hour, she was busy on the third draft of her story.

Maidie burst into the bedroom in the best of tempers.

'I've brought us some Guinness – I need it after all that praying. What have *you* been up to?'

Clara hastily retrieved the pages which littered the floor.

'Inspiration flowing, eh?' she snatched up a page Clara had overlooked. 'Come on, let's have a peep.'

'Please, Maidie,' implored Clara, trying to rescue the page.

'Why . . . what is it? A hot love story?'

'No,' said Clara, almost in tears. 'It's something you'd find awfully boring.'

'How d'you know?' Maidie's face turned suddenly suspicious. 'I'm not educated enough. Is that it?'

'No . . . no . . .' said Clara in agony. 'Of course not. Only I can't bear people to look at things till they're finished.'

Maidie stared. Then to Clara's relief, the suspicious look relaxed into a patronising smile.

'Diddums then. You are a rum kid. Like a rabbit about to eat its young. Come on, have a Guinness. I'm dying for a spot of fun. Shall we ask that stuck pig Jimmy Munroe to have a drink?'

Clara nodded. The elderly young man with the frightened

31

expression was rooming in the same house that week.

'Do him good,' said Maidie. 'He nearly jumps out of his skin when I ask him to pass the mustard. He's terrified of girls. Too pure to be true, my dear. If he were a Catholic there'd be some excuse. But when you don't *have* to be pure . . . well, it's unnatural. I'd like to give him a *real* scare.'

The young man with the frightened look drank his Guinness readily enough and became almost talkative though his expression did not change. Maidie drank several. With each one her spirits rose and her language became less and less inhibited. After supper she suddenly rushed upstairs. Ten minutes or so went by and she did not reappear.

The elderly young man asked Clara:

'Does your friend often drink quite so much Guinness?'

'I've never seen her have more than one at a time.'

'You don't think she might be feeling poorly?'

'I shouldn't think so. She's in tearing spirits.'

'Oh, yes. Ever so cheery,' he said nervously. 'Pardon the suggestion. But don't you think you ought to go up and see if she's all right? She might have come over queer.'

Clara agreed. Before she could reach the door, Maidie bounded through it, dressed only in a pair of black silk stockings and a pink chemise. She had let down her hair which now hung in long golden strands almost to her waist.

James Munroe looked more terrified than ever, but he was not going to be driven out of his comfortable sitting-room.

'I feel like dancing,' announced Maidie gaily. 'Haven't practised for months. Wonder if I can still get up on my points.'

After one or two unsuccessful attempts, she balanced on the tips of her toes, a slender, charming figure. In spite of the pink chemise, her face was a study in angelic innocence.

'Wonder if I can remember a routine.' She skipped a few steps, then stopped.

'Damn,' she said sweetly. 'I'm as stiff as a poker. Can't get my leg up. Come here, Jimmy – hold my foot.'

32

Very gingerly, as if it had been a live shell, Munroe took hold of the small black-stockinged foot.

'That's right. Now lift it up. No . . . higher. Hell, man, don't look so frightened. Haven't you ever seen a girl's leg before? Well, you're bloody well going to now.' She whipped her foot out of his hand and sent it flying up in a head-high kick. 'And again – *and* again,' she panted. 'Now you've got something to write home about.'

The sight of Munroe's panic-stricken face sent her into peals of delighted giggles. Then she relented.

'Poor lamb,' she pouted. 'Was he shocked then? Did naughty Maidie commit a spot of *faux pas*? Well, it'll all come out in the wash as the monkey said.'

Averting his eyes, the unhappy Jimmy collapsed into a wicker chair. Maidie sat down at the piano and regaining her most virginal expression, began to sing:

> 'Hark, hark, my soul,
> Angelic songs are swelling.'

'You sing beautifully,' said the frightened man. 'But aren't you a little cold, Miss Spencer?'

'Maidie to you, and I'm not as cold as I look.' She leapt up from the piano stool and bounded lightly on to Munroe's knee.

'I bet you don't know the difference between a man and a woman, Jimmy,' she said, winding her slim arms round his neck. 'Sweet thirty-five and never been kissed.' She pressed her lips to his recoiling mouth.

After he had, with some difficulty, unwound her, Maidie rushed up once more to the bedroom and returned with an empty Guinness bottle and a rosary. Flinging herself on the floor and waving the bottle in one hand and the rosary in the other, she proceeded to pour out alternate strings of 'Hail Mary's' and unpublished limericks. Munroe, now pale and sweating with fear, dashed out of the room and Clara heard the key turn in his bedroom door. After much persuasion, she induced Maidie to come to bed. Once upstairs, Maidie disappeared into the bathroom, and returned, rather pale but quite sober. She plaited her hair with her usual deftness, exchanging the pink chemise for her white schoolgirlish nightdress and knelt down to say her prayers. When she had finished, she opened her limpid blue eyes and looked at Clara reproachfully.

'You're a good sort, Vere,' she said, 'but I wish you'd take your religion more seriously. I get quite worried sometimes thinking what might happen if I weren't there to keep you straight.'

5

The next day, when they moved on to Gainsborough, Clara found two letters waiting for her in the stage doorkeeper's pigeonhole. One was from Stephen; the other from her father. Stephen's pencil scrawl contained such wonderful news that she entirely forgot her other letter.

'I'll be outside the theatre at Gainsborough on Sunday morning at eleven. We're playing Lincoln this week and I've wheedled Miss Lane into letting me hire a car and drive over. Official reason: get local colour for possible stage version of *The Mill on the Floss*. Real reason: see you. My love – for what it is worth. S.'

It was not till she returned to their digs after the show that she remembered her father's letter, thrust unopened into her coat pocket. She saw that it was a long one and thought remorsefully how faithfully he wrote to her every Sunday, busy as he was, and how carelessly she skimmed through his news. But this time she read the letter attentively and with disquiet. Archie Hughes-Follett was in England and her father had told him the theatres where she would be playing in the next few weeks. She had not seen Archie since she had jilted him nearly four years ago on the verge of their wedding and she had no desire to see him now.

'I hesitated,' Claude Batchelor wrote, 'but it seemed churlish to refuse. I could not help feeling sorry for Archie. He seems rather lost since his mother's death. His job in South America does not seem to have been a success. At any rate he is back in England with no home of his own to go to and, as far as I can see, no definite plans. He has changed a great deal since I last saw him in 1917. In case he should come and see you, I should warn you that, superficially anyhow, you may find him changed for the worse. The war seems to have affected some of the very best in that way. But I am sure that, fundamentally, he is as sound as ever. I was always fond of Archie, as you know, and I was touched by the way he spoke of you: not a trace of resentment or bitterness. Now that he is down on his luck – financially as well as in other ways – I think it would be nice if you could make some little gesture of friendship towards him. I am sure he would not misinterpret it and I feel you owe it to him. Don't imagine that I am blaming you in any way for Archie's present state. The fact remains that, magnificently as he took it, you gave him a great blow when you broke your engagement. I am *sure* he has got over it . . . but equally sure that he needs any friends he can find.'

Weeks of the tour when there had been nothing definite to look forward to had flown. This one dragged interminably towards the distant brightness of Sunday. Though Clara dreaded the thought of seeing Archie again, she would have welcomed almost any distraction to make the slow days go more quickly. Each night she expected to find a letter in his cramped, childish writing but the only other letter that came that week was from her mother. Isabel, too, wrote about Archie.

'Daddy will have told you that your ex-fiancé turned up here last week from South America. He looked untidier than ever; almost dirty, to tell the truth. I am afraid he was also rather tipsy – *so* sad to see a young man from such a background going downhill like that. Poor Philippa Hughes-Follett! It is almost a mercy that she is dead; she would have been heartbroken to see her son in such a state. I *always*, you know, had an intuition that there was some fatal weakness in Archie. More than ever now I realise how *disastrous* it would have been for you to marry him. Daddy still has a very soft spot for that young man, however! I didn't want him to put Archie on your track but you know how obstinate Daddy can be! I implore you not to do anything rash. I know you have a very tender heart, however hard and "modern" you like us to think you are. Women are so dreadfully liable to be moved by pity and though Daddy is sure he has got over everything, *I* believe he's still in love with you. And now, less than ever, would he be a fit husband for my darling, pretty, clever daughter. Even *you* admitted I was right in 1917 and realised your frivolous mother was not such a fool after all. You may have forgotten that day I found you crying your heart out in the Oratory but I never have and never shall.'

Clara had forgotten neither the day nor the conversation with Isabel that had led to her breaking her engagement but she intensely disliked being reminded of it. It was the one occasion in her life on which she had turned to her mother, whom she normally despised, and had found her displaying a most unexpected wisdom and firmness. Clara had long since slid back into her old superior attitude and Isabel into the vain, inconsistent, peevish self which so comfortably justified it. This letter, unlike her father's, had the effect of making her feel a faint, remorseful renewal of interest in Archie.

However, as Sunday came within measurable distance, she forgot all about Archie in preparing to meet Stephen. Examining herself anxiously in the glass, she saw that she had lost some of her freshness in the last three months. Her skin was duller and her eyes looked tired. She began a hasty beauty campaign and made herself take long walks among the warehouses and gabled buildings along the banks of the river where Tom and Maggie Tulliver had drowned in each other's arms.

When Sunday arrived at last, she could only deal with her distractions at Mass by turning her thoughts of Stephen into prayers for him. She kept imploring, 'Please let it come right for us,' without daring to formulate what 'coming right' might mean. Before eleven struck she had passed the theatre a dozen times, forcing herself to walk a hundred yards beyond it either way without looking round or hiding up a side street which gave her a clear view. She laughed at herself for behaving so exactly like Madam Butterfly and even sang softly, 'I without answering, hold myself quietly concealed' ironically imitating Maidie's careful vowels. At last she saw a car drive up and stop in front of the theatre. She sauntered towards it as slowly as possible, not daring to raise her eyes in case the man at the wheel should not be Stephen. She did not look up till she heard the door slam and saw his tall figure in the familiar old trench coat hurrying towards her. She stopped dead with a sudden wild impulse to run away. The next minute she felt his hands on her shoulders and found herself looking up into his face.

'My *dear* Clara!'

'Stephen!'

He looked different, she thought. His pallor was faintly tanned, making his fair hair and moustache seem almost white by contrast.

'How incredibly well you look.'

'Almost indecently fit.' He smiled down at her, tucking her arm under his. 'By Gad, it's good to see you. This calls for a celebration. Damn, they won't be open yet. What shall we do . . . drive out somewhere?'

'Absolutely anything you like,' Clara said happily.

'Perhaps I'd better not use too much petrol. Eliza might get suspicious. After all I'm supposed to be getting local colour in St Ogg's, not roaming the countryside.'

'Eliza?'

'Miss Lane. My boss.'

'Of course.'

'You've no idea of the wangling I've had to do. Naturally she wanted to come along. I invented an eccentric old gentleman who was a great authority on George Eliot and couldn't abide women. Recognise yourself?'

She laughed.

'Character part. Give me time to get into the skin of it, as old Merton Mordish says.'

It was a grey morning yet the prim red streets where she had taken her dull duty walks seemed suddenly flooded with sunlight. Every gable, even every shuttered shop window became beautiful and significant; every passer seemed to look at them with affectionate envy. She could hear Stephen telling her about his parts and the people in his company; she could hear herself laughing and answering but all the time she was saying to herself, 'This isn't a dream. I really am here in Gainsborough on a Sunday morning, walking with my arm in Stephen's.'

At last she became aware in one of the streets leading down to the river that neither of them had spoken for some time. Stephen gently detached his arm.

'I must have a cigarette. Isn't there anywhere in this place where one can sit down?'

She guided him to a bench by the river. Between puffs at his cigarette he looked down at her with narrowed eyes.

'Well,' he said. 'Here we are. Still the same little Clara. Or *are* you quite the same?'

'Do I look awful?' she asked nervously.

'Good Lord, no. Perfectly recognisable. A little *distraite*, possibly.'

'I still can't believe you're actually here.'

'You would if you realised the prodigious efforts I've made to get here. I've not merely perjured myself but I was out of bed by eight on a Sunday morning. I doubt if many men in your life will do as much for you as that.'

'All right. You *are* here. If I can believe you got up at eight, I can believe anything.' She spoke lightly but her heart was unaccountably heavy. It was more of an effort than usual, having been away from him for so long, to keep up the careless note he liked and expected. She wondered if he had the least idea how it hurt her when he suggested there might be other men in her life some day. It was inconceivable to her that she could ever love anyone else. The mere possibility of 'other men' implied something too painful to imagine: the loss of Stephen himself.

She began to ask him questions about his life in the last three months. Once or twice he said impatiently:

'I've told you that already. I don't believe you've listened to a word I've said.'

She knew that she had been too excited by his mere presence to notice what either of them had said as they walked down to the river. This made her self-conscious and for some moments she was afraid to speak at all.

'Absent-minded or sulking?' he asked, pinching her arm rather sharply. 'I can't stand these pregnant silences. I get too much of them with Eliza.'

'What's she like – Miss Lane?'

'My dear, I've told you that too. Very matriarchal but a damn good actress. No doubt you were too *distraite* to hear me say I was going to play Richard II in Oxford.'

'No. That's something I did grasp. I'm terribly excited. It's *absolutely* your part.'

Stephen stared at the river.

'By God, it is. I've longed to play it ever since I was in the O.U.D.S. What a part . . . and what poetry.'

Clara said softly: 'Oh, that I were a mockery king of snow.'

He took it up and went through the whole speech, muting the resonance of his beautiful voice, but making every pause, every inflection perfect.

Clara felt a chill of sheer pleasure run down her spine.

'Stephen . . . if you can do it all as well as that . . . this is going to be *something*. Oh, if only I could come and see you.'

He turned to her with his face alight.

'Aha . . . I've woken you up at last, have I? There's my old crony of the taverns. I was beginning to think I might as well

40

have stayed in my comfortable bed. Listen – I've got an entirely new idea how to work the mirror scene.'

She listened intently for several minutes while he explained and illustrated his idea. She was rewarded by his suddenly flinging his arm along the back of the seat and looking at her affectionately.

'My God, talking to you makes me realise how much I've missed you. No one listens as intelligently as you do. *When* you listen, that is. Have you missed *me*, Clara?'

'What do you think?' she said happily.

'You didn't mention it in your letters.'

'I thought it was too obvious to mention.'

'Hmm. I wondered if some dashing contemporary might have cut out your middle-aged admirer.'

'I wish you'd stop once and for all harping on those ten years.'

'My dear, it's only with you I feel so confoundedly old. With the Lane I feel a positive Peter Pan.'

'How old is *she*?'

'Forty if a day. She doesn't look it on the stage. Remarkable woman. A slight strain, sometimes. Goes in for plain living and high thinking.'

'You sound as if she were trying to reform you.'

'She makes attempts in that direction. Do you know, Clara, I have had precisely two pints of beer since last Thursday? And not a drop of whisky.'

'It sounds like Swinburne and Watts-Dunton.'

'It is rather. However, I intend to relax today. What time do they open in this appallingly smug little town?'

'I've no idea.'

'Very proper. I see life on tour hasn't corrupted you. When I first saw you . . . I thought for a moment the milkmaid had ever so slightly lost her bloom.'

'More than slightly. And probably past recovery,' sighed Clara. 'Touring seems to suit you all right. I've never seen you looking so well.'

'My face hasn't got fat or anything awful?' he asked anxiously.

'Good heavens, no.'

'I shall need all my haggard charm for Richard. And for Wakem if we do the *Mill*. Eliza wants me to play Stephen Guest but I'm sticking out for Philip.'

'I think it's absurd to try and turn the *Mill* into a play. When a thing's conceived as a novel – when all the drama is internal and the whole thing's an accumulation of tiny incidents – it's just sheer mutilation.'

'My dear Clara . . . what eloquence! It must be your father coming out in you. I've always believed you would have made an admirable schoolmistress.'

'Beast. You know I hate people to say that.'

'Have I lost my ancient privilege of teasing you? Actually I agree. But Elizabeth has a fancy to play Maggie Tulliver.'

'At *her* age?'

'I tell you she doesn't look it on the stage. Besides she's got all the technique in the world. Also she's rather the type: intense, humourless, high ideals, touch of fanatical mysticism, etcetera.'

Maggie Tulliver was one of Clara's favourite characters in fiction. She was beginning a spirited defence of her when Stephen interrupted.

'Spare me another literature lesson, dear girl. In my opinion the book's a bore and Maggie's a bore. Maggie's a bore because she's George Eliot and George Eliot was the supreme bore of the nineteenth century.'

'You've *never* appreciated George Eliot,' said Clara, too angry to care whether or not she was boring Stephen. 'I don't believe you've even read her properly.'

'No female novelist is worth reading,' said Stephen. 'Women can't write novels any more than they can write poems. There's only one book approaching a work of art even *signed* by a woman . . .'

'Emily *did* write it,' insisted Clara. This was an old ritual quarrel of theirs.

'Branwell wrote it,' said Stephen, with his most exasperating smile. 'Branwell, who was a drunk of genius. And like Branwell, I propose to make for the nearest pub. Are you coming or do you wish to remain glaring at the Trent and waiting for the eagre to overwhelm you?'

Clara laughed, but not as convincingly as she could have wished. It was nothing new that Stephen should tease her but she was out of practice in hiding the fact that she was hurt. Today, his old joke about women writers went deeper than usual. She had too often rashly imagined this first talk with him after their long separation and hoped that, when they got back to her digs, she might be able to mention, even to show him the story she had written in Nuneaton.

She walked in silence beside him as they hunted for a pub. This time he did not take her arm but strode along, with his hands in his pockets, so fast that she could hardly keep up with him. An east wind was blowing, whipping the ends of her curls into her eyes and raising Stephen's hair in a crest above his high-boned profile. He sang as he walked, in the thin, not quite true tenor that matched so oddly with his resonant speaking voice.

'Then one he singles from the rest
And cheers the happy hen.
With a "how d'you do?" and a "how d'you do?"
And a "how d'you do?" again.'

When they were settled at last in a pub and Stephen had ordered some food and a double whisky, he said:

'You're looking gloomy again. What's the matter?'

'The hen's quite happy, thanks.'

'Hen? Hen?' he frowned. 'Stop being cryptic and have a drink. What do you want?'

'Anything. A Guinness.'

'Quite the old pro, eh? But you'll put on weight if you drink too many.'

'All right. A small gin then. It's Maidie who has such a passion for Guinness.'

'Maidie? Ah yes, of course. Your fantastic room-mate. You wrote me some rather amusing letters about her.'

'Too kind.'

'Women *can* write letters. They should stick to that.'

'I'll remember.'

'Still making masses of money out of those deliciously absurd advertisements? I wish *I'd* got the knack of writing profitable nonsense.'

'Precisely three guineas since the tour started.'

'Pity. I find theatrical life appallingly expensive, don't you?'

'I muddle along somehow. Maidie keeps me in order.'

'Eliza tries to keep me solvent. But I've usually subbed most of my beggarly salary by Friday. You couldn't possibly lend me a quid, Clara dear?'

'I've only got about fifteen shillings.' She emptied her bag on the table. 'You can have that.'

'Forget it. I don't rob children's moneyboxes. I daresay I can manage.'

'Let me pay my share, anyway.'

'I hate it but I suppose I'll have to let you. I forgot this absurd situation when I started ordering doubles. God, it's humiliating at my age. You should have known me when I was a gay captain. But I forgot. You were still in pinafores.'

'How often have I told you I left them off about 1907?'

'Don't be so maddeningly literal. You're still in mental pinafores. I don't suppose you were even aware of the war.'

'Aware enough to have lots of my friends killed in it. Boys who were only two or three years older than I was.'

'Killed,' he said with the sudden moroseness Clara remembered so well. 'They were the lucky ones.' He stared at her almost accusingly; his blue eyes hard and glazed.

She said unhappily: 'I couldn't help it. Being too young and not being a man. I did *try* to imagine it.'

44

'Imagine!' he said bitterly. 'I've seen things you *couldn't* imagine.' He swallowed a great gulp of whisky. Ashamed of her inadequacy, burning with sympathy for all Stephen must have gone through, Clara could not quite stop herself from noticing that his voice and gesture would have registered well on the stage.

She said humbly: 'Of course you're right. I can't imagine it. It's silly even to try.'

With another of his abrupt changes of mood he said:

'Don't look so sad. It doesn't suit you. Come, let the canikin clink. Can we afford another?'

After his third double, he became extremely lighthearted.

'My God, it's good to be with you again, you absurd creature. Trying to look like an actress and sipping your gin like a schoolgirl drinking a particularly filthy cough-mixture. I'm sure you haven't changed since you left that celebrated convent.'

'The nuns would think I'd changed. Considerably for the worse.'

'Rubbish. I doubt if you've got it in you to change. I believe you're immune from experience.'

'Am I as stupid as all that?'

'Very refreshing when it isn't exasperating. There are times when I adore this convent aura of yours.'

'You don't know anything about convents.'

'If you entered one, I should come and rattle at the grill.'

Clara said angrily: 'I'm not in the least likely to enter one.'

'Of course not. They're your church's admirable solution for unattractive females.'

'They're nothing of the kind. Oh, it's hopeless to try and make you understand.'

'Don't try, my sweet. The only time I find you slightly tiresome is when you attempt to explain your religion. Mark you, I approve of religion for women. It's a safety-valve. Poor Celia should have been an R.C. Then she could have complained about me to the saints or gone to confession about me or whatever comforting thing it is you do. At any rate it might have stopped her from making such a fuss. Waiter . . . another double. Hell, is it closing time already? Damn Dora. What a country! In Flanders at least one didn't have to get tight by the clock.'

6

They spent an hour or two of the grey afternoon wandering about the streets of Gainsborough while Stephen made some rough sketches of gables and fluted roofs and the bridge over the Trent.

'I'm only giving Eliza her head about the idiotic *Mill* play because she's letting me do Richard,' he explained.

'You seem to be well in with the management,' said Clara.

'I am, my dear. I know which side my bread's buttered. Eliza's quite likely to take a London theatre next year.'

Clara asked suddenly:

'Did anything come out of your drinks with that man in London?'

'What man? When?'

'The night I went off. When you couldn't get to King's Cross.'

'Oh . . . *that* chap,' said Stephen heartily. 'I'd almost forgotten. No . . . the usual vague promises. Sheer waste of time.'

When dusk fell, they went back to Clara's lodgings. She had bought a few things to supplement the high tea of sausages, bread and butter and cake and bribed the landlady into giving them an extra scuttle of coal for the fire. Mrs Greaves, soothed by Stephen who went out of his way to charm her, became unusually gracious and produced not only her best china but two boiled eggs in woollen jackets.

When Clara came down with her windblown hair freshly combed and wearing a soft green dress that Stephen had once said he liked, he gave her one of his most affectionate looks. At once the sense of disappointment that had haunted her all the afternoon vanished and her heart became as light as a bubble. The ugly shabby room, glorified by the firelight and the presence of Stephen seemed suddenly delightful. She laughed from sheer happiness.

'Ah, that's better,' he said. 'Now you look like my old Clara. I fancied there was a kind of blight on you all the afternoon.'

'East wind, I expect.'

'Yes, indeed. And that terribly smug provincial town. This is the only way to enjoy the provinces. High tea, plush curtains drawn and a blazing fire. What superbly typical digs.'

'Were your Lincoln ones like this?'

'Actually I haven't been in digs for the last few weeks. I've been in loathsome provincial hotels.'

'On your beggarly screw?'

'Not exactly,' he said hesitantly. 'On the house, as it were. Miss Lane wanted to discuss things about the plays. She's very genteel. Doesn't like slumming.'

'I see,' said Clara in a slightly chilly voice.

He reached up his hand from where he sat with his long legs stretched out to the fire and pulled her hair.

'Don't look so fierce. I've had enough of disapproving women.'

'Is Miss Lane fierce?'

'A benevolent despot, shall we say? The company's one big family. But there's no doubt who's the head of it. If she makes a suggestion, it's tactful to agree.'

'What are you? . . . The favourite son?'

He pulled her down so that she was kneeling between his knees.

'The prodigal, on this occasion.'

'And I am the husks and swine? Thanks.'

48

He smiled, stroking back her hair.

'A little pink and white obstinate pig,' he said, kissing her gently. 'And the sweetest of nut kernels.' He stood up and drew her to her feet.

'Come along. I'm dying of hunger. It would be a shocking thing if I were tempted to eat you instead of the sausages.'

He ate ravenously, pausing every now and then to throw back his head and laugh.

'My God, I am enjoying this. I feel as if I were young again and nothing mattered.'

Clara was too excited to eat, but she talked and made silly jokes in an access of absurd happiness. She had never seen Stephen in quite this mood before. Perhaps it was because they were alone together in an illusion of intimacy they had never known in London. They had met in pubs and restaurants and at parties in other people's rooms; even when they snatched an occasional day in the country they had never shared a meal in a room by themselves. The plush curtains shut out all sounds but the hiss of the fire and the faint jangle of Sunday evening church bells. The lamplight softened the sharp lines of Stephen's face; he looked younger, almost boyish as he sat there drinking mahogany-coloured tea, eating everything from sausages to pink sugar cakes and making jokes even sillier than her own. At last Clara fell silent, content to do nothing but watch Stephen's face and hear his voice and laugh. For the first time she felt she could safely give herself up to the delight of being in love with him without always having to be on her guard. It was as if they were living together in a real house . . . almost as if they were married. She sighed with pure happiness.

'Stop smiling at the angels and attend to me,' he said. 'Give me some more tea. Black as you like.'

She poured it carefully from the pewter pot into the cup lavishly adorned with gilt and forget-me-nots, feeling his eyes on her.

'I like watching you pour out tea,' he said. 'So deliciously conscientious like a solemn child presiding at a dolls' tea-party. You know, Clara, domestic life is vastly becoming to you. You oughtn't to be traipsing about with a troop of vagabonds. You ought to be married and have a home and all that sort of thing.'

Her hand shook as she handed him the cup.

'I nearly did get married once. As nearly as possible.'

'I'm exceedingly glad you didn't.'

'Any good reason?'

'Only that we probably shouldn't be having high tea together at this moment. Good enough?'

'Quite.'

'I've got a worse one. Pure dog-in-the-manger. I shall be absurdly jealous of the man you marry.'

There was a knock on the door, though it was not Mrs Greaves' habit to knock before she came in to clear the table. Evidently Stephen's presence put her on her best behaviour. Tonight she made an interminable business of removing the dishes, talking to Stephen to whom she had obviously taken a violent fancy and looking at the pair of them with benevolent curiosity.

When at last she had gone, they sat opposite each other by the fire, hardly speaking. The interruption had broken the spell. Stephen's mood of wild spirits had faded: he sat smoking and frowning at the fire. Clara became conscious of the ticking of the clock. Her sense of timelessness had gone; the precious day was running out. Impossible to recapture that mood; to reopen that conversation. Without meaning to, she sighed.

'Melancholy?' he asked without looking at her.

'A little.'

'So am I. Sunday evening. Now we've stopped talking one hears those infernal church bells. The tintinnabulation of despair. What were we talking about?'

'I forget,' lied Clara.

'I hate the autumn,' he said. 'Remember how we walked in the New Forest last June? You had a dress almost the same green you

50

are wearing now. And the sun shone through the leaves on your hair. Remember that cottage in the clearing and the woman who asked us in to pick strawberries?'

Clara nodded. She wondered if he remembered that the woman had asked them if they were on their honeymoon.

Stephen threw his cigarette into the fire and sang softly in his thin tenor . . .

> 'And while I walked still to and fro
> And from her company I could not go
> But when I waked . . . it was not so
> In youth is pleasure.'

Clara did not look at him. There was a terrible fluttering of hope and fear in her heart.

He said, with a sigh, 'In youth is pleasure. Be thankful you are young, my dear.'

'Why do you always talk as if you were old?'

He assumed his bitter smile.

'Because, as a man, I am finished. Henceforth I only exist as an actor.'

'I can't bear it when you say things like that.'

'Because you're young and sweet and silly.'

'Silly, if you like.'

'You are also a considerable temptation to a middle-aged man determined to do the right thing.'

She looked at him closely.

'Stephen . . . am I being very dense?'

'A little, my dear. It's one of your charms. But it makes things infernally difficult sometimes.'

The sense of hope and fear became almost overpowering.

'Is there something you're trying to tell me?'

'Perhaps,' he said gloomily. 'It may, of course, be entirely unnecessary. I was always rather a vain chap.'

'What do you mean?'

Suddenly he shook his shoulders and sat up.

'Nothing. Shall I read to you?'

'Yes, do,' said Clara with an eagerness she was far from feeling.

'What shall it be? The old *Shropshire Lad*? It's in my pocket as always.'

He pulled out of his pocket the small red battered copy she knew so well and that had been with him all through the war. *The Shropshire Lad* had been the background of all their summer together. He had read it to her in pubs, declaimed it as they paced the London streets in the dusk. All her life she would associate it with Stephen and be unable to read a single line without hearing it mentally in his voice.

She watched him now as he read; his head thrown slightly back so that there was a wedge of shadow under his long thin jaw; his pale lashes dropped over his dark blue eyes. That foreshortened view of his face, so familiar to her since he had a passion for reading aloud, always struck her as masklike. Tonight when she longed for him to talk and not to read, it made him seem infinitely remote.

She glanced carefully at the clock. He had said that he would have to leave at ten and already it was nearly eight. At first she thought he was going to read her the whole sequence. Then, from the way he was turning over pages, smiling and soundlessly shaping words with his lips, she saw that he was choosing the poems very carefully.

At last he looked across at her with a curious expression. She could not decide whether it was angry or appealing.

'Come and sit by me,' he said, indicating the floor at his feet. Then when she was about to move, he frowned and said, 'No . . . stay where you are . . .'

She sat down, beginning to be irritable herself from the strain.

'I don't know where you distract me more . . . over there or close beside me.'

Clara's nerves were so much on edge that she snapped at him.

'Perhaps I'd be less distracting if I went out of the room.'

'I'm sorry. I'm in an abominable mood. Sit wherever you like.'

'I'll stay here,' she said coldly, longing to go and sit with her cheek against his knee.

He shrugged his shoulders; his eyes on the little red book.

'As you prefer.'

She clasped her hands in her lap in an effort to be calm.

'Read to me, Stephen.'

He looked at her then.

'Oh, my dear, why is life so infernally difficult?'

'Is yours being infernally difficult?'

'Infernally.'

'Can't you tell me why?'

'Perhaps . . . at some point. Meanwhile . . . *Shropshire Lad.*'

He began to read, apparently at random. He always read beautifully but tonight there was a peculiar edge to his voice which gave each familiar poem a new poignancy. Listening to him Clara forgot all her resentment. She had been childish she told herself. She was closer to him as he read these words he loved than through talk or even touch. Human contact was difficult for him as she knew; he shied off, suspicious or mocking, from any show of feeling. But the words built up a safe sphere where they could meet. She lay back in her chair, watching him through half-closed eyes, allowing herself the luxury of feeling all her love for him. When he came to 'Into my heart an air that kills,' he shut the book and repeated softly, staring into the fire:

> 'This is the land of lost content
> I see it shining plain
> Those happy highways where I went
> And shall not come again.'

Clara, too, looked into the fire. It was the poem which always moved her most; taking her straight back to the summers of her childhood at Paget's Fold, to that Sussex landscape which she would always see in a peculiar light, at once homely and magical.

The spires and farms would always be those of Bellhurst and the 'blue remembered hills' the downs. But, tonight, Stephen said the last lines with such finality that she came out of her nostalgic dream.

'Stephen.'

'Yes?' He kept his eyes averted.

'You read that . . . as if . . . as if you had lost something in particular.'

'Perhaps I have. Perhaps I never had it.'

'You wouldn't tell me what it was?'

He jerked himself round to face her.

'Some questions are better not asked. Let's have something more cheerful. Here's some good advice for you, Clara.' He pointed an admonishing finger at her as he read, smiling.

'When I was one-and-twenty.'

When he had finished, she smiled too.

'I wonder how many times you've given me *that* advice.'

'But have you taken it? *Have* you kept your fancy free?'

'You'd be the last to know if I hadn't?'

He looked at her curiously.

'Would I? I wonder.'

She shook her head.

'I *am* one-and-twenty. No use to talk to me.'

'Idiot girl. Can't you see I'm trying to be sensible? I don't want you to be miserable and full of regrets at twenty-two. And frankly, I don't want to have regrets myself. Of course I *shall*. Either way.'

Clara sighed.

'I wish you wouldn't always be quite so ambiguous.'

'I'm an ambiguous character. Dense as you are, you must have grasped *that*.'

'I never know what to believe about you. Least of all the things you say about yourself.'

'I'm an actor first and last. That's all there is to it.'

'Oh, *no*, Stephen. There's much, much more,' she said eagerly.

'I hoped you'd say that. You always rise so beautifully.' He held out his arms, 'Come over here.'

She knelt again between his knees. He turned up her face and looked into it.

'I like seeing my reflection in your eyes,' he said. Then, half smiling, he repeated:

> 'Oh, when I was in love with you
> Then I was clean and brave
> And miles around the wonder grew
> How well did I behave.'

'I *have* behaved well, haven't I, Clara?'

She tried to twist her face out of his hands, but he held it firm.

'How bright your eyes are tonight,' he said.

'All the better to see yourself in,' she said, forcing a smile.

'Clara . . . don't tell me those are tears.'

'Of course not.' She blinked them away before they fell.

He released her face and leant back in his chair. His face was troubled.

'Clara.'

'Yes, Stephen.'

'Is it just my middle-aged vanity? Or . . .' He scrutinised her face. 'Or do you really . . . are you really . . .?' The muttered unfinished question ended in a mere movement of his lips.

Clara's heart gave a violent lurch. Unable to meet Stephen's eyes, she stared down at her clasped hands. At last she said in a voice so rigorously controlled that it sounded impersonal:

'In love with you? Yes, I am.'

After the effort of saying it, she felt quite empty. She looked up dizzily, anywhere but at Stephen's face. Beyond his head the room swam out of focus. She became acutely aware of the cramp in her knees, the fire scorching her left cheek, the smell of Stephen's tweed jacket. She felt him take her hands and separate the clenched fingers; she heard him say softly:

'Dear child. Dear Clara. I want you terribly. But, sweetheart, it wouldn't work. For either of us.'

One part of her longed only to give up completely, to throw herself into his arms and forget the long, tortuous game they had played for so many months. Desire, beyond anything she had believed herself capable of feeling, ran through her like an electric shock. Her flesh, her very bones, seemed to be melting. Yet her other part held her in such iron control that her voice sounded dry, almost cold as she asked:

'Why not?'

'I'm a rotten bet for any woman. Least of all, a child like you.'

'As if I cared,' she said fiercely. 'Do you think I'm afraid of being unhappy?'

'That proves what a child you are. You don't know what unhappiness means.'

'Of course.' Her voice was bitter. 'I've spent all my life in a pinafore picking daisies. I forgot. You're the only person who's ever suffered, aren't you?'

He loosened his hold on her hands and looked at her in such surprise that she had an insane desire to laugh. She watched him trying to recover his old mocking look.

'You little Tartar,' he said. 'I'll begin to believe you *are* a woman in a moment. Having just said you love me, you proceed to glare at me as if you hated me.'

'I almost do at moments. But only because you won't see . . . And now you force me to admit . . .' Her lips went too dry to go on. She sat back on her heels, knotting her hands and swallowing hard.

Stephen turned very white. He said uncertainly:

'You frighten me a little. I do love you in my fashion, you know.'

'Do you?' she said sadly, feeling her sudden strength ebb away.

'I suppose I'm too old to have such violent emotions any more,' he said slowly. 'Perhaps I never did *feel* them. Only imagine them when I'm playing a part.'

56

'I could do with awfully little,' she said, managing a smile.

'That's what you think.' He risked a smile himself. 'But you ought to have a great deal. Oh, don't imagine I'm not tempted. I saw a cornflower in Flanders once, flowering away on the top of a parapet. I just had the decency not to pick it and to let it go on flowering away.'

'How do you know it mightn't have preferred to wither in your buttonhole?'

He laughed and pulled her hair.

'I'll remember you long after you've forgotten me. Young girls are always in and out of love.'

'I'm not a flapper. I've had silly flirtations and tried to persuade myself I was in love. But I never have been . . . before.'

'What about this chap you nearly married?'

She said after a pause:

'Archie? That was something quite different. I never even imagined I was in love with him.'

'Sorry for him . . . was that it?'

Clara frowned and said slowly: 'Partly that. It's so hard to explain. He'd been awfully good to me when something horrible happened. I was so absolutely numb and dead after that . . . that thing . . . I didn't think I could really feel anything again. We were both in it. He wanted very much to marry me. It seemed the only thing left . . . to try and give him at least . . .' she broke off. 'Oh, it sounds so disgustingly priggish.'

'I suspect you of a morbid streak of self-sacrifice,' said Stephen. 'Thank heavens you had the sense to break it off.'

'I'm glad now,' she said soberly, finding courage to look at him again.

'You strange child. I almost believe you when you say I'm the first. I'm a very weak character, my dear. When you look at me like that . . . I almost wonder . . .' He paused and shook his head. 'No, it wouldn't do. It wouldn't do at all. You must be firm with me, Clara. It would be sheer madness to ask you to marry me.'

'Would it?' Her heart was beating fast but she managed to speak as calmly as if they were discussing something quite impersonal.

He groaned: 'God knows. I don't. It might be the only sensible thing I ever did. I told you. Life's infernally difficult at the moment.'

'If you'd only tell me why.'

'Better not. Things work out if one leaves them alone. Put your nice little cold hand on my forehead.'

She passed her fingers very lightly over the dry skin stretched so tightly over the bone.

'Your head's very hot.'

He closed his eyes.

'Yes. Go on. It's like being stroked by a flower.'

He pulled down one of her hands and kissed the palm. 'To throw all this away,' he said as if to himself.

'You haven't – yet.'

He opened his eyes and smiled.

'Damn it, Clara. I'm no good at noble gestures. Put up with me a little longer . . . can you?'

'Of course.'

'Good. Come kiss me, sweet and twenty.'

The kiss was a gentle one. Clara's fever had subsided, leaving only tenderness. They sat in silence for a time, her head against his knee.

He said suddenly: 'You've no idea what hell it is being an artist.'

'I suppose not.'

'You're marvellously sensitive – marvellously responsive. That's why it's so refreshing to be with you. But you don't know what it is to feel a power in yourself that must be used or you might as well be dead. It's so damnable to be an actor. A poet or a painter creates his own material. But an actor's got to have a part. He's got to beg and grovel and push for the chance of getting one. Of all the frustrating, humiliating professions.'

She had never heard him speak with such violence. She said consolingly:

'At least you're going to play Richard.'

'I'm going to play Richard. And nothing is going to stop me from playing Richard.'

'Don't growl at me as if I were trying to.'

He kissed the top of her head.

'Silly child. What a pity you can't play my Queen. Delightful little part. And just right for you.'

'Oh . . . I wish I could.'

'No hope,' he said hastily. 'All cast down to the understudies.'

'Is Miss Lane playing it?'

'Good Lord, no. The part's too light and her voice is too heavy. No. Some quite adequate young piece who played it at Stratford. Remember doing Katherine to my Henry V?'

'Of course. What ages ago that seems.'

'Very nice performance. Best thing you ever did. You've got something sometimes though you can be unspeakably bad. Your Mélisande . . . you know that was really rather exquisite. God knows why. You had no technique but at least you had no tricks. I suppose it was moving just because it was so naïve. There's something rather lost and ghostly about you sometimes, my sweet, though you look such a nice solid little milkmaid.'

'I expect the red hair and the white make-up helped,' said Clara, storing up her qualified compliment. 'Daddy didn't recognise me at first. It was the only part he ever liked seeing me in though he can't bear Maeterlinck.'

'Did he see us in *Henry V?*'

'Yes. He thought you were wonderful. But he's frightfully prejudiced. He can't bear seeing anyone kiss me on the stage.'

'Hmm. Good old Freud.'

'Freud?'

'Some Viennese bore Eliza's got a bee in her bonnet about. Let it go.'

'I'm getting practically illiterate,' she sighed.

'Never mind. Intellectual women can be appallingly tiresome.'

'You do despise women, don't you? Women can't think. Women can't write. What *can* women do?'

He pulled her hair.

'I know one who can be rather endearing. Even when she's spitting like an angry kitten. How you hate being teased.'

'I might get broken in to it.'

'Then it would be no fun. Do you think I'm a heartless character, Clara?'

She said slowly: 'I *am* inclined to wonder sometimes. Not that it matters, I suppose.'

'If I laugh at you, don't I laugh at myself? If I torment you, don't I torment myself more?'

Something in his tone jarred on her. The words sounded like a line from a play. He spoke them as if listening to the sound of his own voice; almost as if he might repeat them, trying a different inflection. She glanced up at him without speaking.

'Why the cynical smile, Clara? Don't you believe me?'

'Not entirely.'

'Perhaps you're right. You're an honest wench. Could you make an honest man of me?'

'I'm not all that honest.'

He laughed, putting his arm round her. The clock on the mantelpiece, among the china dogs and nicknacks, began to strike.

'Good God . . . whatever's the time? It can't be ten already.' He stood up, almost pushing her away. 'I'll have to go. I've got to get this wretched car back to the garage in Lincoln by midnight. Otherwise there'll be the deuce to pay in every sense.'

Clara did not try to detain him. Painful as the wrench was, it was also a relief. She was tired and on edge. At any moment her carefully sustained calm might collapse. She might cling to him; even burst into tears.

Instead, she became defiantly practical; finding his coat, putting his matches and cigarettes in the pocket.

'Don't forget your notes and sketches.'

'Wonderful girl. I nearly forgot what I was supposed to be doing in Gainsborough. Hope I've collected enough to impress the management.'

He stood over her, looking solid in the old trench coat which disguised his leanness, and gathered her to him.

'Dear child . . . dear Clara,' he said, with his thin cheek against her hair. 'So difficult to leave. So delicious to come back to. Be patient with me a little longer.'

'Oh Stephen . . . of course.' She pressed her face against his shoulder, trying to feel its warmth through the harsh, stiff material that smelt of benzine and tobacco.

He disengaged her gently and, holding her face in his hands, gave her a long intent look. 'I want to think of you in here . . . in this enchanting, appalling room. With your golden hair all tangled and one cheek as red as if someone had slapped it.'

He moved slowly away from her, singing under his breath.

> 'And from her company I could not go
> But when I waked . . . it was not so . . .
> In you-outh is pleasure
> In you-outh is pleasure.'

His voice cracked on the last note and he laughed.

'Ruined my exit.'

He sketched a mock salute and was gone, closing the door noiselessly behind him. Clara stood staring at the brown varnished panels and the strip of red rep, fringed with bobbles, which still trembled where Stephen's head had brushed them. When she heard the click of the front door, she knelt on the hearthrug in front of the chair where he had been sitting and buried her head in it, stuffing her fingers in her ears to deaden the sound of the starting up of the car.

7

Clara was not surprised to receive no letter from Stephen after that Sunday. He had warned her that *Richard II* was going into rehearsal at once and opened in Oxford in three weeks' time. She restrained herself from writing more than a note when she sent him back the *Shropshire Lad* he had left behind, determined not to intrude herself while he was concentrating on his part.

Refusing to allow herself to write to him only increased her obsession. She carried on incessant imaginary dialogues with him; she recalled every word, every look, every gesture in the attempt to interpret them honestly. Never did she suppose that he loved her as she loved him but she was convinced that she could put up with any suffering, any humiliation if only Stephen would allow her to marry him.

Maidie noticed her abstraction but mercifully made no comment for several days. At last she burst out:

'You're always up in the moon. What is it? That fellow that turned up in Gainsborough? I oughtn't to have left you without a chaperone.'

'I don't think a chaperone would have helped.'

'Hmm,' said Maidie suspiciously. 'You were always vague, God knows. But ever since that Sunday you've been positively soupy.

Almost mental, you look sometimes. Look here, Vere, I'm your pal. If you've got anything on your mind, old thing, you can spit it out to me.'

'It's sweet of you, Maidie. But I don't think anyone can help.'

Maidie looked at her anxiously.

'I say . . . you don't suspect the worst, do you?'

'What do you mean by the worst?'

'Come off it. Or didn't your famous education include the facts of life?'

Clara felt herself flush.

'Oh no . . . I've never . . .'

'Well, that's a weight off your mind, anyway. After all, even good Catholics have been known to fall. I always feel sorry for the ones that get caught. It's another mortal sin if they do anything about it. What *is* eating you then?'

'Wondering what he really feels, I suppose.'

'Is that all?' said Maidie contemptuously. 'I thought it was something serious. One of these days you'll come down to earth and give your fanny a nasty bump.'

The following week the company moved to Birmingham. One night, as Clara was changing for the third act, the stage doorkeeper handed in a card. It was Archie Hughes-Follett's. On the back was scribbled: 'Will you have supper with me after the show? Please say yes.'

'Can I tell the gentleman you'll see him, Miss?' asked the doorkeeper. He winked at Clara with the affability of one who has been well tipped. She said, after a moment's hesitation: 'Yes.'

'Not *him*, is it?' asked Maidie, dipping a hairpin in a heated spoon and carefully renewing a blob of black on one of her long lashes.

'No. Just someone I used to know ages ago.'

'Thought you didn't sound keen. What's wrong with this one?'

'Nothing. Only . . . we were once engaged and I haven't seen him since.'

Maidie swung round.

63

'What an old dark horse you are. *Two* fellows in your life.' She snatched the card and ran a finger over it.

'Classy card. Engraved, not just printed. If you've really done with him . . . you might pass him on. What a knut's name! *Is* he a knut?'

'Quite the reverse. You'd be awfully disappointed.'

'I don't believe a word you say these days, Vere. And I used to think you such a truthful little thing.'

All through the last act, Maidie was in her most mischievous mood. When they were upstage together for several minutes she did her best to dry Clara up by singing under her breath:

> 'I'm Archie the starchy
> The knut with a K
> Pride of Piccadilly
> The blasé roué.'

In the dressing-room she exclaimed with horror at Clara's crumpled skirt and the hole in her jumper.

'How often have I told you . . . be prepared. You look like something the cat's brought home.'

'The worse I look, the better.'

Maidie rolled her big blue eyes at the dresser and tapped her own forehead.

''Spathetic, isn't it, Millie? Almost normal to look at but Mary Rose isn't in it.'

She glanced approvingly at her own trim reflection.

'Now I could go out to supper anywhere and not disgrace a fellow. Instead of which I've got to go home to fish and chips all on my lonesome. I've a good mind to get in first with your Johnnie.'

'You can if you like.'

'Oh no,' said Maidie, pursing her small mouth, 'I never trespass. I'll go and get the boys to walk back with me. I don't like going home alone after dark in big cities. Ta ta.'

She went off singing:

> 'Mary Rose. Mary Rose
> No one ever found out where she goes
> Now she wears undies made of silk
> Comes home at daybreak with the milk.'

Clara had dawdled over her changing, partly because of her natural slowness, partly from reluctance to face Archie. Not that she felt embarrassed or even curious. Her only feeling was one of resentment that he was not Stephen. When at last she opened the dressing-room door, he was just outside, leaning patiently against the damp brick wall of the passage. The light was too dim for her to see his face clearly but his dark red hair was as untidy as ever. He swooped down at her from his immense height, seemed about to embrace her and then dropped his long arms to his sides with one of his old clumsy gestures that she remembered so well.

'Clara,' he said rather thickly, 'Lord, I'm glad you've come. I was afraid you'd given me the slip. I've got a taxi. We may as well go to the Midland. I'm staying there.'

He said little on the way beyond saying that he had seen the show and that it was out of the ark but that she had been simply topping. He seemed uneasy, almost bored; he frequently interrupted her to curse at the driver for not going faster.

'They'll be shut if the blighter doesn't hurry. I must have a drink.'

The Archie she had known four years ago had not been so desperately concerned with closing time. Even when they were seated opposite each other in the great padded dining-room that smelt of cigars, he did not so much as glance at her until he had caught the wine-waiter's eye.

'What do you want? Still like champagne? All right . . . a bottle of 35. But bring me a double whisky right away.'

While he ordered their drinks, she studied Archie's face. After the incisive modelling of Stephen's its bluntness was almost repellent. His features still had the oddly unfinished look they had had at nineteen. Nevertheless he had changed considerably in four years. There were grooves on either side of his mouth; both his skin and the dark red hair which fell more untidily than ever over his low forehead had a dusty look; the eyes she remembered as so clear were yellowish and slightly bloodshot. The hand which held the menu shook a little. It was the unexpectedly shapely hand she knew but the long fingers were deeply stained with nicotine and the nails dirty. Archie had always been untidy: now he looked almost dissolute. He had always treated his clothes brutally. Good though the ones he had on were, they produced an effect of forlorn shabbiness. However, catching sight of herself in a vast gold-framed mirror, Clara told herself she had no right to be critical.

'We look a pair,' she thought, surveying her untidy bunches of hair, her faded jumper with a streak of grease-paint at the neck. The thought filled her with a peculiar dismay.

As if he guessed it he said: 'You're not furious with me for dragging you out like this without warning?'

'Of course not.'

'I thought it was the best way. Take you by surprise. I'm no good at writing letters anyway.'

His whisky arrived and he drained it as if it were medicine.

'God, I needed that. I didn't dare dash round the corner in case I missed you at the theatre.'

'Daddy told you where we were playing?'

'Yes, bless him. I thought you'd rather I turned up this week than . . . well . . . in Worcester.'

She glanced at him kindly for the first time. He averted his eyes and said hurriedly:

'What a nice chap your father is. My God, you're lucky, Clara. You should have known mine.'

She crumbled her roll. 'I was awfully sorry about your mother, Archie.'

He frowned.

'Sweet of you to write. Yes, I miss her a good bit. Of course her heart had been bad for a long time. She didn't tell me at first. But she knew even at Crickleham that it might suddenly give out.'

Clara wondered guiltily whether that had been another secret reason why both his mother and Lady Cressett had been so anxious for them to get married.

She said hastily: 'What exactly were you doing in South America? Did you like it?'

'Loathed it,' he said emphatically. 'What was I doing? Supposed to be learning the job from the bottom in some wretched business Papa had a lot of shares in. The bottom was bad enough but heaven help me from getting to the top. Can you see me in a bowler hat as a company director?'

She smiled naturally for the first time.

'Why ever did you go in for it?'

'No choice. My guardian just shipped me abroad.'

'Guardian? But you're over twenty-one.'

'Hell yes. Nearly twenty-three,' he said gloomily. 'Mamma's dying messed up everything. As long as she was alive, she had control of the money. She let me have all I wanted. But Papa left a frightful will. He hated me . . . Yes, even Mamma admitted it. So he tied up everything so that I can't touch it till I'm twenty-five. I get an allowance of £300 a year and not a penny more.'

'Not too bad for doing nothing. My salary's just half that,' said Clara, with the superiority of the wage-earner.

'It goes nowhere with the sort of things I *like* doing. And I can't get round my guardian. Papa chose my beastliest uncle because he shared his opinion of me. The idea was to drive me into some ghastly job.'

'Well, you'll soon be free of it all.'

'Only if I behave myself according to their ideas. If I borrow so much as a fiver on my prospects, they clamp on the guardian business till I'm thirty. *Thirty* . . . Might as well say till I'm dead.'

'I'm sure we oughtn't to be drinking champagne.'

'It's the first week of the month. Anyway I had a few quid left over from my South American screw when I landed. They gave me a month's salary instead of notice. I made enough at poker to pay for my drinks on the boat.'

'Were you sacked?' she asked diffidently.

'Certainly I was sacked. For being drunk, if you want to know. How the hell my uncle expects me to live on six quid a week with whisky at 12/6 a bottle.'

Still more diffidently, Clara said: 'Whisky's a necessity, is it?'

'It most definitely is.'

They ate and drank for some moments in silence. Never had champagne seemed less festive to Clara. Her parents were right: Archie had certainly changed. She remembered him as an odd creature, clumsy and kind, who did not fit into the grown-up world. Often he had sulked like a schoolboy but never had she seen him in this mood of aggressive bitterness. Tonight he had hardly smiled: in repose, his face was set in lines of angry discontent. She felt a pang of guilt.

'Go on, say it,' he muttered. 'You think I'm a pretty poor specimen, don't you? Well, you're probably right.'

She said uncomfortably: 'Of course I don't. I expect the war . . .'

'The war? Everyone blames the poor ruddy old war. I didn't mind the war. Apart from a couple of scratches I had a cushy time compared to most. Anyway, it took one's mind off things. Don't think I'm being sentimental when I say I jolly well wish I'd been killed.'

'Oh, Archie.'

'Don't worry, old thing. I was only explaining that it wasn't the war. Then I only used to drink in a cheery sort of way and get tight once in a while like anyone else. And afterwards, I chugged along somehow. Mamma was so bucked that I'd survived that she was quite happy to let me mess about in my own way. But since she died and they cut off my supplies and treated me like some sort of mental defective – well, can you wonder it's the only thing that makes me feel human?' He drained his glass of champagne. 'Chin-chin.'

'Chin-chin,' Clara echoed faintly, swallowing the flat remains of her own.

'Fill up. You're drinking like a sparrow.'

She shook her head.

'All girls on the stage I ever knew liked bubbly. But then you never were like anyone else. I can't get over your being an actress. Gosh, I envy you.'

'I always wonder why you didn't become a singer with that voice of yours.'

'Oh, I still sing sometimes. But I'd loathe to be a concert singer. The theatre's the only thing I'm keen on. Used to get up amateur shows in that beastly Santiago. I'm quite hot at lighting effects.'

'You were always brilliant at anything mechanical. Remember your model railway at Crickleham?'

'About all I'm good for,' said Archie gloomily. 'Fixing up models and playing with switchboards.' He sighed. 'Fancy your remembering the old railway. I was crazier about it than any kid when I first fixed *that* up. Then I came to hate the sight of it.'

Clara flushed with shame at her clumsiness. She was the first person to whom he had shown his treasure. He had always said that it was while they were playing with his toy trains that he had first fallen in love with her. And it was by the model railway, two days after Charles's death, that, having refused him once, she had told Archie she would marry him.

She said hastily:

'That very first day at Crickleham, you told me your great ambition was to go on the stage.'

'No one'd look at a great gawk of six foot four as an actor. That stage manager of yours, Lister, quite agreed.'

'Lister!' exclaimed Clara. 'Wherever did you meet him?'

'In the bar, in the first interval. Told him I was a friend of yours and stood him a couple. You don't mind, do you?'

'Why should I?'

Looking at him, she saw, for the first time that evening, the old puzzled, yet eager expression she remembered. Until that moment, she and Archie might almost have been old acquaintances who had met again by chance. He said hesitantly:

'Actually I wanted to have a word with him about you. Your career and all that. D'you know what he said? "If someone could back that kid in a good part that suits her, she might go far."' Archie suddenly banged his nicotine-stained fist on the table. 'Hell . . . when I think of all that cash lying there and I can't touch it for two bloody years. And here you are playing a rotten little part in a rotten old piece that'll pack up in a few weeks anyway. What happens then?'

Clara sighed.

'I've no idea. But if you *had* money, Archie, you don't think I'd let you throw it away on backing me? I'll never be a great actress.'

'I believe in you,' he said stubbornly. 'I believe you could do any ruddy thing if you were given a decent chance.' Suddenly he buried his head in his hands and groaned. 'What the hell's the good of talking? It's even more hopeless now than it was *then*.'

Until this moment Clara had almost convinced herself that he had forgotten their past. Now he raised his head and exposed a face so wretched that her heart sank.

'I swore to myself I wouldn't say a word tonight. But seeing you sitting there is too much. All these years I've been thinking: "What will it be like if I meet her again?" D'you know I almost wish I'd come back and found you were married? Then I'd have known there wasn't an earthly.'

'I hoped you'd got over it all,' she said in dismay. 'I'm sure you have really.'

He shook his head.

'Not a bit of it. Believe me, I've tried. I've gone around with plenty of girls. Damn pretty ones, some of them. But it's no good. There's only one Clara.' He leant across the table: 'I'll tell you something queer. Tonight when we came in here and I saw you properly for the first time I thought for one marvellous moment I was cured. I know I've changed the hell of a lot. But you've changed, too. On the stage, you looked just like the girl I used to know. But off . . . forgive me – you're not quite as pretty as you used to be. In fact, tonight you look a bit of a mess.'

'I know,' she said ruefully.

'But I'm not put off,' he went on. 'I realise now that it's as bad as ever – if not worse. I don't care what you look like. Wouldn't matter if you had smallpox. There can't be anyone else for me ever. It's a rum go, isn't it?'

Clara could only sigh. If Stephen had said those words, they would have meant joy beyond her wildest hopes. Coming from Archie they were meaningless. Yet she felt a deeper sympathy with Archie than she had ever felt before. She said at last:

'Oh, why can't things be simple? Why can't we fall in love with the people who love us?'

'*Are* you in love with someone, Clara?'

She nodded.

'You don't mean he's such an ass as not to love you?'

'He may a little. Nothing like as much as I do,' she broke off, ashamed. 'It's beastly to talk to *you* like this.'

'Don't worry. It's almost a comfort, in a funny way, that you should be in the same boat.'

She felt a sudden kindness, almost warmth towards him. His shabbiness, his air of dissipation no longer seemed repellent. She saw them as the livery of his suffering.

'That's why you look different, perhaps,' he said, 'God, this man must be a fool. And here am I. Nothing in the world I wouldn't do to make you happy. I'm so crazy to marry you, I'd take you on any terms. I wouldn't expect you to love me now any more than I did then.'

'Dear Archie, it would be crazy.'

'For you, yes. Worse than before. At least I had some cash in those days.'

'That's not the reason.'

71

'No. But it would have sweetened the pill. We could have got around, done anything you fancied. Without it, I'd bore you to tears. D'you know I still enjoy playing kid games like we used to . . .' He broke off. 'God, what a clumsy swine. That shows you.'

'It's all right. I hardly ever think about that now.'

But as she spoke, she knew that she had begun to think about it again. When she had been Charles Cressett's governess and Archie used to come over to Maryhall on every possible occasion the three of them had spent their time acting out elaborate spy-games. It was in the course of one of them that Charles had been killed. They were silent for some moments and the silence brought them closer than any words.

'I've been to Maryhall since I came back,' Archie said at last. 'Theresa Cressett sent you her love.'

'How is she?' Clara asked eagerly.

'The same as ever. That woman's a saint. She talks about the boy quite happily now.'

'I don't think I could bear to go there again. Anyway it's out of the question.'

'Not with her. It's only Sir George and . . .'

'Nan? Is *she* still there?'

'Oh yes. For life. I found it jolly hard to be civil to her.' He glanced downwards. 'You still have a scar on your wrist.'

'She was hysterical. She didn't know what she was doing.' Clara paused, remembering the small, furious figure of Charles's nurse stabbing at her with the cutting-out shears. But for Archie, she might be maimed, even dead. 'It all seems so long ago. Like something in another life.'

'I thought that. Yet when I went back this time, it all seemed exactly the same. I suppose I oughtn't to say this. But Theresa still keeps harping on *us*.'

'You don't mean she still thinks we . . .'

'More than ever. You know what she's like. She never gets away from religion for a moment. Thinks you might reform me and do your own soul no end of good.'

'As if I could reform anyone!'

'Well, no one else could. And I'm not going to give 'em a chance to try. I oughtn't to have told you. I'm probably a little tight. Which reminds me, I badly need another drink. You couldn't face coming up to my room? I've got a bottle of whisky there.'

She shook her head.

'It's awfully late. I must go soon.'

'O.K. I'll do without. That shows you how much I feel like going on talking and to hell with the consequences.'

'Say anything you like.'

'Maryhall,' he said slowly with his old puzzled look. 'Something rather queer about that. I said *it* hadn't changed. Of course you and I *have*. But up there I felt as if we *hadn't*. As if I was the old Archie coming chugging up on my motorbike to have tea in the schoolroom with you . . . and Charles. And you were the old Clara, rushing round playing the Schweinhund games with her hair tumbling down. It was so real that I used to find myself having long talks with you.'

He hit his forehead with his closed fist – a gesture she remembered from those days.

'I'm hopeless at explaining. Always was. D'you know when I was telling you that I had that feeling again? You'll think I really am tight and seeing double. But it's as if I *were* double. You too – as if the two of us as we are *now* were here in this beastly dining-room in Brum *and* up there as we were then. Am I mad?'

She looked at him with startled interest.

'If so, I am too. I know that double feeling. I had it after Charles was killed. For months, off and on. I have it now sometimes.' She broke off, frowning. When she went on, her voice was a little out of control. 'I don't believe I've ever been quite real since. Not a whole person. As if some part of me died when Charles did. If I could only go back to before it happened.' She stopped, almost in tears, half frightened by what she had said: half wondering if she really meant it. Archie put his hand over hers and she did not draw it away.

73

For the first time they stared full in each other's eyes. At that moment, his struck her as beautiful. They seemed to have an independent life; as if another, unknown Archie existed in the darkness of those distended pupils.

It was he who glanced away first. Immediately she was seized with revulsion against herself and against Archie. It was as if by those words, by that look she had betrayed Stephen. Her whole body seemed to harden against the ugly young man who sat with his head bent forward, staring at the mess of cigarette ends among the crumbs of his roll. Coldly she noted every detail of his appearance that irritated her: the large, slightly inflamed nose that looked, from that angle, like a clown's; the flakes of scurf on his untidy red hair. When he raised his eyes to hers again, she saw only the discoloured whites and the film that drink had put over them. She drew her hand, which was still touching his, sharply away.

He made a grimace which deepened those new grooves beside his mouth.

'What's up? Now you're looking at me as if I were a leper or something.'

She bit her lip, ashamed of herself, yet all the more irritated with him for having noticed.

'O.K. You needn't tell me,' he said roughly. Some feeling she had never seen distorted his odd, unfinished face. For a moment she felt almost frightened of him.

'I'm no good to you,' she said. 'Or to anyone probably. It would be much better if you'd never set eyes on me.'

'Shut up.' His voice was cold with anger. 'We'd better be going. I'll see you back to your place.'

Walking by him in the darkness, almost in silence, she began to feel remorseful. As they turned into her street, she said:

'I'm sorry, Archie. It sounds so false, I know. But I do wish you could be happy.'

He gave a curious laugh.

'Happy! You're a nice one to talk.'

'Why?'

'Well, you're not exactly happy yourself, are you? Bloody *un*happy, it strikes me.'

Outside the house he stopped.

'Forget all about tonight. Except for one thing . . .

'Yes, Archie?'

'If ever you want me . . . for anything . . . I'm always there. If you don't mind, I may stick around in this town for a few days. Not entirely because of you. I won't even speak to you if you'd rather not.'

'But that's ridiculous.'

'Everything's ridiculous if you ask me. I'd rather you married this chap whoever he is if it made *you* happy. And I'd rather marry you and be unhappy than marry anyone else. Doesn't make sense, does it?'

She said sadly:

'The second part makes sense to me.'

'Poor old darling. We seem to be in it together.'

He had used almost those very words four years ago. Tired and dazed as she was, they produced a peculiar effect. It was as if her mind were suddenly dislocated; as if the world consisted only of this dark doorstep and she and Archie were its only inhabitants. She swayed blindly towards him; he held her for a moment gently and, as gently, let her go.

8

For the rest of that week and all through the next, Archie haunted the theatre but made no attempt to see Clara alone. He left the Midland and took a room in the same house as Lister. When *A Clerical Error* moved on to Coventry, Archie moved with them and again shared Lister's digs. The two became so inseparable that Archie seemed like one of the company. He was backstage at every performance, chatting to the actors in their dressing-rooms or watching the electricians at the switchboard. Clara was amazed at the way he picked up not merely the language but the whole sense of the theatre. He learnt more in two days than she had learnt in two years. Every detail, from lighting to make-up, seemed to fascinate him. He studied each move of the play, the placing of each piece of furniture. Once, when Sam Brilliant was late, she saw him arranging the props table with great efficiency. At first she had thought that Lister regarded Archie mainly as a source of free drinks but, one night, she overheard the stage manager say to Merton Mordish:

'That boy's got something. I thought at first he was just a young ass who fancied himself stage-struck because he was keen on Clara.'

'I agree,' trumpeted Mordish. 'Pity he's so tall. I believe he might have some notion of acting if I had the coaching of him.'

'Can't see him as an actor,' said Lister. 'But I *can* see him being useful on production. Got the hang of the switchboard in no time. Made a damn sensible suggestion about the lighting at the end of Act II.'

He looked round, and, evidently not seeing Clara where she stood in a doorway, said so low that she only just caught it: 'I tell you, Merton, if we didn't look like packing up so soon, I'd sack that cocky idle yid Sam and give Archie a try-out as A.S.M.'

Overhearing this gave Clara a certain sense of guilt. All his life Archie had been looked on as an amiable fool. She asked herself what right she had to feel superior to him. What was she, after all, but a mediocre actress with the knack of writing advertisements and cheap short stories?

During the scene change in the second act she hunted him out and, beckoning him into a corner behind the backcloth, told him what she had heard.

His face lit up.

'You don't know how bucked I feel. Especially at your bothering to come and tell me. Two bits of luck in one day. It's almost too much.'

'What's the other?'

'Something I heard this morning. I've been dying to come and tell you. But I didn't want to make a nuisance of myself.'

The silence on the stage warned them that the curtain would be going up at any moment. She whispered:

'Come round to our dressing-room after the show.'

Maidie, like the rest of the company, had long ago accepted Archie as almost one of them and no longer seemed to regard him as Clara's special concern. That night, however, she observed:

'Your Archie's always in Jimmy Lister's pocket these days. What's Jimmy up to? Trying to get him to put money into a show?'

'He hasn't got any money.'

'He'll have oodles one day, won't he? I guess Jimmy knows

which side his bread's buttered even if you don't. Still, for once I think you showed a spot of sense turning him down. Mark you, I rather like old Starchy even if he does drink a lot more than is good for him.'

'Archie's dying to get into the theatre. I suppose he thinks Lister might help him.'

'Funny ambition for a *boy* of that class. I mean his uncle's got a title, hasn't he? Though . . . pardon my mentioning it, Vere, you'd hardly guess it, would you?'

'Archie was never a snob, if that's what you mean.'

'Snob! He goes a bit too far the other way, if you ask me. Honestly, sometimes you'd think he hadn't been as well brought up as Peter and Trev. You wouldn't think a real gentleman would want to hang round bars all day with a squirt like Lister.'

'I suppose he's always been rather a misfit in his own class. He hates the sort of conventional life he's expected to lead.'

'Unnatural, I call it,' said Maidie, sniffing delicately. 'I don't think you ought to let your own class down.'

She went on removing her make-up in silence for a few moments before asking:

'Is he still keen on you, Vere? It seems to me it's the company he's hanging round nowadays more than you.'

'I'm glad if it is.'

'Did you give him the bird completely?'

'I'll *never* marry Archie,' Clara assured her.

'Most men would go and console themselves. I think there's something queer about that boy.'

Clara asked rather coldly what she meant. However humble she felt towards Stephen, she did not altogether like the implication that Archie's fidelity was so surprising.

'For one thing I don't believe he really likes girls. Don't look so flabbergasted. I don't mean he's like Peter and Trev. But I bet you he's never really got going with one.'

'Well . . . after all . . . he's a Catholic. If you mean what I think you mean.'

'I do and I don't. Some Catholic boys are ever so naughty and some find it ever so hard to be good. But I don't believe Archie's ever been really tempted. I don't believe he's the least bit passionate.'

'Perhaps you'd like to try your Munroe act with him?' suggested Clara acidly.

'Miaow! Puss! Puss!' said Maidie, winking a large blue eye. 'I believe you're jealous. You don't want Starchy yourself but you like to keep the poor chap dangling.' She broke off to call: 'Come in,' as someone knocked at the door. 'Well, talk of the devil. How's our Tiny tonight?'

'Rather braced with life,' said Archie, stooping his tall limp body as he edged through the dressing-room door. He answered with equal affability to his public nickname of Tiny or to Maidie's private one.

'Why? Come into a fortune, old thing?'

'A fortune for me as things are.' He glanced at Clara and patted his breast pocket. 'Guess what I've got in here. A cheque for two thousand ruddy quid.'

'You're kidding,' said Maidie, dropping her hairbrush and staring at him almost respectfully.

'No. Cross my heart.' He turned to Clara. 'Had a letter from my beastly Uncle this morning. Gosh, he hated having to part with it. But he had to. It's something under Mamma's will, not Papa's.'

'Archie, I'm so glad,' said Clara, trying hard not to be envious.

'Lucky pig. I should get him to give you a nice present, dear, before he blues the lot. My advice to you, old boy, is keep enough back to stand yourself a shave and haircut. You need 'em.'

'Spiteful little thing, aren't you?' He pulled one of the golden plaits Maidie was coiling up. 'As a matter of fact, I'm not going to blue it. Well, only a little anyway. God knows I need a bit of fun. And I must get myself some sort of a car. Haven't even a motorbike now.'

'Who gets the change – if any?'

'That's a secret at present.'

'Jimmy Lister, *I* bet,' said Maidie. 'Ba-aa! You ought to have a little blue ribbon round your neck, Tiny.'

'Jimmy's a good chap,' said Archie rather angrily. He glanced at Clara. '*He* doesn't think me such a bloody fool as Maidie does. If we go in together, he'll be in it as much as I will. Anyway I'm not talking . . . yet.'

'Since you're so thick with Lister,' said Maidie, suddenly serious, 'any truth in this idea the *Error* may pack up after Worcester next week? Or s'only a rumour?'

'You'd better ask him yourself.'

Clara forgot all about Archie's mysterious projects. If the rumour were true, she would be free the week after next, the very week that *Richard II* opened. It would not cost much to get from Worcester to Oxford. She began to make hasty calculations. When she next became conscious of the others' conversation, she heard Archie saying:

'Well, it's my last week for the time being anyway. So I want to have a farewell party. Jimmy says we can have it on the stage. Everyone's coming, even Miss Cooke. You'll both come, won't you?'

Only when she saw Archie's expression of delighted surprise and the half-conscious movement he made towards her did Clara realise that she must, in her excitement, have smiled at him as if he were Stephen.

The party on the Saturday night had a noisy, slightly desperate gaiety. Their notices had gone up the night before. Though they were not entirely unexpected, most of the company had hoped that they might book up for a few weeks more. For many it would mean a time of acute anxiety wondering if and when they would get another job. Clara, with a home to go to and the prospect of seeing Stephen so much sooner than she had dared to hope, felt too guilty to enter into the 'eat and drink for tomorrow we die' spirit of it. All the others, even Archie himself who was already so much more part of the company than she had ever been, had something to lose. She was the only one to whom the end of the tour came as an unmitigated relief.

Though she talked and laughed and danced with all comers, she remained a little detached and felt the rest were aware of it. All round her old feuds were being forgotten in the common anxiety of the prospect of being out of a job. People who only a few hours before had been saying the most spiteful things about each other were exchanging addresses and recommending agents. She saw the astonishing spectacle of Maidie and James standing with their arms round each other's waists and overheard the even more astonishing tributes Merton Mordish was paying to Brett Wilding.

'You know, old man . . . and I'm weighing every word I say . . . it would be criminal if you gave up playing juvenile for ten years at least. *Anno domini* doesn't mean a thing when you've got the *touch*. Given the right part, you could knock spots off Gerald.'

She was conscious all the time of Archie's presence, more conscious than he seemed to be of hers. She even caught herself out feeling a childish pique because he was not paying her any particular attention. He danced with her only once and during the dance talked only company shop. It was almost impossible to believe that only ten days ago he had been imploring her to marry him on any terms. She had been touched by that devotion she could not return. Though for his own sake she wanted him cured of it, it had been a comfort to know that someone felt for her as she felt for Stephen. Had his outburst in Birmingham been no more than a mood of drunken self-pity? Since he had become so passionately interested in the theatre, though he spent so much time in bars, he was, in fact, drinking less. Tonight he looked more like the boy she remembered four years ago. Yet there was a difference. Perhaps because he was being the success of the evening, his odd, blunt features no longer gave the impression of being unfinished. Lit up with excitement, his face was amusing, even attractive. For the first time in her life she saw

Archie as someone with whom other girls could conceivably fall in love.

Peter and Trevor came up to her as she was sitting momentarily alone on the canvas-covered steps of the set they used in the last act.

'Tst . . . fancy *you* being a wallflower, dear,' said Peter, putting his arm round her. 'You should have brought your knitting. *So* important to look as if you didn't care.'

'Tell us the facts, Clara,' said Trevor. '*Such* rumours are going round. They say Archie popped the question in Brum and you turned him down. And now he's come into a fortune and you're wishing you'd said "yes".'

Peter interrupted Clara's muddled attempt to explain.

'Of course she isn't. She's got other fish to fry. I saw you that Sunday in Gainsborough. Oo la la!'

'I didn't see you.'

'I know you didn't, dear. You were so occupied in gazing into somebody's eyes, you cut me dead. Don't blame you. The *most* marvellous-looking man.'

'*I* remember,' said Trevor. 'Peter raved about him. I got ever so jealous.'

'Too distinguished for words. That slightly hollow look.' He gave Trevor a malicious glance. 'A *real* blond, like that Norwegian chorus boy. Years older of course. But fearfully romantic-looking . . . that "I've got a secret sorrow" expression. Are you the secret sorrow, Clara?'

She said lightly: 'He looked just the same when I first met him.'

'I know the type,' said Trevor. 'Beware of them, Clara. They're absolute icicles, dear.'

'You got a touch of Norwegian frost-bite all right,' said Peter.

He began to sing, eyeing them alternately:

'The gipsy warned me
The gipsy *warned* me

82

He said to me "My child

He's a bad man . . . a very *bad* man!"'

Clara laughed and joined in.

'But I just calmly smiled.'

'Stop it you ruddy amateurs,' shouted Jimmy Lister. 'Maidie's going to oblige with some *singing*.'

Maidie had seated herself at the piano and was playing chords on its tinny keys. People stopped shrieking and laughing and sat down on the furniture of the set or on the stage itself. Archie propped himself against the piano, whispering to Maidie. Clara heard her say:

'Don't be bashful, Tiny. After all, you're paying for the drinks.'

She nodded at him and went into the prelude of 'If you were the only girl'.

Clara had forgotten how astonishingly good Archie's voice was. It rang out true and rich, without a tremor or a hint of forcing, so that for some moments she was lost in the sheer beauty of the sound. When Maidie joined in the duet, her pure clear notes were like silver against the gold of Archie's. Clara was fascinated by these two voices, each perfect of its kind and each so unexpected in the singer. The voices, singing the absurd song with the utmost seriousness, seemed as remote from Archie and Maidie as two angels. Yet they belonged to these two strange creatures; they were perhaps more truly Archie and Maidie than the selves they presented to the world. All round her, people had assumed unfamiliar faces. Lister's coarse, shrewd features wore an expression of innocent yearning; Mordish had a look of inspired anger like an old priest reproving the devil; Trevor, pale as wax, seemed, with his closed eyes and lips parted in a faint smile, just to have died an edifying death. Everywhere faces perhaps unknown to the owners were revealed through the familiar masks.

She wondered what face she herself was assuming as she became, like the rest, involved in the dated, potent song. If 'Tipperary' would for ever call up the marching privates of '14–'18, 'The Only Girl' was the eternal theme song of the subaltern on leave. Innumerable 'only girls' had pressed their bobbed or piled-up hair against a khaki shoulder to the sounds of it in the soft lights of Ciro's or the Four Hundred. Innumerable 'only boys' had played it over and over on scratched records in their dugouts. Clara could remember her father vamping it on the piano on Sunday mornings in Valetta Road; the only song he had learnt since he came down from Cambridge twenty years before the war. He had picked it up from his subaltern ex-pupils and sung it till so many of them had been killed that he could no longer bear the tune. She remembered how he had once liked to sing it with her, looking at her with a glint in his eyes that forced her to play up to him as she sang. Once, afterwards, he had sighed and said: 'Cheap sentiment, I grant you. Yet what, after all, but the universal aspiration of the human race? The garden of Eden. Plato's divided creatures eternally seeking their lost halves.'

Archie and Maidie, gazing into each other's eyes, slowed down to their last bars. Clara felt a double twinge of envy and jealousy. Envy of Archie for being able to do one thing supremely well was mean, but rational. It was harder to scold herself out of the jealousy which was not only mean but unreasonable. However, as the last notes thinned away, Archie turned his head and looked straight at her with such fervour that she knew his feelings had not changed. Her absurd relief made her more ashamed of herself than ever.

When the song was over, she made no attempt to join the people who rushed up to him, slapping him on the back and extravagantly praising his singing. Some minutes later Jimmy Lister came across to her.

'You know, Clara,' he said, pinching her bare arm. 'I think you're making a big mistake.'

'What about?'

84

'You needn't be upstage with me. Archie and me are pals. He's told me all. Damn nice chap, Archie.'

'I know.'

'What's more, he's got a bloody marvellous voice. Many a pro's making good money whose singing isn't a patch on it. He's dead keen to go into musical comedy or revue. But what manager's going to give a great hulk of six foot four a try-out even as a chorus boy? No, his only hope is to be in a position to put himself across in his own show.'

'But that's impossible.'

Lister laid a finger against his nose.

'I've got ideas. Long-term policy, you might call it. Here and now he's got a bit of cash. Don't look sniffy, dear. I know, better than you, that two thousand quid doesn't go far in show business. But I might be able to get him in on the ground floor of something good. A real investment. I'd be prepared to go in with him though I couldn't put up any cash. Archie could work under me and be getting experience all the time. Then, when he comes into the big money, he could put on his own shows, and not as a ruddy amateur.'

Clara said doubtfully:

'I should have thought it was awfully risky.'

'You've got to take some risks in this business.' He gave her a truculent look. 'That's women all over. Bloody wet-blankets. No imagination. I was thinking of your good too, as it happens.'

'Mine?'

'Well, you want to get on, don't you? I'll be quite frank with you, my dear. You're quite promising and not bad-looking when you take a bit of trouble. But I don't see you going far unless you get a bit of a push. That poor mutt's crazy about you. If you've any sense, you'll stick around while the iron's hot.' He put his arm round her and breathed whisky into her face. 'I think you're quite a juicy piece myself. But what a ruddy little icicle! You'll never get on in the theatre if you're so stand-offish.'

Lister suddenly dropped his arm. Clara saw with relief that

Archie was standing beside them. By now he was a little unsteady on his feet and his eyes were beginning to look glazed.

'No offence meant,' said Lister. 'Just telling this little girl she was a naughty, obstinate little girl who doesn't know what's good for her. Doesn't appreciate her Uncle Jimmy.'

'Doesn't appreciate me and never will,' said Archie, swaying slightly and propping himself on Lister's shoulder. 'Four bloody years I've been in love with that girl.'

'Trouble with you, old boy,' said Lister solemnly, 'you don't know how to handle women. Never let 'em get you down. Above all, never discuss business with 'em. Petty minds. No imagination. Can't see further than the ends of their silly little noses.'

Clara moved away. Archie made an attempt to follow her but Lister held him back. She felt a sudden disgust with the whole world of the theatre. Picking her way through the gabbling groups, she wondered how, only a few minutes ago, she could have found those tipsy faces touching, even beautiful. Now her only desire was to get away from them and be alone. The prospect of having to live with them for even one more week seemed suddenly unbearable. Then she thought that, at the end of that week, she would see Stephen and nothing mattered any more.

As she put on her coat in the dressing-room, she remembered that Stephen belonged, far more than Archie, to the world of the theatre. But he was working with people who cared only for their art; he was outside the vulgar scramble where people pushed and exploited and traded on others' love or trust to make big money, to have their name in lights. As she slipped behind the back-cloth, on the way to the stage-door, Archie was singing 'The Only Girl' again. The wonderful voice sounded a little thickened and unsteady. She had forgotten, till that moment, that he had sung that song the first day she met him. Suddenly, almost like a hallucination, she saw that other Archie, slouching beside her in the park at Crickleham in his uniform slacks and a pair of unlaced tennis shoes, singing with impersonal fervour:

'I would say such – wonderful things to you
There would be such – wonderful things to do
If you were the only girl in the world
And I were the on – ly boy.'

9

It was a raw damp November morning when the company arrived at Worcester for the last week of the tour. Clara could not help recalling that golden afternoon, four years earlier when she had arrived there full of hope and excitement to begin her new life at Maryhall. As she stepped out on to the platform she glanced along it apprehensively as if she feared or expected to see some remembered figure. When a boy in a tweed overcoat dashed through the gates, she had a moment of panic. He was just sufficiently like Charles to bring up his image with painful sharpness.

She loitered at the bookstall, staring unseeingly at piles of magazines, to put off the moment of going out into those too-familiar streets and trying to replace Charles's image with Stephen's. But her mind was stuck in the past; she could barely conjure up Stephen's face.

She was interrupted by a painful dig in the ribs from Maidie.

'If you want to buy something, for goodness' sake buy it. I'm famished and it's miles to our digs.'

Clara hastily bought the *Saturday Westminster* she had forgotten to buy in Birmingham. As she picked it up, she had a feeling that there was something unusual about this particular number. But she was too frightened of Maidie even to glance at it.

As they tramped the half-mile to their digs, Maidie said unexpectedly:

'That green paper's the one you sent your tale to, isn't it? The one you were so coy about in Nuneaton.'

'Yes.'

'Ever hear any more about it?'

Clara shook her head: 'No. What's more, I never shall. I did something idiotic.'

'Would you believe it?' said Maidie sarcastically. 'What was it *this* time, may I ask?'

'I only put my address for that week.'

'Well, write, soppy. She'll forward letters.'

'There won't be a letter,' said Clara with gloomy certainty. 'Just the returned manuscript. Still, as it's my only copy . . .'

When they arrived at their digs, the paper slipped from under Clara's arm as she put down her suitcase. Maidie retrieved it, gave it a scornful glance, then suddenly whistled and thrust it under Clara's nose.

'Look at that, you silly old Wurzit.'

Unable to believe her eyes, Clara stared at the list of contents and read: "The Hill of Summer" – Clara Batchelor.'

Forgetting everything, she snatched the paper and standing there, still in her hat and coat, read every word of her story. Though she was used to the curious transformation effected by print, it appeared at first to have been written by a stranger. Convinced at last that it was hers, she found some parts far better and others far worse than she remembered. One paragraph drove her to a furious exclamation.

'What's biting you *now*?' Maidie asked.

'How *could* I?' Clara muttered, 'Of all the ghastly sentences!'

'Committed a spot of *faux pas* in your grammar? Well, they've printed it, haven't they? If this paper's so bloody educated . . .'

'Not the grammar. The adjectives!' wailed Clara.

'I shall use some adjectives about you in a minute. For heaven's sake, sit down and eat your kippers. Then you'd better write off straight away about that money. What'll they pay?'

'No idea. Two guineas perhaps.'

'Wish someone'd pay *me* two guineas for writing down my girlish thoughts. Nice work when you can get it, as the charwoman said to the tart.'

Clara floated through the remaining hours before the show in a state of bliss. For the first time in her life, she dared to think of herself as a writer. Even Stephen could hardly fail to be impressed by her appearing in a paper which published Coppard and De la Mare. She was planning to send him a marked copy when she remembered that she did not know where his company was that week.

There was no letter from him at the theatre. She told herself it was unreasonable to expect two miracles in one day. She reminded herself that each week of the *Richard* rehearsals would be more harassing than the last. Nevertheless, she was disappointed and vaguely disturbed. Not one sign had she had from him since their Sunday in Gainsborough.

That night in the dressing-room, Miss Cooke said with a sigh:

'There are some houses with such beautiful gardens in this neighbourhood. How much I wish I could see some of them. Crickleham Park, of course, is one of the show places of the county.'

'It's very impressive,' said Clara. 'I knew it when Archie and his mother lived there.'

'What ... Archie Hughes-Follett who was with us in Birmingham and Coventry? How very interesting. What a pity he did not come on to Worcester. He might have been kind enough to get me permission to see the park.'

'I'm sure he would. If he knows the people who have it now.'

'Such a good-hearted boy I thought. Well, it can't be helped. Actually I prefer gardens not quite as grand and formal as the Crickleham ones must be. A friend of mine often talks of the most exquisite small place she once visited near Worcester. It belonged to a very old Catholic family – the Cressetts. I wish I could recollect its name.'

'Maryhall,' muttered Clara, feeling her skin contract under her make-up.

'*That* was it. Do you know that house too?'

Clara made a vague sound and concentrated on applying carmine to her lips.

'My friend told me,' went on Miss Cooke, deftly pencilling her crow's feet, 'about a dreadful tragedy there some years ago.'

'Go on, tell us,' said Maidie.

'I daresay Clara has heard about it.'

Clara said nothing. Her hand shook so that she could hardly hold the stick of grease-paint.

'*I* haven't,' said Maidie. 'I like a nice gruesome tale.'

'It's nothing to laugh about, my dear. The only child – the heir – was killed accidentally while playing some game. It was during the war. I know his poor mother had gone to London to meet Sir George Cressett who was coming home on leave. A governess, quite a young girl, was left in charge of the boy. People said that, instead of looking after the child properly, she was flirting with some young officer when it happened.'

Clara stared at her own reflection. Her crimson upper lip looked like a grotesque scar above the lower which had gone so white as to be almost invisible. She said shakily:

'I don't think it happened quite like that. I . . . I knew the girl.'

'Clara dear, I'm so sorry,' said Miss Cooke with concern. 'I had no idea . . . I should never have referred to it if I'd dreamt . . . It should be a lesson to me not to listen to rumours. Poor young thing . . . she must have suffered dreadfully.'

Clara said nothing. She was aware of Maidie's eye on her; an eye that, propped open ready to have red spots planted in its corners, looked enormous and accusing like the painted eye that adorned a text at Paget's Fold. 'Thou God seest me.'

She remembered that she had told Maidie that she had once been a governess. But Maidie merely observed:

'Ever so sad for everyone. Still, accidents will happen. You know what kids are.'

That night Clara gave such a shocking performance that Lister told her roughly that if the tour were not finishing, he would have sacked her. Back in their digs, Maidie said only:

'You'll never be an actress, old dear, if you let your private upsets interfere with your work.'

'I know,' said Clara meekly, feeling immense gratitude to Maidie for not asking the questions she was so obviously dying to ask. 'I'm beginning to wonder whether I ought to go on with the stage at all.'

'Heard from that fellow lately? The Gainsborough one.'

'Not a word.'

'Aren't men the giddy limit? Still, there are other fish in the sea.'

'There's only one person I'll ever want to marry.'

'We've all heard that one.' Maidie's voice was scornful but not unfriendly. 'It's like the measles. Better get it over while you're young. Trouble with you is you don't know the first thing about men.'

'I'm sick of being told that,' said Clara peevishly. 'When I was in my 'teens I had a friend called Patsy who used to keep saying the same thing.'

'And me thinking I was your first friend who had a spot of commonsense. Pity neither of us could pass it on.'

Clara said nothing. The evening had left her raw. Tears that were half anger, half nervous misery came into her eyes. She bit her lip savagely in the effort to stop them running over. Not for anything would she let herself break down in front of Maidie. But Maidie suddenly flung an arm round her shoulders.

'You're really hot and bothered, you poor old Wurzit, aren't you? Don't mind me. It's only my bit of fun. I know how it feels, believe it or not. That's why I prefer 'em bald and grateful nowadays.'

Clara had to laugh. Maidie gave her a friendly slap.

'That's better. Never say die, as the monkey said. Seriously, you should think twice before you chuck old Starchy out for good and all. He's a decent boy even if he does drink the hell of a lot. I wouldn't mind having a shot at reforming Mr Archibald Hughes-Follett Esquire myself.'

'Maidie . . . Why, only a week or two ago you were saying . . .'

'I can change my mind like anyone else, can't I? I hadn't heard him sing then. That voice does funny things to me.'

'Why don't you have a shot then? He likes you awfully.'

'Who cares?' said Maidie. 'He ought to be in a museum. Only living specimen of the boy who can only love one girl.'

'I hope you're wrong.'

'Sucks – I believe you get no end of a thrill out of Archie's soupy devotion. Still maybe there's a catch in it. I've never known there not be.'

'What kind of a catch?'

Maidie turned her big blue eyes up to the ceiling.

'Something I'm too pew-er to mention let alone to try to find out.' She sang demurely:

> 'He's more to be pitied than censured
> He's more to be helped than despised.

And don't you forget it, Vere, next time the poor sap pops the question.'

10

Two nights later, the stage doorkeeper produced a letter for Clara. In her disappointment that it was not from Stephen, she scarcely glanced at it. Tearing it open idly she was confronted with an unmistakable handwriting, upright and impersonal as a nun's. Intent, a little frightened, she read:

'My dear Clara,

Archie is keeping me company for a few days while my husband is away and Nan has gone off to nurse her sister in Hereford. I do not know how you feel about coming to Maryhall but it would give me so much pleasure to see you again. Archie is driving into Worcester tomorrow (Thursday) when, he tells me, you do not have a matinée. If you would care to come over for lunch, he would pick you up at the theatre at 12.30 and return you in plenty of time for the evening performance. I shall understand perfectly if you do not feel like coming but I hope very much that you will.

Yours affectionately,
Theresa Cressett.'

Clara slept little that night, trying to make up her mind

whether to go or not. She understood that tactful first sentence only too well. It would be painful to go to Maryhall again in any circumstances, but to be smuggled into that household, to which she had once had the illusion of belonging, would be humiliating. She suspected that Lady Cressett was offering her a kind of test. If she refused, it would be another proof of her cowardice. She both longed and dreaded to see Charles's mother again. When at last she made up her mind to go, she knew, with a pang of self-contempt, that she could not have brought herself to face it without Archie.

He arrived next morning in the car she remembered so well. The sight of it brought back, not only Charles, but the whole background of Maryhall. Nothing could have been more typical of the Cressetts' orderly economy than that sober dark green Wolseley which had not been new in 1916 but whose paint and fittings shone with the patina of constant care. Even Archie himself looked well-groomed. He had had a shave and a hair cut; someone had evidently cleaned his shoes and pressed his clothes.

As he tucked the musquash rug round her knees (there was a new neat darn in its cloth border which she would have recognised anywhere as Nan's), he put his hand on hers for a moment.

'It's marvellous of you to come. Theresa's set her heart on it for some reason. Frankly I thought it was asking a bit too much of you.'

'What about you?' she asked gently.

He frowned, as he started the car with the expertness she had forgotten.

'Oh, I'm quite used to it now. But the first time, well, I guess you'd rather be on your own. Having me around might make it worse.'

She said truthfully:

'Without you, I couldn't have faced it at all.'

He said, with a look of such radiance that she turned her head away ashamed:

'That's the most wonderful thing you've ever said to me.'

She was grateful that he spoke little during the six-mile drive. It was almost exactly the same time of year as when they had last driven along that road. The same wintry sun lit up the sallow fields and the pollarded willows by the Severn. That last day, they had driven in the other direction and she had been grateful for every milestone that took them further from Maryhall. Now, as the Malvern hills loomed larger and she began to recognise fields and houses, it was as if she were being drawn backwards through time as well as space. To avoid the landscape, she glanced at Archie's profile, set in lines of unusual resolution. That was how it had looked at the inquest. Against her will, she wondered whether Stephen Tye would have been so recklessly anxious to take all the blame on himself. To remind herself that Archie was inferior to Stephen she asked with a touch of patronage:

'Still stage-struck? Or have you thought better of Lister's great plans for your future?'

'By no means,' he said, keeping his eyes on the road. 'Going to look him up as soon as I get back to London. But the last day or two . . . Well, you know how it is at Maryhall. One gets talking to Theresa.'

Clara did not answer. She felt suddenly vulgar and diminished. It was Archie who next broke a silence which had become uneasy. Turning to her at last, he enquired:

'Have *you* any plans?'

'No. I suppose I only asked about yours because . . .'

He dropped one hand from the wheel and touched hers.

'I understand, old thing. You'll feel better once you've seen Theresa. *She's* just the same.'

She said wretchedly: 'I'm sure. But *I've* changed.'

'Hang it all, one expects people to at our age. What about me?'

Clara frowned.

'I don't believe you have. Not in yourself.'

'Theresa wouldn't agree. She used to think I was one hell of a good boy. Now I'm sure she believes I'm skidding down the road to ruin. Drink. Gambling. Won't stick to jobs. She probably suspects Women with a capital W too. There, for once, she'd be wrong. But it doesn't make the least difference to the way she treats me. So *you've* got nothing to worry about.'

'I'm not so sure. If you're different, it's only on the surface. But I feel I've changed deep down. Very much for the worse, too.'

'Can't say I've noticed it.'

'Probably hardly anybody would. But she might. She knows things about one before one knows them oneself. My badness – or whatever it is – mayn't *show*. If it did, everyone might be so horrified that they'd run away from me.'

'Rot,' said Archie, slowing down so suddenly that Clara was flung forward. 'Sorry, darling. Even if it weren't rot, I know one person who wouldn't.'

Clara stared at the road and realised, with a thrill of terror, that they were less than a mile from the lodge. She wanted to cry out that she couldn't face it, but her lips twitched too much for her to make a sound.

Archie said suddenly:

'I've been reading "The Hill of Summer". I liked it terribly.'

'You liked it?' she said, too astonished to be civil. 'I'd have thought it would have bored you stiff.'

'I bought the paper because I saw you reading it in Brum. Found most of the stuff too heavy going. But I read your story three times. Pleasure, not duty.'

Clara promptly decided that 'The Hill of Summer' must be far worse than she supposed.

'Have you read any other stories of mine?'

'Rather. We had *London Mail* in the Club in Santiago. But – of course I don't know the first thing about writing – they didn't seem anywhere near the same class. Frightfully clever and all that. Can't think how you do 'em.'

'But "The Hill" seemed different?'

'Oh, absolutely.'

'Why? How?'

'Don't ask *me*. Hang it all, I'm not literary.'

'I'd *really* like to know.'

'Well . . . if you insist . . . I'd say anyone with the brains to do that sort of thing could have done the *London Mail* ones.'

'Perfectly true. And the other?'

'I'll only drop a brick.'

'*Please*, Archie.'

'Right. First, I thought no one but you could have written it. Second, I didn't think even you could write anything which got me so much.'

They were the first words of praise Clara had heard. She was so grateful that she was almost as pleased as if they had come from Stephen. Perhaps it was even more reassuring to know that she had impressed anyone as simple and honest as Archie. She looked at him with affection.

'*No* one could say anything handsomer than that.'

'Good egg. I'll tell you something rather odd. I used to be rather keen on poetry when I was at Beaumont. Don't suppose I've so much as opened a book of poems for years. But the other day I started rummaging in the Cressetts' library and found old Marvell. I used to like some of his stuff a lot.'

'Oh yes?' said Clara politely. She loved Marvell but, at that moment, she only wanted to talk about her own work. 'I don't suppose I shall ever write poems again. I used to write the usual rubbish at school of course.'

'Must be damn difficult. But it was reading "The Hill" that made me want to read some poetry again. Rather queer, eh?'

'Rather interesting.'

'You know, old thing, you ought always to write things like "The Hill". Sheer waste of time for you, that other stuff.'

Clara's pleasure gave way to panic. She muttered in a furious, jerky voice:

'You don't understand. One can't turn it on like a tap. That story was probably a fluke anyway. Also, you seem to forget I haven't got a private income.'

'Now I *have* put my foot in it. Sorry, darling.'

She said nothing, ashamed and a little frightened by her out-burst. She was shaking all over as if she had been insulted or unfairly attacked. At last she managed to murmur grudgingly:

'*I'm* sorry. I'm developing a filthy temper.'

'Forget it. My fault. Bull in the china shop as usual.'

He slowed down the car almost to walking pace. They were within fifty yards of the gates of Maryhall. A woman was stand-ing in the road outside the lodge, waving to them.

'Archie – look – it's Lady Cressett.'

A moment later, without knowing how, she found herself in Theresa Cressett's arms and being kissed on both cheeks as the nuns used to kiss her at Mount Hilary.

'My dear Clara . . . I'm so very, very glad you could come.'

The two of them walked up the drive together while Archie went ahead in the car. However hard she tried not to glance at them, Clara could not help being aware of familiar landmarks: the shrubbery where she and Charles had had their hut; the rose-garden that had once been a cockpit and where a few late roses still bloomed; the blue-faced stable clock peering over the shoul-der of the plum-coloured house. It was almost exactly the same time of year as when she had last seen Maryhall: she had, for a moment, the illusion that nothing had changed. She could have sworn Lady Cressett was wearing the identical grey-green tweed suit she remembered so well. Her hair was still piled above her pale, dim-eyed, Flemish-looking face in the elaborate way that had seemed old-fashioned in 1916. She talked gently as they walked, keeping the conversation to impersonal things. There had been a meet at Maryhall last week and the lawn had been rather cut up; the Severn had flooded badly last year; they had won six prizes at the flower show; they were thinking of putting up a new greenhouse.

As they approached the house, a collie advanced to meet them. Clara felt Lady Cressett's hand tighten for a moment on her arm as she said quietly:

'You remember Hero? He's quite a staid middle-aged gentleman now.'

Clara felt a catch in her throat and knew that the unavoidable moment had come. She remembered Charles's cherished and bullied Hero as barely full-grown. The illusion vanished. She put out her hand to the dog, almost expecting him to snarl at her.

'He's not forgotten you,' said Lady Cressett. 'Look – he's grinning. You remember Clara, don't you, old boy?'

Clara's eyes began to sting as Hero stood on his hind legs, pawing at her and trying to lick her face. Of all the things she had been so careful to steel herself against, she had forgotten Charles's dog.

'Down, Hero. Don't worry,' said Lady Cressett. 'And come along, my dear. You must be dying for some food.'

11

A parlourmaid whose face Clara did not know waited on them. Otherwise nothing was different. Pine logs hissed on the open hearth; the dining-room still smelt of beeswax, herbs and woodsmoke. There had been a bowl of the same red dahlias the last time she had sat at that table with its patina of three centuries of polishing. Then she caught sight of the silver mug Charles had always used, standing on a sideboard among Sir George's trophies. After that, her eyes kept reverting to it and she found it hard to make conversation. Everything she thought of saying seemed to have some connection with Charles or to be so obvious an avoidance as to be worse. Lady Cressett came to her rescue.

'Fancy your acting in *A Clerical Error*. I took Charles to see it one Christmas when they did it in Malvern. He thought the curate was a priest and was terribly shocked when he got engaged. Of course Nan's a Protestant but such a High one that Charles hadn't quite grasped the difference.'

Clara brought herself to enquire after Nan. Lady Cressett gave her that faint smile of approval she remembered so well.

'Very much the same outside,' Lady Cressett glanced over her shoulder and, seeing the parlourmaid was absent, went on: 'But *inside* there's a great struggle going on. You must pray for her. You know how . . . well . . . resolute Nan is in her loyalties.'

'Yes indeed,' said Clara. The face of Charles's nurse, thin and white under the smooth red hair, rose in her mind as she had last seen it, twisted in hysterical rage.

'Resolute is putting it mildly,' said Archie. 'She's the most obstinate woman I've ever met.'

'She has the defects of her qualities,' said Lady Cressett. 'That's what makes it so hard for her to take the final step. She feels it would be disloyal to her own Church.'

'Is she really thinking of becoming a Catholic?' Clara asked.

'It's only a question of time. Imagine how Charles must be praying for her in heaven. When you think she couldn't deny him anything on earth.'

Archie said:

'If there's one thing I can't imagine, it's Nan admitting she might have been wrong.'

'That's what my sister Monica used to say. She's dead, Clara, did you know? Of course she'll be praying for Nan too.'

'When she can spare time from arguing with St Paul about women's rights.'

'You're a very irreverent young man, Archie. If that's how the Jesuits brought you up, I'm glad we meant to send Charles to Downside. As to Nan, when she *does* come in, she'll put us all to shame. Those fierce, all-or-nothing people often turn into saints once they're converted. "God seeks and loves courageous souls." St Theresa said that. Nan's nothing if not courageous.'

Clara felt herself blush. She knew what St Theresa went on to say about cowardly souls and was painfully conscious of being one. Nor was she 'aided by humility', the only virtue in which cowards were likely to excel.

The three of them had their coffee in the drawing-room whose green panelled walls and gilt garlands Clara had admired on her first evening. Her eyes wandered nostalgically over the lute-backed chairs, the Sheraton tables tidily littered with snuff-boxes and porcelain, the miniatures of generations of Cressetts.

When the heads of the other two were turned, she nerved herself to look into the bright, impudent brown eyes of the page of Charles the First's court. Their likeness to those of his last descendant was too vivid to bear. She looked away and became aware of an unfamiliar frame on a table. Lady Cressett, catching her glance, said gently:

'It's a snapshot we had enlarged. We hated that stiff professional one with his hair plastered down and his tie straight.'

Clara had identified that snapshot. Now, the boy's upturned face grinned at nothing; the hand which had been clasped in her own had been retouched and furnished with a cricket ball. This wiping out of her image gave her such a sense of being utterly banished from Maryhall that her mouth went dry. She tried to say something and choked.

Lady Cressett said quickly:

'I like the original much better. It's in my Caussade that I read every night. Monica took the two of you without your knowing. Charles and his beloved "Spin" . . . Ah, Clara dear, don't.'

For Clara had burst into loud, blubbering tears like a child. Archie leant forward and put a hand on her heaving shoulder.

'My darling old thing . . . try not to.'

It was a minute or two before she could stop crying.

When she had recovered herself, Lady Cressett said:

'Shall you and I take a turn in the garden, Clara? It's such ages since I've seen you.'

Never would Clara have been gladder of Archie's presence. As she drew back at the door to let Lady Cressett pass first, she shot him a despairing look which he returned. Lady Cressett caught this interchange and smiled.

'You two,' she said. 'It's hard to realise you're officially grown-up. I'm only stealing her for a little while, Archie.'

Clara's tears had wholly restored her to the present. As she walked with Lady Cressett along paths bordered by yew hedges and over lawns from which the day's fall of leaves had been swept into neat piles, she was aware of differences. Maryhall, however slowly, however minutely, had changed in four years; she saw it as a real place and no longer the fixed landscape of a dream. It was Lady Cressett now who kept reverting to the past.

'That tree really ought to come down but he did so love climbing it.'

Or: 'His rosebush only produced two roses this year. It's a miracle it ever produced any since he planted it practically upside down.'

They were skirting the wall of the kitchen garden when Theresa said hesitantly:

'Could you bear it if we went in? I couldn't for a long time. Now I've come to love it again. I come here every day to say my rosary.'

Clara had not the courage to refuse. After the first pang, she felt no more than a dull sadness as they paced between the box-edged beds.

'I thought it would help even if it hurt,' said Lady Cressett.

Clara made a vague sound.

The other went on: 'Of course *we* shall always feel it. The human loss. That's inevitable. But *he* is happy with God. Sometimes, you know, it is as if he were quite near me. Not when I'm *trying* to feel it. But sometimes, when things are difficult and dark, quite unexpectedly, I have a flash of realising what we know by faith – that the blessed do watch over us. After all, it's part of their joy in heaven to help the people they loved on earth.'

'Yes, indeed,' said Clara, embarrassed. It came over her how much she had lost that sense of commerce between heaven and earth which had seemed so natural at Mount Hilary and Maryhall.

'Clara,' Lady Cressett said after a pause. 'Do you mind if I'm very indiscreet?'

'Of course not.'

'Only because I'm very fond of you. For your own sake, not just because you were so devoted to Charles. I wonder so much what you are going to make of your life.'

'I wish I knew.'

'You're a changeable child, aren't you? The last time you and I had a talk, you were quite seriously considering becoming a nun. Now, here you are on the stage. Do you feel you've found your vocation at last?'

Clara shook her head.

'I doubt if I'll ever be more than a bright amateur. If I were a real actress, I wouldn't mind drudging round the provinces for years.'

'But it's beginning to pall already? Ah well, perhaps one of these days you'll give it up and get married.'

Clara sighed.

'Perhaps.'

'Forgive me, my dear, but I'm afraid I've been plying Archie with questions. I've had so little news of you for years. I gather there is someone whom you care for very much.'

'Yes,' muttered Clara, as if confessing a fault. In the atmosphere of Maryhall, her love for Stephen seemed disordered, almost guilty. She laughed rather artificially. 'But I don't know if he does. Enough to risk marrying, that is.'

Lady Cressett asked gently:

'Supposing . . . just supposing . . . he didn't? Would that prevent you from marrying anyone else ever?'

'How can I tell? I just can't imagine wanting to.'

'No one can at the time. Yet, you know, Clara, I've seen girls who thought their hearts were broken make very happy marriages with someone else. Happier, often, than ones who have married men with whom they were very much in love.'

Clara said, rather irritably:

'You seem to take it for granted that I shan't.'

'No, no . . . of course I didn't mean that . . . I only said "suppose". If you've really found the right person this time and he feels the same . . . men are often slower than we are at making up their minds . . . I wish you all the joy in the world. Is he a Catholic, this man?'

'No.'

Lady Cressett sighed.

'My poor child. I've known some happy mixed marriages but not many. A man will promise anything when he's in love. But once married – I've seen it happen so often – he may object very strongly to carrying them out. That can lead to such terrible conflicts and bitterness. It's the Catholic wife who suffers most.'

'Isn't that looking rather far ahead?'

'Not too far surely, if you're so certain you'd say "Yes". And if he's holding back, isn't it very likely just because he's not willing to have his children brought up Catholics?'

Although – or perhaps because – these probings came nowhere near the heart of her trouble, Clara found them painful. Blind to everything but the dazzling hope of Stephen's allowing her to marry him, she had never even considered the religious side. Faced suddenly with these questions, she felt a chill deeper than the resentment of having her love treated like a legal abstraction. The fact that she had never faced them herself seemed to prove how frail her hope must be. Fear made her insolent. She said, with a particular smile and voice that always maddened her father:

'Even you could hardly expect me to ask quite such a leading question.'

Lady Cressett's pale, rather heavy face twitched for the first time in the nervous tic her sister used to call 'the tombstone of Tess's temper'.

'I expect I deserved that. Rushing in where angels fear to tread.'

'I'm sorry,' Clara said sincerely. 'It's sweet of you to bother about me at all.'

'Rubbish. I only hope it all comes out right. I'll pray for you. In the long run, it's the only thing any of us can do for each other, isn't it? And you must pray too. Of course I'm sure you do.'

They walked in silence for some moments. At last Clara said:

'I'm afraid I'm not very devout. I don't mean I've lost my faith.'

Lady Cressett squeezed her arm.

'Of course you haven't. Don't think I don't realise how difficult it must be for Catholic girls these days. When I think of the sheltered lives Monica and I led at your age! Even if we'd gone out and worked as you wonderful young things do, I'm sure things would have been easier then. The whole atmosphere seems to have changed since the war. It's no longer just a question of Catholic or Protestant. One hears more and more of people who believe in nothing.'

'Oh, I do believe. At least I go on taking it for granted that I do.'

'Now, now Clara,' said Lady Cressett with a touch of sharpness. 'None of that bad old habit of yours. Even in your teens you were much too introspective. Always questioning yourself and trying to analyse every little thought and emotion. Of course you believe.'

'But it all seems so remote. I don't seem to feel any fervour any more.'

'Feelings don't matter. There's probably much more merit in keeping up one's bare obligations when they've become a dry duty than in doing all sorts of extras because one's *feeling* pious. On the stage, I daresay it's difficult even to get to Sunday Mass.'

'Oh no. It's always been possible.'

'Splendid. I shall quote you to Archie as a good example.'

'Archie? Why?'

'You know what men are. They so easily get slack when there's no one to keep them up to it. It's not deliberate. Archie admits he sometimes just can't bring himself to get up in time. Of course, as you probably know, there's often a reason for that in poor Archie's case.'

'Yes. But I don't care what Archie does. He's a million times better than me in every way.'

Lady Cressett laughed.

'I believe you're a great deal fonder of Archie than you admit.'

'Of course I'm fond of him.'

'Just now, when we were in the drawing-room, you seemed so much of a couple that for the moment I forgot that all is supposed to be over between you.'

'It *is* over,' said Clara hastily.

'It seems such a pity,' Lady Cressett sighed. 'Of course you were both such babies *then*. It's obvious that the poor boy's fonder of you than ever, you naughty child.'

'It's not my fault. I didn't *want* to see him again. If Daddy hadn't put him on my track . . .'

'Your father likes him very much, doesn't he? And Archie seems devoted to him.'

'Oh yes. They dote on each other.'

'And what does Mr Batchelor think of the other one?'

Clara stiffened. Her father was the last person in the world to whom she could have admitted her feeling for Stephen.

'He thinks he's a very good actor. But he hasn't the least idea . . .'

'Oh . . . an *actor*.' Lady Cressett's voice was politely chill.

Clara said with a touch of malice:

'After all, Archie wants to go on the stage. Hasn't he told you?'

'I don't take that very seriously. It's just a notion he's got because you're on the stage at the moment. Also it's the one thing that would most annoy his uncle. You'll see . . . when he comes into his money in two years' time, he'll buy a nice place in the country and settle down sensibly. Let's hope he finds a nice girl to settle down with.' She pinched Clara's arm. 'Don't you hope he will?'

'Of course. Though I'm not sure that Archie *is* the settling down sort. Any more than I am.'

'Oh . . . oh,' said Lady Cressett. 'I knew a girl not so many years ago who longed for a place like Maryhall and a nursery full of children.'

Clara sighed.

'I know,' she said slowly. 'Back here with you, I could almost imagine wanting it again. You told me once I was like a chameleon. It's true. I change all the time according to where I am and the people I'm with.'

'Pity someone can't pick you up and put you on the right colour.'

They had arrived once again at the door of the walled garden. Lady Cressett stopped, with her hand at the latch, looking not at Clara but down the box-edged path. Clara knew by her expression that she was praying. It was not till they had closed the door behind them that she said:

'Charles was so fond of you both. You must forgive me if I can't help hoping that, in spite of everything . . . Yet I've no right to wish this or that. Nothing matters, does it, except that things should come out the way God wants them to?' She smiled. 'And that's so often just the opposite of the way *we* think best.'

Clara said nothing. She stared across the lawn with the cedar and the weeping-willow to the parti-coloured fields sloping down to the bend of the river, trying to replace them with the land-lady's parlour where she had last seen Stephen. It was always hard for her to imagine life going on in any place other than the one she was in at the moment. Already it seemed unthinkable that, in a few hours, she would make up her face in a crowded dressing-room, prance and giggle through her silly part and eat sausages with Maidie over a gas fire.

Lady Cressett smiled:

'That was a long thought, Clara.'

'Not worth calling a thought,' said Clara, smiling too. 'Just a chameleon's automatic reflex.. They have nervous breakdowns, don't they, if you change their backgrounds suddenly?'

'There's Archie coming to meet us. Poor boy. We've been out nearly an hour.'

Clara looked towards the soberly elegant plum-coloured house in its setting of clipped yews and flagged terrace. The sky, grey all the morning, had cleared in the west. The sun, already dipping towards the crescent of rising woods behind the house, warmed their last leaves to the cock-pheasant tints she remembered. Tree and lawn, brick and stone, were washed with soft colour and shadow in the muted light. Once again she saw Maryhall as the symbol of order and tradition; of a life oriented beyond time. As Archie's tall figure strode towards them, she saw his face, too, in a transfiguring light. For a moment she wondered whether, if she had never known Stephen, the two of them might not have been able to build up a Maryhall of their own.

Lady Cressett said softly:

'Whoever you marry, Clara, remember that the man and the woman are only the beginning. One doesn't always realise that when one's young. A Catholic, most of all, has to look beyond. To the children. To the family as a whole.'

Clara said nothing. Though it was only Stephen that she wanted, the words faintly stirred some part of her that seemed to have no connection with him.

Lady Cressett smiled.

'If you could love my boy so much, think what it will be when you have some of your own. You have so much capacity to love . . . too much to spend on just one person.'

Clara was startled.

'Capacity to love? No . . . no. . . . I'm much too selfish. I mean . . . if I really had . . . it would be there all the time, wouldn't it? I'd be able to love *anyone*.'

Lady Cressett patted her cheek.

'Then you'd be a saint, my dear.'

Clara sighed. She knew more than the other suspected of what Theresa Cressett's life had been. She knew that Charles's father, like Charles himself, turned cruel if he were thwarted in the least thing. Theresa had lost her only child and the fact that she could not have the others for which she longed had been turned into bitter reproach by the husband whose one passion was Maryhall itself and the carrying on of his name.

What she had built up required qualities Clara did not even begin to possess. This home, this atmosphere whose spell Clara now felt again, was not something ready-made. It had been created and sustained by endless patience and daily small renunciations of self-will; by a love which expected no human return.

Clara said, almost with anguish:

'Oh . . . if only . . . only I could be like you.'

'Nonsense,' said Lady Cressett emphatically. 'Nobody's meant to be like anyone else. What's the point of God going to all the trouble of making every one of us unique if we go and spoil it all by trying to copy each other?'

The next moment, Archie was upon them. As he fell into step beside them, he gave Clara a quick questioning glance.

'Feeling all right now?'

She nodded.

'I was sent to tell you both tea was ready. Then I suppose I ought to be getting Clara back to Worcester.'

'I've arranged for Milburn to drive her,' said Lady Cressett.

'I say, Theresa. I thought I was going to,' protested Archie.

'I forgot to tell you. Lydia Coles 'phoned to say she was coming over after tea. She'll be so disappointed if you're not here. After all, she was one of your mother's best friends.'

'Oh, very well,' said Archie gloomily. 'Will you be going straight back to Valetta Road when the company packs up, Clara?'

Clara flushed.

'No. I'm going to Oxford.'

'For long?'

'I don't quite know. A week at the most.'

'Tell me the address. I'm getting a motorbike and sidecar in a day or two. I could easily pick you up there and run you back to London.'

Clara felt herself flush deeper still.

'I don't even know where I'll be staying.'

She forced herself to look up into his face. He had gone white and she knew that he had guessed.

He said with a strained smile:

'Well, that's napoo then. Have a good time in Oxford.'

On the drive back to Worcester, she could not shake off a weight of sadness. Revisiting Maryhall had aroused so many feelings she could not quite analyse. Sitting there in that familiar car, behind Milburn's rigid green back, she had an odd sense of being banished from that world even more definitely than four years ago. When she had first heard that Archie was not coming back with her, she had felt an irrational disappointment along with her relief. Now she began to wish he were there, if only to stop her from remembering his stricken face as he said 'Well, that's napoo then.'

She turned her mind with a definite effort to Stephen. Nearly three weeks had gone by without a sign from him. The fact that for the first time she did not know where he was playing this week gave her a feeling of panic. Never had she been so utterly cut off from him.

It was only four days now to his first night. If there were no letter for her that evening, she would risk sending him a note to say she was coming to Oxford – no more. She would have to send it to the theatre: he would be sure to be rehearsing there on Monday before the actual performance. But which theatre? Suddenly she remembered having seen an Oxford paper on the station bookstall when she had bought the *Saturday Westminster*. If there were no announcement of the play, at least it would give the names of all the theatres and she could send a note to each.

She asked Milburn to stop at the station and was just in time to buy the *Oxford Mail* before the bookstall closed. Back in the car, she opened it at random, searching for the theatre column. The first thing that caught her eye was a blotched photograph of Stephen himself. Beside it was one of a handsome, middle-aged woman with smooth dark hair and earnest eyes. Over the two pictures ran the heading – 'Stage Romance'.

At first these words conveyed no meaning whatever to her. Then she read the caption below the two smudged, smiling faces.

'An additional interest will be created in Mr Stephen Tye's performance of the title role of *Richard II*, which opens at the Playhouse next Monday, by the fact that he has just married Miss Elizabeth Lane, manager and leading lady of the company. Miss Lane is a firm favourite with Oxford audiences and we regret that she will not be personally appearing in *Richard II*. However, she and her husband plan to appear together in many future productions, including *Antony and Cleopatra* and a stage adaptation of *The Mill on the Floss*.'

PART II

1

On the morning of her wedding, Clara woke up with the sense of continuing a dream. She had refused overnight her mother's offer to help her to dress. When at last she forced herself to get out of bed, she pottered aimlessly about her untidy bedroom and was so reluctant to put on her white dress and veil that her father kept coming up to rap impatiently on the door.

In the end, it was he who nearly made her late for the ceremony. As they waited outside the Oratory, he discovered that one of his gloves was split. Before Clara could stop him, he leapt out of the hired car, hailed a taxi and disappeared. She sat there, as if in a trance, while strangers pressed their faces against the glass to stare at her and an agitated verger gesticulated from the steps. When at last he returned, he panted, as he pulled on his new gloves:

'Must think me mad. Thank God you're still here.' She wondered if he had really expected her to run away. Her will was too paralysed even to formulate the wish.

As they paced up the aisle, she was only hazily aware of organ music, turning heads and the candle-lit altar at the foot of which stood a tall red-headed man, so unfamiliar in his formal clothes that at first she did not recognise him. She had dreamed so often in the last years that she was in a church, about to marry Archie

Hughes-Follett, that this walk up the aisle might have been mere repetition. The only detail which made her suspect that, this time, it might be happening in fact was the trembling of her father's arm. As they advanced slowly towards the altar, it was she who seemed to be supporting him.

When she and Archie made their vows, she recovered enough sense of reality to feel awed. They stood side by side muttering, like children who have forgotten the answers in catechism class, while the old priest patiently prompted them. She heard the two of them make those tremendous promises which bound them for life and thought with panic: 'Do we really know what we are doing?'

She tried to follow the magnificent liturgy of the Nuptial Mass but the print swam before her eyes. All she could do was to pray distractedly that at least she would not make Archie unhappy. As she prayed, she was overcome by the sense of her own emptiness and fickleness. Only a few months ago it would have seemed impossible that she should ever stop loving Stephen. Now she could hardly remember what that love had felt like. She had soon reconciled herself to the first fierce pain of loss; what still came back in all its nakedness, often at the least expected moments, was her utter humiliation. This enduring sense of shame had become dissociated from Stephen himself. She no longer bore him any resentment; she had gone to see him play Richard II when the company had come to Croydon, only a few weeks before her wedding, and had critically admired his quite remarkable performance. Afterwards, she had accidentally run into him and his wife and had even felt a touch of cynical affection at his relief when she acted better than she had ever done on the stage. She had noted with amusement that Elizabeth Lane had watched him anxiously while they talked, with false heartiness, of old friends at the Garrick; she had even caught a covert glance of something warmer than gratitude from Stephen himself. But all this had done nothing to heal the deep hurt to her pride. That had remained and been gradually transformed into the conviction that, even if she could bring herself to take the risk of falling in love again, she would be quite incapable of doing so.

The great petitions of the Nuptial Mass brought home to her her utter inadequacy. What right had she to suppose that she could make Archie happy by marrying him? All she could do was to implore forgiveness for what suddenly seemed to her a shocking presumption as the priest prayed that she should be as pleasing to her husband as Rachel, as wise as Rebecca, as faithful as Sara. Only at the last blessing, when he prayed that they should see their children's children, did she lose the awful sense that she was treating a sacrament as if it were an empty formula. Though she dreaded the thought of Archie's making love to her almost as much as she dreaded the pain of having children, there, at least, was something real to which she had committed herself and where she was determined not to cheat. She gave an inward cry for grace to overcome her repugnance and cowardice and glanced upwards wanting, for the first time, to see Archie's face. But though she had often, during the ceremony, been aware of his eyes on her and avoided them, this time it was his that were averted. She saw only the kind red face of the old priest, smiling at them as he pronounced the words, as if adding a human blessing to the divine one.

Once the service was over, she relapsed into her dreamlike state. At the reception, she felt as if she were playing an unrehearsed part with surprising ease. Cousins ignored since childhood; friends whom she had not seen for years; unknown relatives of Archie's appeared like a well-drilled crowd on the stage. Only one person seemed not to be playing her part with conviction. Under her gay new hat, her mother's dark eyes were rimmed with red and her mouth drooped with a sadness more appropriate to a funeral.

While Clara was changing in the hotel bedroom, which gave her more than ever the sense of dressing for another act in a play, Isabel for a moment destroyed the illusion by bursting into genuine tears. Clasping Clara in her arms, she had sobbed: 'Darling . . . darling child . . . Oh, I hope . . . I pray everything will be all right.'

Arrived at Brevisham, the superbly inappropriate house which Archie's Aunt Sybilla had lent them for their honeymoon, they were once more involved in the ritual play. The butler and the housekeeper were waiting at the top of the steps to congratulate them; the house was full of white flowers. Later, when Clara descended the wide shallow staircase, in a new evening frock, aware of candlelight and slyly smiling servants behind the open door of the dining-room, the sense of being on the stage became overwhelming. It was a relief to her to see that Archie felt exactly the same. During dinner, while they ate out-of-season food and drank champagne, they tried to behave as if they had been married for years, under the eye of a butler who had known Archie as a schoolboy. When at last they were left alone, Archie blew out his cheeks with such a comic sigh that she laughed naturally for the first time that day.

'Gosh, I don't think I could go through all that again even for you, my sweet. I say . . . couldn't we bolt? Go to a pub or a nightclub or something?'

'We can't. Your aunt would never forgive us. After all she *has* been awfully kind.'

'That's the worst of Sybilla. When she's got a generous fit on, there's no holding her. When she hasn't, she wouldn't fork out so much as a dry biscuit. And of course she's only doing all this to spite Uncle Stanley. She hates him like poison.'

'Why?'

'Because he hates her, I suppose. For one thing because she's always taking up with weird religions and groups and so on.'

'But her husband . . . your uncle . . . was a Catholic, wasn't he?'

'Uncle Gerald? Gracious, yes. All the Hughes-Folletts are. I believe she used to go on at him a lot. Uncle Stan said she talked him into his grave. Gerald was the fool of the family of *that* generation but Uncle Stan had a weakness for him.' Archie frowned. 'Pity he hasn't transferred it to me.'

'I thought he was rather sweet at the wedding. I admit he looked formidable.'

'Well, as he couldn't actually stop me from getting married, he had to put a good face on it.'

'Did he want to stop you?'

'Naturally, he thinks I'm a young ass not to wait till I've got my cash or what *he* calls a decent job. But I wasn't going to risk losing you again. Suppose you'd changed your mind?'

He caught her left hand and kissed the ring on it.

'My wife. I simply can't believe it.'

'Neither can I.'

'Wish we could just have got into the old motorbike and side-car and hopped off to nowhere without making plans. I can't stick Brevisham. These big houses bore me stiff.'

'I think it's quite fun for a little,' said Clara. 'You forget I'm not used to luxury.'

'You shall have as much as you like if you can stick me for two years. But you won't want a sort of ghastly formal life will you, darling? I thought it'd be fun to spend the cash on amusing things – *when* we get it. Not on servants and great boring houses and all that sort of rot. Still . . . if you want 'em . . .'

'I've no idea what I shall want in two years' time.'

Archie gave her an odd look.

'I know what I want now . . . this very minute,' he said in his most serious voice.

'What?'

'To dance with you.'

Clara had an obscure sensation that was partly relief, partly dismay. It lasted only a moment; by the time Archie had opened the gramophone and put on a record of *Avalon* it had gone.

Brevisham, built by a Hughes-Follett with a passion for Scott, was a fantastic example of nineteenth-century Gothic. From out-side it presented a vast front of still raw pink brick and yellow stone adorned with crenellated towers, crossbow slits, ogives, iron grilles and huge oak doors studded with nails. The largest of these opened into a stone-flagged hall with stained glass windows and an organ loft. Sybilla Hughes-Follett had furnished it with huge chintz-covered chairs and sofas and strewn its chilly flags with white fur rugs. A concert-sized grand piano stood on a daïs at one end, banked by tubs of hydrangeas; a log-fire hissed in the carved stone fireplace. The general effect was that of a brand-new school chapel converted into the lounge of a luxury hotel. Archie rolled back some of the rugs and they began to dance, their feet rasping softly on the stone floor.

'I'm the least little bit tight,' he announced at one point. 'Hardly surprising when you consider how much champagne I must have swallowed today out of pure funk – Forgive?'

'Of course. It doesn't show, anyway. I feel slightly hazy myself.'

'It's all right as long as one stops there,' said Archie earnestly. 'And I'm going to, from now on.'

'You've been wonderful these last weeks.'

He held her closer.

'I wasn't going to take any risks. Don't even feel I want the stuff, now I've got you.'

The slight haziness seemed to disconnect Clara from her body. Her limbs moved smoothly and rhythmically, following Archie's lightest indication of their own accord.

'You're dancing marvellously,' he said. 'We've never gone so well together. Wish we could just go on dancing all night.'

'I wish so too,' she answered truthfully. 'Don't let's talk.' Dancing with him in this relaxed, dreamy state, she felt closer to him than she had ever thought possible. Never before had she been in close enough harmony with him to realise how well he danced. All his clumsiness vanished as soon as he moved to music; his subtle changes of step and rhythm, now that for once she could follow them instinctively, seemed to speak a language her body understood and which affected her almost as much as his singing.

When at last, suddenly exhausted after the long, glittering, unreal day, she said she wanted to go to bed, he looked, for a moment, almost angry. An odd expression, at once sullen and aggressive, clouded his face. Then he recovered his smile and kissed her.

'You must be almost dead. Run along, my darling old thing. I'll just go and have a nightcap. Positively only one.'

She had lain for some time in the great scrolled and gilded bed before she heard him moving about in the dressing-room. By the time she was aware that he had come into their bedroom, her eyes were closed and she was almost asleep with the lamp on. Rousing herself with an effort she saw him standing by the bed, looking more like an overgrown schoolboy than ever in his pyjamas. His red hair was tousled; his arms were so long that his lean wrists protruded from the sleeves as if he had outgrown them. But there was nothing boyish about his filmed, haggard eyes. He stood staring down at her so strangely, almost accusingly, that she sat up and asked:

'Is something wrong? Are you ill?'

'Ill?' he said vaguely and thickly. 'Not in the least ill. Perfectly all right. Didn't mean to wake you. Sorry.'

The next minute he lurched forward and fell on his knees by the bed and buried his head in his hands. He stayed thus, without moving, for so long that Clara at last touched him on the shoulder. He lifted his head and stared at her blindly. His face was flushed and swollen.

'Archie,' she said gently, shaking him a little. 'What's the matter?'

'Nothing's matter. Only saying prayers. Must say prayers.'

She saw then that he was drunk. She did not feel angry, only helpless and a trifle frightened. With difficulty, she managed to persuade him to get up and helped him into the bed beside her. He lay heavily on his side, his head turned from her and buried in the pillow. But just as she bent across him to put out the light, catching the fumes of whisky from his half-open mouth, he looked at her, with a flash of recognition in his filmed eyes.

'Clara . . . darling Clara,' he whispered. 'Didn't mean . . . Couldn't . . .' The whisper became inaudible. He gave a grunting sigh, like a man in pain. The next moment he was fast asleep.

2

After a while, Clara herself slept but lightly and uneasily. At intervals she woke, aware of the unfamiliar heat and weight of someone lying beside her. The darkness was already thinning, so that she could see the outlines of the furniture in the great three-windowed room, when she fell into a heavy doze. She dreamt that her father came and rapped impatiently at the door, exactly as he had done while she was dressing for her wedding. Just as she was going to call to him, she realised with horror that she was in bed with Archie. Overcome with shame and guilt, she crouched under the sheets, silent. The knocking grew more imperative; it sounded threatening. Then she remembered with relief that Archie was her husband. Her father had no right to be angry. She called nervously, 'Come in, Daddy,' and, in the effort of doing so, woke up. Someone was indeed knocking at the door, but softly and discreetly. Clara called more confidently, 'Come in' and a maid entered with a tea-tray.

'Good-morning Madam. Shall I draw the curtains? Mr Archie is still asleep, isn't he?'

'Good-morning,' said Clara, smiling at the maid with passionate gratitude for not being her father. 'Yes, please draw them.'

The sight of the trees and a distant sunlit rise broke her wretched sense of isolation.

'It's nine o'clock, Madam,' said the maid, putting down the tray. 'Would you and Mr Archie like your breakfast in bed or downstairs?'

'I'll wait till he wakes up and ask him.'

The maid smiled slyly:

'Mr Archie's not usually an early riser, Madam. Will you ring when you want breakfast or your bath run?' On the tray was a letter in her father's writing. Seeing the words, 'Hughes-Follett', she wondered what he could possibly want to say so urgently to Archie. Then she grasped that it was addressed to herself. She stared for some time at the envelope before she brought herself to open it. The small fact that her father would never again address her in her maiden name made her realise, for the first time, that she was actually married. Even when she had convinced herself that she was no longer Clara Batchelor but Mrs Hughes-Follett, she still hesitated to open her letter. When at last she did so, the 'Dearest Clara' dispelled the obscure anxiety that persisted from her dream. If he had been angry, it would have been only 'Dear'.

Dearest Clara,

I had a childish fancy to be the first person to write to you in your married name. This is only to send my best love and all my blessings to you both.

I must apologise again for my absurd behaviour outside the church. I cannot think what possessed me. I knew, even at the time, that no one would have minded in the least, even if they had noticed it, the fact that the bride's father had a split in his glove! To think that, at such a moment, when you must have been nervous and overwrought, I should have distracted you and nearly made you late for the ceremony, fills me with shame. I can only say "mea culpa" and offer the feeble excuse that I was a little overwrought myself.

Let me say once more – to both of you – how delighted I am to have Archie for my son-in-law. How providentially

it has turned out in the end! Bless you again, my dearest
child . . . may I say, my dearest children?

Your affectionate father,

C.F.B.

She read the letter two or three times as she drank her tea.
After the unreality of yesterday it seemed to link her once more
to her old self. However disjointed her life might be, however
much she was haunted by the sense that everything she under-
took was doomed to failure, she remained Claude Batchelor's
daughter. In marrying Archie she had perhaps made up to him
for all the times she had disappointed him in the past.

The letter, she noticed, contained no reference whatever to
her mother. This was so unusual that it brought home to her how
deeply divided her parents were on the subject of her marriage.
She tried to assure herself that her mother's disapproval meant
nothing to her. Nevertheless it was faintly disturbing that anyone
so vague and variable should have held firmly to the same opinion for four years. Even more disturbing had been Isabel's unusual
silence. When, for the second time, she had announced that she
was going to marry Archie, Clara had expected protests, even
tears. There had been none. Her mother had merely said: 'I'm
sure Daddy will be delighted. It's what *he* always wanted.' Only
for that one moment yesterday had her unnatural calm broken
down. She told herself that now it was positively her duty to
ignore her mother. Henceforth only *he* mattered: her loving,
admiring father who was so certain she had done the right thing.
Forgetting that, only a few minutes ago, she had been reduced to
guilty panic by his mere presence in a dream, she gave a satisfied
smile.

As she sipped her delicious tea and looked out on sunlit lawns
and trees in their fresh spring green, she felt a rush of gratitude
that was almost like love to Archie, still heavily asleep. This
marriage had restored her to her father; henceforth the three of
them were bound in a new tie from which her mother was

excluded. She thought how passionately Claude had wanted a son; how passionately she herself had wanted a brother.

She stared at Archie's flushed sleeping face and half-open mouth. What would her father have thought if he had known that her husband had been drunk on his wedding night? She turned back to that pathetic, rather pompous letter. Why was it so reassuring to her disturbed mind? Why did it seem like absolution for a sin she had forgotten to confess? What she had most dreaded in marrying Archie had not happened. She had dreaded it yet obscurely wanted it, as if that unknown, violent contact with another person would break down some barrier in herself. Suddenly she laid the letter against her hot forehead, as if it had some secret meaning which could only be communicated by touch.

3

Four days later, Archie too had a letter. He glanced through it impatiently; then his face darkened.

'Whatever's the matter?' Clara asked.

'Hell,' he said without looking up. He was studying it carefully now and frowning with the effort to take it in.

'Bad news about the Lister thing?'

'Pretty grim,' he nodded.

Clara had long ago given up trying to follow the financial tangles of the enterprise in which Lister had persuaded Archie to invest three-quarters of his legacy. The idea was to found a club with a small theatre attached. Lister had not himself put any money into it but had agreed to run the theatrical side for a salary and a percentage of the takings. Archie, in return for his capital, was to be paid £400 a year for the vague job of 'General Secretary' but would in fact spend most of his time working under Lister.

At first the plan had seemed fairly reasonable. She believed that Lister was too shrewd to be involved in something with no hope of success. But, after her only meeting with the man behind the scheme, she had begun to have doubts. She had met Bell in a bar with Lister and Archie and had asked him one or two questions. Bell's answers had been either evasive or patronising. Later, Archie had told her apologetically that Bell was a temperamental chap and hated talking business to women. After that, she had only been able to gather from Archie the vaguest idea of what was going on. However, he was so happy and excited about the plan that she had kept her misgivings to herself. Less surprised than he, she was able to ask quite calmly:

'What's gone wrong?'

'Can't quite make out. Something about their not being able to get a theatre licence unless they make some structural alterations.'

'Surely Bell went into all that before he started the rebuilding?'

'Maybe they've changed the rules or something. He keeps saying "unforeseen circumstances". Anyway, what it boils down to is they need more cash. Everything's going to take a bit longer than they thought and they've got to find money for a mortgage instalment.'

'I thought they'd bought the place outright.'

'Well, it seems they had to do some wangling. Someone else who was coming in let them down and they had to borrow.'

'They can't have any more of yours.'

'They certainly can't,' he said quietly. 'I had a slight shock when I saw my bank manager the other day.'

'But, Archie,' she said aghast. 'It can't *all* have gone. Five hundred pounds is an *enormous* amount of money. You can't have spent it all in a few months.'

'Oh . . . there's a bit left,' he said hastily. 'Oh, yes . . . quite a bit. Must be. But you know, even though I've mostly been staying with the family, it's damned hard to live on six quid a week if you're going to have any fun at all. Then there were odds and ends like the old motorbike and sidecar. Oh . . . and a quarter in advance on the Chelsea house.'

It was Clara's turn to feel guilty. During their engagement she had let him take her out and give her presents without worrying whether he could afford them as he could when his mother was alive.

'I ought to have restrained you,' she said. 'I'll be good from now on. I'm awful at managing money myself.'

'Don't worry, darling. As I say, there's a bit left. And I didn't fritter it all. That two hundred was really an investment.'

'*What* two hundred?' she asked, with sudden apprehension.

'I forked it out to buy the option on some play by a friend of Bell's.'

'You never told me.'

'I was going to. It only happened a week or two ago. Getting married put everything out of my head. Had to make up my mind in a hurry because Bell said there was another management keen as mustard to get it. Decent of him to tip me the wink. He swears it's an absolute winner and that I'd be mad to lose the chance.'

'Does Jimmy agree?'

'Actually, he hasn't read it yet. I've only glanced at it myself. I terribly want your expert opinion. It's translated from German by some foreign chap whose English struck me as a bit wonky. I thought maybe you might be an angel and knock it into shape a bit. We may make pots out of it some day.'

'Some day,' sighed Clara. 'But what's our situation now?'

'It certainly looks a bit critical, darling. Still I'm sure we can wangle something.'

'What's the worst that could happen?'

'It won't, of course. But if they can't raise any more cash, the whole thing may go phut. Including my job.'

'Have they any hopes?'

'Well, frankly no. They want me to approach Uncle Stanley.'

Clara's heart sank like a lift.

'Archie . . . you know he wouldn't. He loathes the idea of your having anything to do with the theatre.'

'He wouldn't in the ordinary way, the old swine. But Lister says Bell's worked out a very hot notion. Something no chap with a head for business could resist. Hang it all, it's my money. Fairholm doesn't stand to lose a cent. Even he could hardly want to see everything I've put into the Club go down the drain.'

'You're jolly brave to tackle him.'

Clara tried to sound cheering but she had a foreboding that, even if Lord Fairholm agreed – and nothing could be more unlikely – the Club was doomed.

'Shouldn't dream of trying if we weren't right up against it. If it were just me alone, I'd probably say to hell with it all and cut my losses.'

Clara smiled at him across the breakfast table. The porcelain and fine linen seemed suddenly to have become symbols of unattainable security. The Georgian silver winked smugly in the morning sun.

'Don't worry just because of me,' she said, her spirits rising as if in defiance of Aunt Sybilla's wealth. 'Even if the Club should fail, we'll manage somehow.'

Archie's angry, worried face relaxed for the first time.

'You're a wonder,' he said, reaching out a long arm and gripping her wrist. 'What a girl to have in a crisis.'

Clara felt a hypocrite. She knew very well that she was not being brave. She could smile, simply because the prospect of anything real, even a disaster, had revived her. The artificiality of Brevisham was beginning to get on her nerves. Something of Sybilla Hughes-Follett's own boredom had communicated itself to the place. Left a childless widow at forty, she had spent the last fifteen years fighting off this boredom by constantly changing houses, friends and religions. Brevisham was still a fairly new toy but, like all Sybilla's lavishly redecorated interiors, it suggested a stage set which might be demolished at any moment. Sometimes, when she and Archie came in to those restaurant-like meals, Clara was almost surprised to find the servants and the furniture still there.

'Some honeymoon,' said Archie, looking considerably less cheerful than Clara. 'The ghastly thing, darling, is that it looks as if I'll have to go up to London today. I've simply got to sort this out with Bell and Jimmy.'

'I'll come with you.'

'I say – will you?' His face lightened, then clouded again. 'But where can you go? I'll have to hang about in bars for hours. Probably have to stay the night if I'm to get hold of Uncle Stanley.'

'I shan't butt in on your conferences. You seem to forget we've got a house of our own now.'

'Good Lord. I'd almost forgotten. At the worst, we've got a roof till June. But won't you be bored to tears all alone?'

'Not as bored as I would be here.'

'I say . . . I'm simply longing to get into our own place. What about you?'

'More than anything,' she said truthfully. 'I suppose we couldn't? . . .'

They looked at each other questioningly. Then Clara shook her head.

'No. It would be too rude to your aunt. After all, she *has* been awfully kind.'

'Hang Sybilla. It's you I'm thinking of. I wanted you to have a bit of comfort.'

'I've had so much, I feel bloated. And if we are going to be ruined, it seems sillier than ever living in this sort of way.'

Archie groaned.

'When I think of all the things I'd like to give you . . . Lord I hope I haven't really landed you in a mess. If this job *did* go phut we wouldn't have a penny. But it just *can't* happen. I'll get Fairholm to fork out some of my cash if I have to wring his neck to get it.'

'We've still got your three hundred a year. Lots of people haven't that.'

'Doesn't leave more than about a quid a week after the rent's paid.'

'I'll go back to doing advertisements. I made £250 one year. If I went on the regular staff instead of free-lancing, I might get quite a lot more.'

'Shut up,' said Archie fiercely. 'That's one thing I won't stand for. You're not going to slave at something you loathe just because I've let you down.'

She said, in sudden panic:

'We've got the house till June. Oh, Archie, I just couldn't bear to let it go. I'd do anything rather than lose my little house.' She added hastily, '*our* little house'.

He looked at her rather ruefully.

'You adore that place, don't you?'

'Yes, I do,' she admitted. 'Don't you?'

'Oh yes. Rather. Even if I do feel as if I'd bump my head on the ceiling. But then I'd adore any place where I could live with you. Theatrical digs – Tithe Place – Brevisham . . . it's all one to me.'

She wanted to say, 'To me too'. But before she could get the words out, he came over and kissed her.

'You shall have your precious house. Anywhere where you can put up with your ghastly husband a little longer.'

'Really, Archie. We haven't been married a week and you talk as if I were threatening to run away.'

'You'd be justified,' he said sadly. 'You know that, old thing.'

She kissed him with remorseful affection, saying softly what was almost the truth:

'I'm quite happy. I don't want things to be any different.'

4

A few hours later, when Archie dropped her at the little box of a house in Tithe Place, Clara felt the first positive pleasure she had known since they danced together the first night at Brevisham.

She had discovered the house one afternoon in late February. She had been wandering about London on one of the many restless, discontented days of the interval between the tour and the wedding. During those early months of 1921, living once more in Valetta Road with her parents and her grandmother, she had felt like a traveller waiting to start on a journey. She had not particularly looked forward to it: there were moments when she would gladly have cancelled it. But she had committed herself and there had been nothing to do but idle about at home, neither inhabiting the present nor dreaming excitedly about the future.

Her preparations for her marriage had been sketchy and listless till the final rush of buying clothes. This time she had been able to afford only a minimum. Knowing that her father was short of money, she had felt guilty about his paying for the expensive wedding which neither she nor Archie wanted but which his pathetic pride demanded. He had been distressed when they had decided to take a small furnished house or flat to save trouble. To him it seemed almost immoral that a young couple should not begin life among their own furniture. But Clara and Archie had one trait in common: neither of them took the least interest in domestic details. All that they wanted was to walk straight into something ready-made that would give them the minimum of trouble.

That particular afternoon she had had no intention of house-hunting. She had been walking blindly, taking any turning at random, till she somehow found herself in the King's Road. She knew Chelsea hardly at all but she remembered that a friend of Stephen's called Clive Heron lived there. He had known Stephen in the army and Clara had been both amused and impressed by him when the three of them had occasionally spent an evening together in the Garrick School days. Wanting to forget everything connected with Stephen, she had not thought of Heron for months. Now, suddenly, she remembered his address and found her way to Paultons Square. She stood outside his house and was almost on the point of ringing the bell when she realised that, at this moment, he would almost certainly be at the Home Office. At once relieved and disappointed, she walked slowly through the square, charmed by the small Georgian houses. Suddenly it occurred to her how delightful it would be to live in Chelsea and she began to explore its back streets with a growing sense of excitement.

It was a mild afternoon with a foretaste of spring; crocuses were pushing up in paved gardens and window boxes; the pale sunlight made the cream and white and grey stucco-fronted houses look like an eighteenth-century print. One crooked row, where the houses changed colour and character at each bend, particularly charmed her. The variety was so utterly unlike the uniform terraces of West Kensington that she might have been in another town, almost another country.

She began to walk slowly and stealthily; peering in at windows. Even the curtains fascinated her after the dreary tiers of serge, brocade and lace in Valetta Road. Some were brightly coloured: orange, magenta or jade; some mere pieces of printed stuff carelessly draped. Now and then they were even of dirty yellow lace with an aspidistra behind them. The windows at which she stared longest, had no curtains at all and through them she could make out dim shapes of easels, jars full of brushes and canvases piled anyhow against the wall. Through one such, which was open, she saw the back of a man actually engaged in painting a picture. The smell of turpentine affected her as once the smell of the theatre had done. Without stopping to think why, she stopped and stood, clutching the railings in a kind of ecstasy. At the same moment, further down the street, a piano burst out, firm and confident, in the first movement of a Mozart concerto in C major which she particularly loved. Hearing the piano, smelling simultaneously the turpentine and the damp earth of a window box and seeing an almond tree in flower at the corner of the street she had one of her rare timeless moments when everything came together and seemed to have a significance beyond itself. The moment passed; the tree, the music, the man painting the picture resumed their separate identities. But it had left her with a discovery. Chelsea was not merely charming or 'old-world' or unlike West Kensington: it was a place where people worked. If she could only live there, feel this atmosphere all round her, she might be able to begin to work properly herself. As if to confirm it, the pianist began patiently playing a phrase over and over again. Tears of joy came into her eyes; she found herself praying incoherently: 'Oh, God . . . let me work like that one day. Oh, God, don't let me be just a messy amateur.'

At the end of the street was an extremely small house with a 'To Let' board . . . Clara boldly rang the bell and interviewed the owners. To her disappointment, they were not artists but a young couple, slightly older than herself and Archie, to whom she took an instant dislike. The wife was harshly good-looking in a brassy way and the two of them conveyed a curious impression of being at once rather too smart and indefinably seedy. Clara was not yet expert at recognising the peculiar stamp of those who live by small sharp practices.

She fell in love with the house at sight. The small rooms with their light distempered walls and sparse, gay furniture were as unlike Valetta Road as possible; indeed unlike any place in which she had ever lived. She was horrified to find that the rent was four and a half guineas a week – more than three-quarters of Archie's allowance. But Mrs Woods pointed out that there was a separate studio which she could easily let for a pound a week. Painters and sculptors, she asserted, were simply fighting for studios in Chelsea.

The 'studio' turned out to be a stone-floored wooden shed with a dirty, broken skylight. But Clara was in too ecstatic a state to notice details. She was so dazzled by the idea of possessing a studio, as well as a house in Chelsea, that she was already planning to use it herself as a workroom. She summoned just enough shreds of commonsense not to commit herself then and there. In spite of Mrs Woods's assurance that there were half a dozen people after it, 38 Tithe Place had still been to let in April.

Archie had signed the lease a fortnight before their wedding and during that time Clara had gone over to Tithe Place on every possible occasion. The pleasure of turning the key in her own front door was one that never failed, even though she had soon discovered certain flaws in her dream house.

The rooms were even smaller than she had fancied. An ingenious arrangement of mirrors gave a deceptive sense of space, as she found out when she tried to add a few objects of her own. There were no shelves and no room to put even the smallest bookcase; the fresh light covers concealed the hardest of cheap and ill-sprung chairs; the gay rush mats, strewn with apparent negligence, were calculated camouflage for holes in the carpets. The basement, which contained a dark little dining-room and a kitchen with a battered, rusty gas-stove and a cracked sink, smelt of mice and mildew.

However, the fact that the house was so tiny gave her a good excuse for leaving the bulk of their wedding presents at Valetta Road. Both she and Archie felt oppressed by those elaborate clocks, silver bowls, dinner services and cases of cutlery which they were sure they would never need even if there had been any room to put them. Since she was making yet one more new beginning, it was more fun to travel light; unencumbered by objects chosen by people of her parents' generation. Nevertheless, there was something about the atmosphere of 38 Tithe Place which faintly disturbed her. She decided that, since they were not yet actually living there, it must be because it still seemed to belong to the Woods whom she disliked more each time she saw them.

Today, as Archie carried in their luggage, she thought she would really begin to inhabit the house and make it her own.

'Don't know when I'll be back, old thing,' he said as he kissed her goodbye in the hall that was so low that his head almost touched the ceiling. 'But you bet it will be the very first minute I can get away.'

As he reached the bottom of the steps, he turned, ran up again and caught her in his arms just as she was shutting the door.

'I just can't believe it,' he said. 'To think I'll come back tonight and find you here in our own house. Let's wash out Brevisham, shall we? After all, this is where we really begin.'

When he had gone, Clara wandered from room to room without attempting to unpack. All she wanted was to savour the intense pleasure of having, for the first time, a place where she could do as she chose. Even her father had no right to come here unless she invited him. At Valetta Road, though he had long ceased to be an alarming figure, her heart still jumped with the old apprehension when she heard his latchkey turn in the lock. Now, the click of a key could only be Archie's. Whatever she might come to feel about Archie, she was convinced that she could never be afraid of him.

Sitting in one of the Woods' broken-springed chairs, she closed her eyes in the effort to take in this enormous change in her life. It was Archie who had made all this possible. She felt again that glow of gratitude that was almost love. Her father had been so disturbed at the mere suggestion of her living alone or even sharing a flat with another girl that she had not had the courage to defy him. It occurred to her that, if she and Archie had been brother and sister, no one would have minded their setting up house. Slightly shocked at the thought which was so nearly a wish, she opened her eyes and stared at her wedding ring to remind herself that they were husband and wife.

In his remorse after that first night, she had had difficulty in persuading Archie to drink so much as a glass of sherry. Once convinced that he was forgiven, he had been as gay as a schoolboy let off a punishment. She had an odd sense that, in the last three days, she had grown older and Archie younger. There seemed a wilder disproportion than ever between the implications of the Nuptial Mass and their actual behaviour. They were like two children playing truant from school. At Brevisham, Archie had wanted to spend most of the day playing invented games such as they used to play with Charles at Maryhall. But though she tried hard to enter into the spirit of them, she easily grew bored. She had managed to hide her boredom but there were moments when she wondered how long she was going to have to keep up the part of Wendy to Archie's Peter Pan.

One tiny episode had shaken her far more than the tragicomedy of their wedding night. For hours one morning she had fetched sticks and stones for Archie while he dammed a stream with the absorption with which he used to work his model railway. When at last he had finished his dam, he had turned to her with shining eyes.

'There, my girl,' he had said, holding her to him with a masterfulness unusual in him. 'You haven't married a dud after all. That dam will hold against the deluge.'

Suddenly, she had had to use all her self-control not to pull away some of the stones and release the imprisoned water. The impulse was so violent that for a second she had almost lost consciousness. And in that second she had had a kind of instantaneous dream in which she was a railway engine driven by Charles Cressett and Archie.

As if it were dangerous to think too much, she jumped up from the chair. Immediately she was conscious of the number of mirrors in the tiny space. Three different angles of her head and shoulders and one full-length figure sprang towards her. The little room, with its holland covers and primrose walls and arty rush mats, seemed to close in on her. For a moment, it was an effort to remember that this house was the symbol of her new-found freedom and not a room in a horrible story she had once heard where each day the walls of a prisoner's cell drew imperceptibly nearer together. She turned towards the window and looked out into the sunlit street. On the corner of the opposite pavement was a high oblong block of red brick which suggested a town hall. It had such a secular air from the outside that she had only recently discovered that it was a Catholic church. Now its uncompromising bulk, which interrupted the row of charming dwarf houses and partly blocked the light from her own, seemed both a relief and an irritation. It was like the intrusion of a firm Nannie into the nursery. The intrusion allays panic but it reduces the magic palace once again to toy bricks. She was about to turn away, like a sulky child, when she noticed a man walking along the stretch of pavement in front of the church.

He was tall and heavily built, with a rather impressive head which struck her as vaguely familiar, as if she had seen it photographed somewhere. There was something impressive too about the way he wore his shabby old jacket and torn, open-necked shirt. What interested her most was that he carried a large canvas under one arm and a frame over the other. Here was proof that she was really living in Chelsea where it was as natural to see painters walking about bareheaded carrying their pictures as to see bowler-hatted bank clerks carrying despatch cases in West Kensington.

She watched him reverently as he crossed over to her side of the street. Forgetting that she was visible, she gave an admiring smile. The smile was not for the man himself but for his profession and she was dismayed when he stopped dead under her window and smiled too. He was so tall that their eyes were almost on a level; his were grey and bright as a boy's though there were crow's feet round them and he was evidently much older than herself. There was an oddly youthful delicacy too about the features of his plump, full-moon face. His smile, which made dimples in his fleshy, but not flabby cheeks, was so unabashed and cheerful that she had to go on smiling herself. Then, suddenly, she turned away and hurried into the passage. The sitting-room was so small and the window so large that there was no hiding in it. She stayed for a minute or two in the dark, narrow hallway, half-excited, half-afraid. Perhaps in Chelsea people thought nothing of ringing strangers' door bells. It would not do to be stuffy and conventional as if one were still living in West Kensington.

She longed to meet this painter – any painter – but she wished she had not smiled at him like that. Something about him strongly suggested that he put only one interpretation on smiles from strange young women. After a few moments she ran upstairs to the bedroom and peered cautiously from behind the curtain. The man was still in the street, moving away very slowly and looking back hopefully over his shoulder at every other step.

When he was out of sight, she felt suddenly exhilarated. She decided she must stop mooning about from room to room and do something about organising her new life. The house, though tidy, had an indefinable air of neglect. When she went to the dressing-table to take off her hat, she found an even film of dust on the mirror. Evidently the charwoman whom they had taken over from the Woods had not come in every day as she had been paid to do. There had been no time to warn her of their sudden return. Had she meant to leave everything to the last day, banking on their not finding her out?

Clara felt cheated and angry. Though she was aware of knowing little more about housekeeping than Dora Copperfield, she resented being treated like a fool. However, perhaps she was being unjust to Mrs Pritchard. Supposing she were ill – so ill that she would be unable to come back for weeks? Clara had no intention of sweeping and dusting and scrubbing. She decided she had better put on her hat and go round and see what had happened.

Congratulating herself on having been businesslike enough to have made a note of the address, she set out full of virtuous zeal. But by the time she found the house, which turned out to be nearly a mile from Tithe Place, she felt considerably less efficient. Mrs Pritchard, a youngish woman, with paste slides in her bobbed hair, who bore an odd resemblance to Mrs Woods, was smoking a cigarette in her open doorway. Mrs Pritchard assured her that she had been ever so poorly the last few days but would be round at nine sharp tomorrow though she wasn't really up to it. No one could have looked less like an invalid but Clara could not meet the challenge in those sharp green eyes. She thanked Mrs Pritchard meekly, dared not mention the money and walked away as fast as possible, aware of those sharp eyes boring into the back of her head.

Even when she was back again in Tithe Place, she was still conscious of Mrs Pritchard's contemptuous stare. Used to the friendly servants at Valetta Road, who thought nothing too much trouble for 'Miss Clara' and who were as honest as the day, it had not occurred to her that a daily help might become a tyrant. She could not get rid of her because the Woods had made it a condition that she should be kept on. Indeed, she began to wonder whether the woman were not a kind of spy for their landlords.

To try and convince herself that the house was, after all, theirs for the time being and she was free to do as she liked, she unpacked and arranged her clothes and the few wedding presents they had brought over. She even daringly changed the position of some of the Woods' furniture and put away some of their ornaments, replacing them with her own books. By the time she had finished and gone out and bought some flowers, it was late in the afternoon and dusk was beginning to shadow the windows with blue. She began to look forward desperately to Archie's return.

She sat down, lit a cigarette, and her mind wandered back to the painter. How she envied that man, looking so happy and assured, not caring in the least that his jacket was old and shapeless and his shirt torn. How she wished she could be like that, really free, caring only for one's work and utterly absorbed in it. She had already convinced herself that he must be a very good painter. Why hadn't she had the courage to speak to him? Perhaps at that very moment he had been looking for a studio. Hadn't she, after all, a studio to let? True, she had meant to use it herself for writing. But how stimulating it would be to have a real painter working just across their tiny courtyard. There was something, she was sure, about the smell of turpentine and linseed oil that would make her *want* to write – to work hard for hours every day like that pianist down the road, not just mess about with unfinished beginnings or bring off a fluke now and then like an amateur. She would put up a 'To Let' notice tomorrow and see what happened.

Forgetting all about Archie, forgetting that she was tired and hungry, she ran out to the 'studio' to examine its possibilities. It was smaller than she had supposed at first and, now that the Woods had piled empty crates of beer bottles and two tin trunks in one corner, one really could not think of it as anything but a large shed. Moreover, there were no means whatever of heating or lighting it. It had been a warm spring day but the 'studio' had a cellar-like chill and its stone floor numbed her feet through her thin shoes. Shivering as she walked through the small paved yard, bordered by a strip of earth in which grew a sooty laurel and three anaemic, fading hyacinths, her spirits sank again almost to zero. No one could paint there; no one could even write there. She made a final tour of the house, though she knew every detail of its three pairs of box-like rooms by heart. Where *had* she supposed she was going to write? The only solid table was in the basement dining-room, the one dark spot in the house. The sitting-room was unthinkable; the spare room too small to house even a school desk besides the bed; there was, in fact, nowhere but the bathroom that had enough floor space to put an extra table and chair. Ending her tour in the kitchen, she realised again that she was remarkably hungry. There was nothing in the larder and, if she and Archie were to have any breakfast, she must go out and hunt for some food.

By luck, she found a tiny shop, almost like a country grocer's, still open. As she walked back laden with tea, butter, bread, eggs and condensed milk, she remembered guiltily that she had not left a note for Archie. He had counted so much on finding her there when he got home. It was not till she turned into Tithe Place, that she realised how much she herself was counting on finding him in. When she saw that the windows were dark, she could hardly bring herself to turn her key in the door.

Fumbling without success for the switch in the passage, she could have sworn she heard someone moving on the upper floor. She called weakly: 'Archie – is that you?' There was no answer. When at last she found the switch she was trembling all over. She forced herself to go upstairs but there was, of course, no one there. Afraid to pull the curtains, she turned on the lights in all the six rooms and installed herself in the little sitting-room staring out into the street and hoping that every male figure that moved into the circle of the lamp at the corner might be Archie. At last she could bear being alone no longer. Leaving all the lights on, she dashed out into the street and across to the church. She rattled vainly at the handle of the iron-studded door. It was locked. She stood with her cheek against the door, praying incoherently, trying to feel the presence of the Blessed Sacrament behind it. After a few minutes she grew a little calmer and found courage to cross the road again. A man was now standing where she herself had stood in the window. Unable to make out his face against the light, she had another rush of terror till she realised that it could be no one but Archie.

Archie said thickly:

'Where the hell did you get to? Had the wind up. Lights on all over the show. No Clara. Whass it all mean?'

Clara tried to explain but he was too drunk to take it in. He collapsed heavily on to the tiny sofa and tried to pull her on to his knee. She avoided him and sat on a chair against the wall, as far away from him as was possible in the box of a room.

'Can't bear touch me, eh?' he said belligerently. 'Think I've had a few? An' why shouldn' I have a few? Bloody well needed them. Nice day I've had. Come home and what do I find? Wife gone. First money gone. Then wife gone.'

'I've not gone. Oh, do *try* and tell me what's happened.'

'Nothing's happened. Tha's the point. Ab-so-luly nothing – Napoo. Sunk.'

'You mean your uncle won't—'

He blinked at her, suddenly solemn.

'Not a bloody penny. There's a nice bloody uncle for you. Very offensive about my frien's – I took exception. Poor old Bell. Simply wouldn' listen proposition. *Water*tight prop'sition. And my money, mark you. Who the hell else's? Eh? Tell me that if you can. It's free country, isn't it?' His voice rose aggressively again. 'Well go on . . . tell me . . . is it free country or not?'

'Yes . . . I suppose so.' She had never seen him in a state approaching this before.

'Glad you agree something I say. Think I'm a bloody fool, don' you? But you've got to admit chap's got right to his own money if it *is* free country. Jimmy agrees. Bell agrees. Nice chaps – absoluly dead right. And now where are we? Three poor sods . . . all . . . utterly . . . sunk.'

He rambled on incoherently. At moments he forgot who she was and argued angrily with her as if she were his uncle or commiserated with her and invited her to drown it in a short one as if she were Lister or Bell. At others he would be conscious of her again, now remorseful, now resentful.

Sometimes it was:

'Only girl in the world. Married her on false pretenshes and now look at the bloody mess I've made. Went away and I don' blame her.'

Sometimes:

'How the hell d'you expect me to do anything when you think I'm utter dud? Don't argue – You know you do. Only got to look at your face. Never believed in me: never for one second. Old Jimmy was right. Never listen to a woman. Wet-blankets one and all.'

It was like a nightmare sitting there in the bright little room with this man who looked like Archie and spoke in Archie's voice but with whom she could make no contact. Anything she said, any questions she asked seemed to reach him in some form other than intelligible words, as puzzling or even threatening gestures. Sometimes when she spoke, he smiled at her foolishly: sometimes he put up his arm as if to ward off a blow. Once he lurched over to her, grabbed her by the shoulders and began to shake her. The pouring out of this incoherent talk seemed to fuddle him more and more. He was both more absurd and more frightening than Stephen had been at his worst. Stephen, even when he could hardly stand, had always retained a certain charm. He might no longer be able to identify Clara or anyone else but he created a kind of fantastic world and invited anyone who was with him to share it. If he was pugnacious, he behaved like Don Quixote riding at the windmills; if he was melancholy, he declaimed poetry or apostrophised the lamp-post, on which he proposed to hang himself, with articulate eloquence. Right up to the moment of his final collapse which was always sudden and silent, he remained recognisably the same person.

Paler than ever, his eyes glittering, Stephen drunk had something of the air of a fallen angel. Archie drunk seemed almost sub-human. As he sat hunched up with his long arms dangling almost to the floor, his thick, low-growing hair falling forward over the big nose, now red and swollen, he suggested Caliban.

At last, after one of his long, mumbling tirades, she could bear it no longer. Her head was aching with the strain of trying to make any contact with him. She had eaten nothing since their breakfast at Brevisham and the fumes of stale whisky made her feel sick. She tried to make her escape but, before she could get to the door, he made a dash at her and wrapped her in his arms. He held her so tightly that she could make no movement beyond turning her head away. If he kissed her at the moment, she thought she really would be sick. Suddenly, he crumpled up, slithered to his knees, still clutching her fast round the waist and burst into loud, blubbering sobs.

'Don't go . . . Darling girl . . . Only girl in world . . . Don't leave me . . . Don't run away . . . Can't live . . . Absolutely can't live if you go.'

She managed at last to get him into the little spare room next door and heave him somehow on to the bed. He gave one or two deep grunting sighs and fell asleep, breathing heavily and painfully like a patient under an anaesthetic. She found rugs and blankets to cover him and put a jug of water beside him. These small practical tasks broke her sense of nightmare. He lay there so ugly, pitiful and defenceless that she could no longer feel frightened or even angry. She bent down and kissed his cold damp forehead and the half-open mouth twitched in a wry smile.

She went upstairs to their own bedroom where the light had been burning all those hours. As she went to the window to draw the curtains, she saw the great dark bulk of the church opposite against a sky full of stars. But now she no longer resented its presence. She leant her hot cheek against the glass. The tears pricked under her closed eyelids but she was too exhausted to cry. After some minutes, though her head throbbed and burned, she felt calmer. She forced herself to look for some sheets and made up one of the two beds. Tired as she was, it was some time before she fell asleep. She tried to put some order into her spinning thoughts. From what she had gathered from Archie, there could be little doubt that there was no hope for the Club. He had indeed talked wildly of new people who could be interested, even shouted once or twice that his uncle would be sorry for having missed a bloody wonderful chance, but she had no reasonable hope left. She must pull herself together, think of a plan, get some work before they were literally penniless. But her mind refused to bite on anything concrete. The future appeared only as a menacing, impenetrable wall. She gave up at last and let small jagged images project themselves on the screen of her closed eyelids; her father's agonised face when he had returned with his new gloves; Charles Cressett grinning at her in one of his fiendish moods; Archie drunk; Archie sober; Archie smiling as he left her twelve hours ago saying 'This is where we really begin'.

6

Clara had been married for two months. Having for the first time no definite occupation, she could not establish any order in her life. The fact that Archie had none either, and was even more untidy and impractical than she was herself, was rapidly reducing her to a slattern. Day by day she grew more inert and apathetic, weighed down by a sense of guilt but too listless to pull herself together.

Archie had tried desperately to persuade some member of his family to put up the money to save the Theatre Club but everyone, including Aunt Sybilla, had firmly refused. Now that the scheme was dead and buried, he continued to spend most of his time in bars and drinking clubs with Lister and his friends. His excuse was that, if he 'hung around with the boys', sooner or later something would turn up. Sometimes he came back fairly sober; more often drunk. Twice she had had to bail him out of Vine Street. His moods varied between wild optimism and penitent pessimism. Already she was almost immune to both. Meanwhile another quarter's rent would soon be due for the house. She knew that Archie was spending far more than his allowance. The odd cheques they had been given as wedding presents had long ago been cashed and frittered away. For the past week or two she had been imploring Archie to tell her how much, if anything, still remained of his legacy. But he kept evading the question, saying that things were rather complicated at the moment and a lot of chaps owed him quite a bit of money and it would be time to start worrying when one of his cheques actually bounced.

This sense of insecurity, instead of bracing Clara to try and make some money herself, completely unnerved her. Once, when there was a chance that Lister might have been able to fix the two of them up in a touring company she was panic-stricken. Not only was she convinced that she would never be capable of acting again, but she could not face all the reorganisation this would mean. They would have to give up the house which she clung to though there were times when she almost loathed it. Even the thought of packing her clothes was an intolerable burden. She was as relieved as Archie was disappointed when this scheme, too, came to nothing.

There was a positive reason, as well as sheer inertia, which compelled her to try to stay on in Chelsea. At least she could wander about the streets and feel that people were working all about her. This was more often torture than comfort for, far from catching any infection of diligence, she became more and more incapable of writing anything, even the simplest letter. Original work was impossible. She told herself that, in any case, she had no right to attempt it until she had made some money. Her advertising firm was beginning to press her for some overdue pieces of copy. Day after day she sat down at the ricketty dining-table in the basement, the only table big enough to work on, only to find herself at the end of an hour with two sentences begun and scratched out. Then she would take up the paper, hoping to warm herself up by reading other advertisements and find, at the end of another hour, that she had read everything in it down to the Stock Exchange prices till her mind was more fuddled and inert than ever.

Archie was out so much that she found herself more alone than she had ever been in her whole life. Yet she made no effort to seek out any of her old friends and took to putting off people at the last moment when they invited her out. She did not know what obscure impulse drove her to isolate herself in this way but, once she had formed the habit, she could not break it. The more she was alone, the more she became conscious of her own emptiness. Sometimes she even doubted whether she existed at all. Once this sense of non-existence was so acute that she ran up from the basement to the sitting-room full of mirrors almost expecting to find nothing reflected in them. But her face stared back at her anxiously from various angles and she was horrified to see how much she had changed in a few weeks. It was not merely that, in the sunlight, she had a dulled look as if there were a film of dust all over her skin and hair but that there was a vacancy in her expression that frightened her. She found herself addressing her reflection as she used to do when she was a child. 'Really, my dear,' she said severely, 'you look as if you weren't in your right mind.'

After that, Clara bought herself a stout black notebook, exactly like the ones her father always used for writing his lecture notes, and began to keep a kind of diary. Writing in it gave her the illusion that she was at least producing something. If she was going to talk to herself, it was surely better to do so on paper. She might even discover something curious or useful in the process.

All sorts of odd things went into this secret book: reflections on her own character, severe exhortations to herself, scraps of conversation overheard in the street, descriptions of rooms or faces; dreams, speculations about religion and life, curious names which she might one day use in a story. She knew that the notebook was cheating. Sometimes she was so disgusted with the triteness or the flatulence of much that she wrote in it that she was tempted to destroy it. Suppose anyone who had ever credited her with a crumb of intelligence, let alone talent, were to read it? The thought was insupportable to her vanity. Nevertheless she continued to make entries at fairly regular intervals, offsetting the indulgence of this 'pretence' writing by refusing to allow herself to erase even the most shaming passages. It would do her good, she told herself savagely, to realise to what maundering idiocy she could descend.

Occasionally she and Archie lunched on Sundays at Valetta Road. When they did so, they made such an effort to appear a care-free modern couple that they almost deceived themselves. Clara, who might have been slouching about for days in the same crumpled frock, would dress and make up with as much care as if she were dressing for a stage part. Archie would shave, put on a clean shirt and only accept a second whisky after much pressing from her father. For an hour or two Clara would regain her sense of continuity enough to believe that the paralysed drifting of her days in Tithe Place would not go on for ever and that her life was not irremediably broken. Seeing Archie and her father's genuine affection for each other, her heart would warm to both of them. Stimulated by this and by the meaner wish not to let her mother have the satisfaction of knowing that her marriage looked like being even more of a failure than Isabel had predicted, she would behave to Archie with unusual sweetness. Archie, who never bore grudges, would respond at once so that by the time they left, arm-in-arm, Clara had almost convinced herself that, this coming week, things would definitely take a turn for the better. So far, however, they had not done so.

The last Sunday of June was Clara's twenty-second birthday: they were both invited to lunch at Valetta Road. That morning Archie was feeling so ill after a night out with Lister and the rest that he could barely open his eyes, let alone get up, by the time they were due to start. Reluctant, not to leave Archie to his hangover but to face her parents without him, Clara went alone. As she walked to the bus she thought rather bitterly of the difference between this birthday and her last. Her father, always punctilious about special anniversaries, had made an occasion of her twenty-first. There had been a dinner party of a dozen people with wines carefully chosen by Claude, including Château Yquem of her birth year, 1899, as well as the ritual champagne. He had also given her a cheque for fifty pounds. How much more she needed fifty pounds this year with the rent for Tithe Place due in a few days. What a fantastically large sum it had seemed at the time and how quickly it had melted, mostly on dinners and drinks for Stephen. She had not dared to ask Stephen to the party but she had asked his friend Clive Heron, the man who lived in Paultons Square and whom she had not run into since she came to Chelsea.

As she walked despondently along the King's Road, wishing she could put the clock back a year, a man's voice said:

'Well, are you going to cut me dead?'

She looked up, only half-surprised and altogether pleased, to see Clive Heron himself. Her first reaction was relief that, for once, she was decently dressed and made-up; her second that this was a good omen for a birthday which had begun so gloomily.

'How extraordinary,' she said, smiling up at him. 'I was just thinking about you.'

'*Most* extraordinary. *Very* queer,' he said in the mock Bloomsbury voice he used except when he was unusually serious. 'Now *why*, may I ask?'

Though Clara had only met Heron at intervals during the two years since she had first met him and he was reputed to be a 'difficult' person, she had always been completely at ease with him. In the intervals she was apt to forget his very existence but, as soon as she saw him again, she always felt a peculiar pleasure. She felt, too, as if they were resuming an interrupted conversation.

'Because it's my birthday.'

'Your birthday,' he said gravely. 'Dear me. Already? I have hardly recovered from your last birthday. Your father's wines completely metagrobolised me. Are you having another orgy?'

'No. It's all going to be rather dismal.'

'Come and have a drink. I was just taking a pre-prandial stroll to the Six Bells.'

'I'd love to but I daren't. I've got to lunch with my family and I'm late already.'

'Vexatious. Now I suppose I shall have to turn round and accompany you to your bus.'

'You needn't. I know it's agony for you to change your plans.'

'True. But I get an exquisite pleasure from occasionally mortifying myself. Besides, it appeases my eternal sense of guilt.'

As he turned and walked in her direction, Clara wondered why anybody who always appeared as gay and reasonable as Clive Heron should suffer from a sense of guilt. Probably it was only one of his amusing affectations. Looking up at him, she thought again how unlike anyone else he seemed. Dressed as usual with meticulous neatness and extreme conventionality, he always struck her as a creature who, in attempting to adopt a protective colouring which would make it invisible, merely emphasised its strangeness. Tall and preternaturally slender, there was something birdlike about the movement of his long legs and the quick turns of his small head that made his name oddly appropriate. He had a way, too, in talk of suddenly pouncing on something that interested him, like a heron spearing a fish.

'You are remarkably silent,' he said, after a moment. 'What have you been up to all this time?'

She told him that she was married.

'Yes, yes,' he said impatiently. 'I know. Stephen said something to that effect.'

'I didn't know he knew. Do you often see him?'

'Hardly ever. I can't stand that ghastly woman his wife. What a fool he was not to marry you. I told him so roundly. Of course it would have been disastrous.'

Clara laughed. 'How do you know?'

'I know everything. Surely you realise that by this time? Far more infallible than any of your Popes.'

'Are you speaking *ex cathedra*?'

'Certainly. However, no doubt you've married someone equally unsuitable.'

Since for some reason she was always compelled to be frank with Clive Heron, she answered:

'Yes.'

He darted her a look from the clear, light-lashed eyes which gleamed so intelligently behind his pince-nez. She could not imagine Heron's face without those pince-nez. Poised precisely on the bridge of his elegant nose – all his features were small and delicately finished – they seemed as much part of him as a bird's crest.

'I could have *told* you so. *Why* didn't you consult me?' he groaned.

'Because I can never bring myself to the point of ringing you up.'

'Precisely. Neither can I. That's the trouble with both of us. Hopeless neurotics. Yet I constantly get very near the point.'

'I got as far as your doorstep one day. In fact that's probably why I'm now living two streets away from you in Tithe Place.'

'Tithe Place.' He heaved a sigh. 'Really, then, there's no excuse for not doing something about it. Not that it *really* makes things any easier. I can't bear dropping in or being dropped in upon. I should still have to brace myself to use the telephone. Still, I am prepared to go to considerable lengths to see you. Ring me at the Home Office. *Yes-ss. You* ring *me.* We'll have a nice dinner together and moan about the *horrors* of the universe. The fair white scroll of the universe on which God so misguidedly scrabbled the history of mankind.'

'Here's my bus,' said Clara regretfully.

'Dear me, yes. A bus,' he said, looking at it over the tops of his pince-nez. '*Very* portentous. You had better mount it.'

As she did so, he gingerly raised the hat which looked so much too big for his small, shapely head, revealing the impeccably neat reddish gold hair which, she knew, caused him nervous misery to ruffle.

'All in perfect order,' she said reassuringly from the step. 'But *do* put it on again in case.'

'The *only* person who understands about my traumatic hair. Goodbye, now, goodbye. Write down all I said. And . . . oh, dear yes, remember me to your astonishing father. Has he any of that Château Yquem left?'

The bus started with a jerk.

'I'll bring you a bottle some day, if he has,' said Clara, almost falling off the step into Heron's arms. He pushed her upright.

'Don't titubate. I'm too frail to cope with titubating women.'

The bus suddenly stopped again. Heron said furiously:

'Why can't the beastly thing make up its mind? Machines have no right to be neurotic.'

The noise of the engine starting up again made it impossible for Clara to catch some admonition he called from the pavement. It began 'Why on *earth*' and ended with something which sounded remarkably like 'marry *me*'. But this, she decided, was impossible. One of the things about Clive Heron that made him seem to belong to a different species was the difficulty of envisaging him married to anyone. Not that he suggested a dried-up bachelor: on the contrary there was an extraordinary freshness about him which made him look considerably nearer twenty than thirty. He took, moreover, an ardent and analytical interest in the love-affairs of his friends. Stephen, who had known him first in the army and had a great affection for him, said he was too much like a cat ever to attach himself to anyone. Stephen had also been unflatteringly surprised that Clive Heron had apparently taken a fancy to Clara at their first meeting. Clara knew that he liked her and that something about her – she had no idea what it could be – seemed to please and amuse him. But never, in her wildest moments, had she ever considered the possibility of his falling in love with her or she with him. Even if he had used the words 'marry me', they could not conceivably have any personal reference. Next time she saw him, she would ask him exactly what he had said. Knowing Heron's habit of vanishing, though he seldom left London, as completely as if he had gone on a world tour, it might be months before she had the opportunity. The fact that he lived only three minutes from her own house made it almost more unlikely that she would run into him by chance. Not that he would consciously avoid her now that they were near neighbours, but, he hated unexpected meetings so much that she could almost fancy that he had the power of making himself invisible to avoid them.

She realised, when she almost overran the point where she had to change on to the West Kensington bus, that she had been thinking about Clive Heron longer than she had ever thought about him before. She realised, too, that these thoughts had been curiously comforting. When at last she rang the bell in Valetta Road, she felt more light-hearted than she had done for months.

7

Inevitably the birthday lunch was strained. Old Mrs Batchelor kept enquiring curiously what was the matter with Archie and would not let the subject alone. Finally, Isabel lost her temper and said:

'Probably Archie was drunk last night and Clara is too loyal to say so. After your own experiences one would suppose you might have learnt a little tact.'

There was a painful silence. Claude, always hurt by any reference to the fact that his adored father had at one time been a heavy drinker, turned white with anger. Clara's grandmother laid down her knife and fork, sniffed and fumbled for her handkerchief. Only her mother, with ostentatious calm, went on eating.

'Really Isabel,' Claude said at last. 'That seems to me quite unjustified.' He turned to Clara. 'Please tell Archie how *very* sorry I am he could not come. You might add how much I appreciate his unselfishness in letting you desert him when he is feeling so ill. You must go back and look after him as soon as possible. But, before you go, my dear, could you spare me just a minute or two in the study?'

Though no painful interview had taken place in the study for several years, Clara's heart still sank at those words. Back among the shelves of old books and neatly labelled black files, sitting in the huge faded green armchair her father had used at Cambridge and staring at the dusty casts of Plato and Athene, she felt once more an apprehensive child. It was the first time she had been alone with him since her marriage. Though she no longer feared his disapproval more than anything else in the world; though, ever since her re-engagement to Archie, he had treated her with the utmost gentleness; something of her old sense of guilt returned as he seated himself at his desk, sucking at his pipe and absently jabbing a fountain-pen in and out of a bowl of shot as he often did when worried.

For a moment she thought he was indeed angry. He was frowning and his jaw was thrust forward in the way she had always taken as a storm signal. Only once before had she known him angry on her birthday. That was an occasion at Mount Hilary which she could still hardly bear to remember.

The nuns had confiscated the beginning of a novel she had been writing in secret. They had given her no chance to explain that she had made her characters behave as badly as possible in those opening chapters because she meant to convert them all sensationally in the last. Without telling her, they had sent the manuscript to her father and even threatened to expel her. The day he came down to deal with this situation happened to be her birthday. Summoned to the parlour at an unusual time, she thought his visit was a delightful birthday surprise. But, as she was sliding excitedly over the slippery parquet to greet him, she saw the expression on his face. It was so thunderous that she had stopped dead; her knees trembling so much that she could not take another step. He had been in no mood to listen to explanations even if she had not been too paralysed to attempt them. The things he had said to her that day had been so terrible that there was a blank in her mind about the end of the interview. She could not remember his going away; she had nothing but a confused recollection of sobbing in the chapel all through Benediction and being put to bed in the infirmary. The next time she saw him, he had been quite genial and had made no reference to the object of that terrible visit. Neither of them had ever mentioned it since.

As she sat there now, waiting for him to speak, she realised that it was the eighth anniversary of that incident. She had a sudden absurd notion when he cleared his throat, rather portentously, to speak, that he was going, at last, to refer to it. Suppose he were going to give her, after all these years, a chance to explain? Suppose he were actually to forgive her for what had outraged him in what she had written, in all innocence, at fourteen? Might that relieve the appalling guilt and self-mistrust which overcame her every time she tried to write anything which was not merely confected? In the last two months, this guilt and impotence had spread to anything she wrote at all: to advertising copy, even to letters; to anything, in fact, designed to be read by others. Only the black notebook, though it contained much that might make her reasonably feel guilty, was exempt from the blight, simply because it was secret.

All her father said, however, when he spoke at last, was:

'Forgive me, my dear . . . you have every right to be offended if I am wrong . . . but was there any grain of truth in what your mother suggested just now?'

Clara's mind had wandered so far that she could not at once bring it into focus. She frowned, trying to remember precisely what it was that Isabel had suggested.

'Oh . . . about Archie, you mean? As a matter of fact she guessed perfectly right. But I didn't want her to know.'

'I appreciate that. I admire your loyalty very much. Very much indeed. You can be sure, Clara, that nothing you choose to say will go beyond this room.'

'I'm sure it won't. Still I don't think there's much point in saying anything.'

'Perhaps you're right. And I respect your silence. Yet would you mind my asking one thing?'

'Of course not.'

'Then is today exceptional? Let us say last night rather. That sort of thing happens now and then to any young man. I'm afraid it happened to me quite frequently at Cambridge. And, I regret to say, occasionally even after I was married.'

'It happens a good deal, yes.'

He sighed and bit the stem of his pipe.

'I can't tell you how sorry I am to hear that. My own impression was that Archie had taken himself in hand quite remarkably. All through your engagement . . . and on the few occasions when he's been here since your marriage . . . I've never seen him anything but perfectly sober.'

'He was wonderful for months before we got married. It's only since—' She stopped suddenly.

He gave a half-smile.

'Come, come. Let's hope there's no connection! But seriously, my dear, don't you think that it's time Archie got a proper job? It seems to me obvious that these shady theatrical people he goes about with – I wish to God he'd never heard of that infernal club – are doing him no good at all. Isn't it time you used your influence to keep him away from that crowd?'

'I couldn't if I tried. Archie *likes* those people. And he's determined to get into the theatre by hook or by crook.'

He said, eyeing her rather sternly:

'The last thing I want to do is to hit you when you are down. And I have nothing but admiration for the pluck with which you have taken this blow. I have never heard you reproach Archie, though I believe you were sceptical from the first about this disastrous business. All the same, Clara, I must point out that it was through you he met these people. Also, if you hadn't gone on the stage, I doubt if he would ever have had this insane idea of becoming an actor.'

She said with some heat:

'That's absolutely untrue. He talked about it years ago. The very first time I ever met him, in fact. Long before it ever entered my head to be an actress. I suppose you'll blame me for his drinking next.'

'Nonsense. I know very well it began in South America. I attribute it entirely to the shock of his mother's death and finding himself alone in the world.' He paused and glanced tenderly at the photograph of the distinguished-looking, white-bearded old man who had once been an unsuccessful village grocer. 'My poor beloved father . . . *his* trouble began with the shock of my sister's death as a baby. And no doubt with Archie . . . the shock of losing nearly all his capital – not to mention the salary those swine promised him . . . accounts for this relapse.'

He broke off, as if not quite convinced by his own words. Clara, darting a sidelong glance at her father, intercepted an equally hasty one from him. Averting their eyes, they both spoke at once.

'I'm sorry, Clara . . . what were you saying?'

'No . . . no . . . go on. Nothing at all important. I mean . . . I daresay you're right.'

He squared his shoulders and pulled fiercely at his pipe which had almost gone out.

'Things can't go on like this. Archie must pull himself together and make a fresh start. And you must help him.'

'But how?'

'I am sure Lord Fairholm would do everything possible to find him another post.'

'What . . . abroad?' she said aghast.

'Not necessarily. Nor would it matter if the salary was not very impressive. He has, after all, his allowance. The great thing is that he should have a regular job.'

'Nothing would induce Archie to ask his uncle for anything. He's definitely quarrelled with him. Anyhow, Archie would refuse point blank to work in an office. And I absolutely see his point of view.'

'Then may I ask how the two of you propose to manage? His private income barely covers this preposterous rent you are paying. That house was an absurd extravagance even when

Archie supposed his income would be more than double what it is. Now, it is sheer folly to keep it on.'

Conscious that her father was perfectly right, she bristled defensively.

'Oh, we'll manage somehow. You seem to forget that I'm quite capable of making money. I made £250 the year before I went on tour. I could probably make even more if I set my mind to it.'

'I don't deny it. But I should like to point out two things. First . . . that I never expected you to contribute one penny of anything you made to the household expenses here and you never saved one penny of it for the future. You had all that to spend on anything you fancied and I am afraid it gave you very unrealistic ideas about money. Your mother and I had exactly £250 to live on – for everything – the first year we were married.'

'Yes, I know,' said Clara peevishly. 'What was the other thing?'

'That I am sure Archie is far too fundamentally decent to wish to depend on his wife's earnings. Moreover . . .' He hesitated and cleared his throat. 'There might come a time when, even if you were contributing something, you might no longer be able to go on working.'

'Isn't that looking rather far ahead?' she asked flippantly. 'After all it's not much more than eighteen months till Archie comes into his money. Presumably I shan't be entirely decrepit at twenty-three.'

He stiffened.

'A good many things can happen in eighteen months in the life of a young married couple. Particularly if they are Catholics, as, thank God, you both are. That is why it is so essential that you should not dip into whatever is left of Archie's capital.'

Clara felt her face assume the supercilious little smile he hated. She said pertly:

'Why don't you give all these awful warnings to Archie? After all, it's really up to him, isn't it?'

He flushed a little.

'I'm sorry if you think I'm prying into your private affairs.

After all, you are my only child. It's only natural that I shouldn't want to see you make a mess of your life.'

'Have I complained?' she asked coldly.

'Never for one instant. I can't say how much I admire your loyalty.'

It was Clara's turn to flush.

'I'm sorry, Daddy, I'm being rather beastly. I know you're only trying to be helpful.'

He sighed:

'If only there were some way that I could be of some help.'

On a reckless impulse, she took him up.

'Actually you could. Only I expect it might be rather a nuisance for you.'

His face brightened . . . 'Yes?'

'Well, as a matter of fact, we *are* awfully hard up at the moment. I've got various things on hand not quite finished. Even when they are, it'll be some time before I get paid and it comes in in driblets. You couldn't possibly lend me the money for this next quarter's rent? I'll pay you back, I promise.'

The moment she had said it, she realised her folly. To cover up the blunder, she launched on a lie.

'I mean . . . I'm sure Archie has all that and . . . much more in the bank still. But after what you said about not dipping in . . . I agree . . . it would be *much* more sensible not to.'

Her voice trailed away. She was quaking inside in case he challenged her. Never before had she tried to deceive him on such a scale as this. She watched his face anxiously but could not immediately read his expression. He scratched some figures on his blotting-paper, then shook his head.

'I'm very sorry indeed, my dear child, but I am afraid it's quite impossible. By my reckoning, you are asking me to lend you something over sixty pounds. I have to admit that I don't possess such a sum or anything like it. I don't get this term's salary from St Mark's for another three weeks and every farthing of that is earmarked.' He smiled ruefully. 'Now you see the results of mismanaging money. Having never managed to save anything myself, I am a shocking example for you to avoid.'

Clara felt ashamed. She knew very well that, all his life, he had given away money and helped his many poor relations so that, though he made a good deal by his coaching and his classical text-books, he had constant anxieties about money. Her mother was extravagant and he himself loved occasional outbursts of entertaining or present-giving. If he was hard up at the moment, Clara knew that it was because he had spent considerably more than he could afford on her wedding. Yet, though she was ashamed, she also felt obscurely and unfairly resentful.

She said, none too graciously:

'Forget it. I'm sorry I suggested it. But you did ask if there was anything you could do.'

'And I meant it. But, my dear child, I honestly don't think it would be helping you to encourage you to go on living in that furnished house. You could get an unfurnished place for a quarter of what you are paying now.'

'I daresay. But we haven't any furniture.'

'I'm sure we could spare you quite a lot. And I think Archie would be wise to break into the nest-egg for that. It would be a real economy in the end.'

Clara said quickly: 'Moving's out of the question. We have to give the Woods three months' notice.'

Though already she half hated Tithe Place, the thought of leaving it, still more the idea of having to take any definite action, threw her into a panic.

'You could sub-let. Incidentally there's a very pleasant little maisonette going in Baron's Court Road for £40 a year.'

'I'm sorry, Daddy. I simply couldn't *bear* to live in West Kensington. I'd rather live in a *garret* in Chelsea.'

This time he was really angry. He said sarcastically:

'I'm sorry you were forced to live for so many years in the slum that was good enough for your parents.'

'I didn't mean that.'

'Hmm. I presume you mean you prefer the atmosphere of art for art's sake and all that rot? I'm beginning to wonder whether you're not considerably more to blame than poor Archie. I can assure you this isn't at all the life I envisaged for both of you. What's more, I'm sure Archie detests it as much as I do. The boy's a gentleman and is probably longing for a quiet, decent life. No doubt you fill the place with short-haired women and long-haired men. Archie has all my sympathy if he prefers the public house.'

Through her own resentment, Clara dimly guessed that there was pain as well as anger behind this outburst. But she could make no allowances for this. She broke out almost hysterically:

'If I'd known you were going to do nothing but carp at me and criticise me, I wouldn't have come here at all today. All my life, you've wanted me to think as you thought and do what you wanted and made me feel guilty if I didn't. Why shouldn't I live as I want to? I'm not asking *you* for anything.'

Oblivious of the fact that she had just asked him for sixty pounds, Clara felt possessed by a glow of righteous fury. She felt she was defending something immensely precious almost at the risk of her life. Never had she spoken to her father like this. Yet, even as she raged, she was conscious that she had no idea what it was that she was defending with such vehemence. He turned and stared at her with his jaw dropped and his face working. At that moment, the study door opened and her mother looked in smiling.

'Clara, darling, Zillah's made you such a charming birthday cake. She'll be so hurt if you don't come and look at it before she goes out for her afternoon off.'

She looked at their two faces.

'Whatever is the matter with you two? I could hear your voices all along the passage. Really, Claude, you look as if we were back in the old days and you had been scolding Clara for not doing her homework properly. You must remember she's a married woman now.'

Profoundly grateful for the interruption, Clara jumped up and followed her mother.

Outside, Isabel whispered to her:

'Darling . . . was that a rescue in the nick of time? Was Daddy being horrid and unsympathetic? He *can* be when he talks about duty and all that. Men so seldom understand what women feel.'

Clara said offhandedly:

'We were only having a rather boring discussion about houses and so on. Nothing in the least dramatic.'

8

The next day Archie was penitent. Instead of going off at mid-
day as usual to meet Lister, he took Clara to lunch at a cheap
little restaurant in the King's Road where the waitresses wore
orange smocks and there were check cloths and earthenware
pitchers on the tables.

'You can't be more fed up with me than I am,' he said. 'I didn't
even give you a present. Not because I forgot. A temporary
breeze at the bank.'

'Do tell me the worst. Have we *anything* left?'

'I haven't blued the lot, if that's what you mean. Things need
a bit of wangling at the moment, that's all. Thank heaven, the
old pittance is due this week.'

'So's our next quarter's rent.'

He started.

'Hell. It *can't* be. Thought we had ages yet. The Woods will
jolly well have to wait. Serve 'em right. They're bloodsuckers
anyway.'

'I tried to borrow the money from Daddy yesterday. He hadn't
got it.'

'Gosh, I wish you hadn't done that. I can hardly look him in
the eye as it is. When I think of my own beastly relations –
rolling in money and too mean even to lend one a fiver . . .'

Clara, still resentful from the day before, said:

'He wouldn't either in his present mood. Not to *me* at any rate.'

'What do you mean?' he asked suspiciously.

'Oh – you've entirely cut me out with Daddy. You're the blue-eyed boy and I'm the unscrupulous woman who's ruined you.'

'Don't be so sarcastic.'

'I'm not.'

'Then you're just pulling my leg. I feel rather awful because I touched him for a fiver myself last time we were over. Of course I'll pay him back. Did he say anything about it?'

She shook her head.

'He *wouldn't*,' said Archie. 'He's too damn nice. Greatest sport I ever met except one of the J's at Beaumont, old Sam Sissons.'

'He isn't always as nice as you think. He can be beastly sometimes. And very unjust, too.'

'That I simply can't believe.'

'It's perfectly true. As true as the fact that the rent's due and we owe the laundry over four pounds, not to mention various other bills. Also we still haven't paid Mrs Pritchard for last week.'

'Go on. Rub it in. You've every right to, I suppose. But . . .'

'But what?'

'I can't bear it when you look like that and use that acid sort of voice. It's not like you. You used to be so sweet.'

'I've always told you I wasn't sweet. And even if I ever had been . . .'

'You'd be as sour as a lemon after being married to me for two months? Thanks.'

'Archie, truly I don't *want* to be a beast. But things are getting me down. I just don't seem to know where I am any more.'

'They're getting me down too. And one of the things that's getting me down most is seeing you look so utterly miserable most of the time. I feel such a guilty swine that the only thing seems to be to go out and get blind.'

He looked so wretched that she said remorsefully:

'I expect it's my fault too, being miserable. I don't know what's come over me lately. I feel as if everything had got jammed up inside and out. I can't get up the energy to do anything . . . even to write my silly stuff for Rapson's. I'm tired and depressed and irritable all the time – for no reason.'

'Plenty of reason.' His low forehead, under the untidy red hair, crinkled into a deep frown. 'The way things have turned out, you must wish I'd never come barging back into your life.'

Almost frightened, since she had fought hard against the thought for weeks, reminding herself constantly about 'for better, for worse', she stretched across the table and touched his long, nicotine-stained fingers. Trying to puzzle out something, she herself frowned as she said gently:

'No, I don't. It's just that I don't seem to be able to fit things together any more. Or perhaps because *we* don't seem to fit in anywhere. Do you remember years ago – we'd only known each other a few weeks then – saying you and I were two of a kind?'

'I remember all right. The day I gave you my revolver and you didn't want to take it. God knows what I thought I meant . . . if anything.' He sighed. Clara could find nothing to say. She took one of the cigarettes from his crumpled packet of Gold Flakes and asked him for a light. Mechanically, he struck a match but, instead of lighting her cigarette, let the flame burn itself out. He took her left hand, absently removed the cigarette she held and began to twist the wedding ring on her finger.

Almost accusingly, he said:

'It's getting too tight. At Brevisham, it was so loose it nearly fell off.'

'I know. I've been getting steadily fatter for weeks. All my skirts are getting tight too.'

He dropped her hand, as suddenly as he had taken it, and lit the cigarette he had removed from her fingers. After a puff or two he said, as if to himself:

'I wonder. If we could have gone to Maryhall instead of to that beastly Brevisham . . .'

Clara said nothing. Her mind shot off on one of its tangents. They could not have gone to Maryhall because Charles's father could not have endured her being there. Yet, if Charles had not been killed, would there ever have been any question of her marrying Archie? Where did any chain of circumstances begin? What had led her, step by step, from that afternoon in the walled garden to be sitting here, facing Archie across a check tablecloth littered with crumbs and cigarette ash and bound to him for life?

She looked into his eyes as if she could find the answer there. They still recovered their clearness almost at once if he kept off drink for a day or two. The lids were still pink and puffy from his last bout but, once again, she saw in the eyes themselves that extraordinary beauty she had noticed in Birmingham. She could only describe it to herself as 'unfallen'. The contrast between that innocence and her own growing sense of being somehow inwardly corrupt was so painful that she had to look away.

'Buck up, my darling old thing,' he said. 'Our luck's bound to change sooner or later. Actually I met quite a useful bloke in Mooney's on Saturday.'

'Chance of a job?' She tried to sound hopeful.

'Well, no immediate prospect. Actually we weren't discussing jobs. Though this chap's well in with the Craven and Ellis management. No, the main thing at the moment is he's got a friend who wants to buy an Indian and sidecar. I'm meeting them both for a drink tomorrow.'

Though Archie had used his motorbike, the first thing he had bought out of his two thousand, very little lately, Clara knew how he treasured it. She realised things must be desperate.

'Archie . . . must you really sell her? Isn't there any other way to raise the rent?'

'Blast the rent. I certainly wouldn't sell her for that. No, I'm going to buy you a decent birthday present. I meant it to be a surprise but I thought even the prospect might cheer you up a bit.'

'Dear Archie . . . Truly I don't want one. I'd far rather . . .'

'But *I* want to. And I shall,' he said doggedly. 'You mayn't believe it and most people might think I've a damn queer way of showing it. The fact remains that I happen to love you.'

She stared at the fading marigolds in the mock peasant jug.

'I don't deserve to be loved,' she sighed. 'I really believe I'm a kind of monster. Not a real person at all.'

'Shut up. I can't stand it when you talk like that.'

'It's true,' she persisted, finding a curious relief in attacking herself. 'Look at the way I've let people down all my life. Look at the people I've disappointed . . . and worse than disappointed. My father. Lady Cressett. Now you.'

'Me?' He stared. 'How do you make that out? Surely it's the other way round. I've let you down good and hard, haven't I?'

'I *don't* make it out,' she said. 'Yet I believe somehow it's my fault. I believe Daddy was right. Perhaps that's why I blazed out at him.'

'Absolute rot,' he said. 'I don't even see what you're getting at. I'm right out of my depth. All these heart-searchings are too subtle for me. I used to have the hell of a time at Beaumont when we were supposed to examine our consciences every night. Easy enough if I'd had a fight or passed round sweets in chapel. But how the hell was I to know if I'd been "diligent in setting my neighbour a good example" or provoked another to sin?'

Clara laughed for the first time.

'We used to have that one. I expect we took it straight from you. I used to drive myself nearly mad with scruples. My bugbear was "Have I wasted time in idle day-dreaming?" I used to wonder if thinking up stories counted.'

'My God, it's good to hear you laugh again,' he said. 'Talking of stories, that's something I *have* got on my conscience. I don't believe you've done any of your own writing for ages. I know you've been hammering away at some of those beastly advertisements again.'

'Well, we need the money, don't we? As a matter of fact, I've gone so stupid I can't even do *them* now. I ought to be hammering at them this very minute instead of sitting here.'

He groaned 'And you say you've let *me* down. That's just the one thing I didn't want – that you should have to go on drudging away at that wretched stuff. To think I've got two hundred quid tied up in that play. I'd sell the option tomorrow though Jimmy swears I could make a packet if I held on. Just a question of smartening up the script a little.'

'You wanted me to do that, didn't you?'

'My darling old thing . . . I just haven't had the face to ask you . . .'

On an impulse, she said:

'I'll read it as soon as you like. And I'll gladly do some tinkering if it would give you a better chance of selling it.'

His face became radiant.

'Would you really? My God, you're a sport, Clarita. I know it's like putting a race horse in a coal cart. When I think of that marvellous story of yours . . .'

She broke in morosely:

'Forget it. I'll never write anything decent again. I know that for certain.'

'Don't say that. Believe it or not, it hurts.'

In the bitterness that swept over her almost like physical nausea at any reference to her writing, Clara hardly heard him. She muttered as if to herself:

'Amateur's luck. Exactly what Stephen said about my bringing off Katherine and Mélisande.'

Archie said jealously:

'You were in love with him when you wrote it.'

'What on earth has that got to do with it?'

'*He* let you down all right.' He flushed darkly. 'My God, there are moments when I could almost kill that man.'

'Don't be absurd. I've told you over and over again he doesn't mean anything to me now. I've seen him. I've proved it.'

'I believed you when you told me you'd go on loving him whatever happened.'

'I believed it too. That ought to show you how absolutely unreliable I am.'

'For once *you* don't see what *I* mean. It's not just jealousy. I hate him because he's done something to you. You're not the same person.'

'I'm not *any* person. That's the point. I never was and never will be. The sooner you realise that, the better.'

The anger left his face.

'Talk all the nonsense you like about yourself. Won't make the slightest difference to me. I'm quite content with what little bit of you I've got.'

The orange-smocked waitress who had been hovering impatiently for some time approached with the bill. Archie fumbled desperately in all his pockets and produced two shillings and a threepenny bit.

'I say, old thing. Frightfully sorry but can you come to the rescue? Thought I had lots more than this on me. I cashed a cheque at Mooney's only the night before last.'

Luckily Clara had a pound note that her mother had given her for her birthday. It was all the money she had.

'Pay you back tonight, cross my heart,' he said. 'Means I'll have to nip up to Mooney's though to cash another cheque. If I take a taxi, I'll just get there before closing-time.'

'Why Mooney's and a taxi? Your bank's just along the road.'

'Yep. Only it *might* be safer to postdate it a bit. The barman at Mooney's knows me.'

Clara could not help saying:

'He certainly ought to by now.'

9

For the next fortnight Clara forced herself to work several hours a day. By some extraordinary stroke of luck, the rent account did not arrive. What was almost as great a relief, Mrs Pritchard, who had been coming more and more irregularly, disappeared altogether. The fact that Archie's cigarette case and Clara's silver brushes disappeared too seemed to guarantee that she would not return. They were both delighted to get rid of those hard, prying green eyes and of the difficulty of scraping together fifteen shillings every Saturday. Grateful for these respites, Clara resolved to make a fresh start. Perhaps if she tackled what was to hand without fussing and fretting, heaven would take pity on her and Archie. She polished off six long overdue pieces of copy for the advertising agents and plunged into the revision of A Night in Vienna.

It was difficult to imagine why anyone should want to produce such a stale, feeble, back-broken play as it turned out to be. Nevertheless, turning it into recognisable English demanded just enough ingenuity to give her the illusion of working. It even gave her a certain satisfaction of the kind she used to feel when she had produced a passable Latin prose for her father. Having something concrete to do gave some shape to her days and restored her sense of continuity enough to keep her from slipping back into inertia. She locked the black notebook in a drawer and felt no need to write in it.

The change in Archie was startling. He paid only short occasional visits to the Leicester Square bars and when he did, drank only beer. With excited optimism he began to build a model stage in the 'studio' and to design sets and lighting effects. Instead of wandering about the house in his pyjamas most of the morning, unshaved and chain-smoking cigarettes, he was often at work on his models before breakfast. Sometimes Clara could almost pretend to herself they were two struggling young artists; the fact that they couldn't pay the rent when the demand did arrive and that lately they had lived mainly on buns and chocolate, now seemed rather romantic. When they walked down the King's Road, hatless and untidy, she thought they looked a typical Chelsea couple.

Once she caught sight of Clive Heron, carrying a neat despatch case and evidently on his way back from the Home Office. She waved from the other side of the road but he appeared not to notice. However, she was quite sure that he had when he promptly reversed his direction and darted up a side street.

'What made you think you knew that man?' Archie enquired. 'You gave him the fright of his life.'

'I do know him. His name's Clive Heron. He's a Civil Servant.'

'He looked that type,' said Archie, with contempt. 'Why the hell did he cut you? Thought we looked too disreputable, I suppose.'

He squeezed her arm affectionately.

'Good heavens, no. He'll have some fantastic reason of his own. If you think he's just a conventional bore, you're absolutely wrong. He's about the most amusing and original person I've ever met. I like him immensely.'

'You do, do you? I'm not exactly conventional myself. But I call that little exhibition just now plain bloody bad manners.'

'It wasn't. It was extremely funny. All the funnier as the last time I saw him – it was only on my birthday – he was imploring me to ring him up.'

'Was he indeed?' Archie did not sound at all amused. 'And are you going to?'

'Probably not. We hardly ever do meet in fact, though I've known him since my second year at the Garrick. It's become a kind of joke. We keep saying we must do something about it but we can't make the effort.'

'Hmm.' Archie's voice was still suspicious. 'Sure it wasn't me he was running away from? Is he an old flame?'

Clara laughed.

'If you knew how funny that was! Even as an *idea*!'

'It doesn't strike *me* as so uproariously funny,' said Archie stiffly. 'Anyway I don't think I much care for this precious Pelican or whatever his ruddy name is.'

In spite of the heat, which showed no signs of breaking, Clara managed to keep going fairly hard on A *Night in Vienna*. Even in the basement dining-room, the coolest room in the tiny house, the rest of which was like a slow oven, her hand sweated so much that it stuck to the paper. It was so hot that the water from the cold taps ran permanently tepid; the grass between the flags in the yard was as dry and yellow as old cornstalks; the leaves of the parched laurel drooped motionless, like strips of painted tin. Tired and limp as she was, Clara worked on with a persistence which surprised her. She felt that, if once she stopped, she would never get up the energy to start again. She managed to suppress the knowledge that what she was doing was not only futile in itself but unlikely to bring them back any fraction of the two hundred pounds Archie had spent on the option. In spite of everything she drove herself on, determined to finish it as a point of honour. At least, her working produced an extraordinary effect on Archie. If she were to give up, she was sure he would relapse too.

One afternoon, when she was halfway through the last act,

the two of them went into one of the little shops that sold paint-ing materials. While Archie was choosing some odds and ends he needed for his model stage, the tall heavily built man who had smiled at her through the window on that first afternoon in Tithe Place, came into the shop. Archie was standing at the far end of the counter, with his back turned. The stranger gave Clara a quick smile of recognition, followed by a long, brooding stare. He was evidently about to speak when Archie called to her:

'Come and give me some advice, darling.'

At the same moment, the owner of the shop, deserting Archie, bustled up to the newcomer and said deferentially:

'Ah . . . Mr Marcus Gundry, sir. It's a long time since I had the pleasure of seeing you here. Thought you'd given us up.'

Trying to place the name, which, like his face seemed vaguely familiar, she remembered she had seen it on a poster of an exhi-bition of pictures by Duncan Grant, Matthew Smith, Mark Gertler and other painters the mere mention of whom made her father fulminate.

Forgetting Archie's appeal for advice, she stayed to listen rev-erently while Marcus Gundry joked with the proprietor and ordered some tubes of paint ('Viridian' . . . she must remember that for her notebook), three brushes and a gallon of turpentine.

The painter had a rich voice which matched his size and his ample gestures. The proprietor asked if he were exhibiting with the London Group and he answered that he was sending in three pictures. When it came to adding up the bill, he laughed; 'I'm broke. Put it down to me, will you, Mr Steen?' and the other laughed back: 'I quite understand, Mr Gundry. Only too pleased to oblige you again.'

Clara had crept up so close, in order not to miss a word, that when Gundry swung round to leave, he knocked into her and dropped some of his tubes. As they both bent down to pick them up, he whispered: 'Third time lucky, perhaps?' Eyeing Archie's back, he added: 'Husband?' Clara nodded. He smiled. Two round dimples appeared in his firmly padded cheeks, making him look like the conventional jolly monk of Victorian pictures. He muttered 'damn' under his breath and said aloud:

'I say, *please* don't bother. Awfully kind of you. Entirely my beastly clumsiness.'

Archie had turned round to see what was happening. Gundry stood up and included all three in a sweeping, mischievous glance. As he opened the shop door, booming 'au revoir', he drooped his eyelids and fixed Clara once more with that intent, brooding stare. This sudden change of expression transformed the whole aspect of his face. The jolly monk vanished: there appeared instead a mask, at once sensual and sad and curiously Napoleonic in cast.

On the way back to Tithe Place, Archie said:

'Do you know *him* too? That chap who was throwing his weight about in Steen's?'

'Marcus Gundry?' Clara spoke the name with proprietary pride. 'Of course not. He's an *extremely* well-known modern painter.'

'Never heard of him.'

'I don't suppose you've ever heard of Sickert or Duncan Grant.'

'Right as usual. But I wouldn't care if he was Michelangelo. I didn't like the way he looked at you.'

'The other day you were complaining because someone *didn't* look at me.'

'This is entirely different. Civil Servants are harmless. But all these Chelsea painters are bad lots.'

Clara said irritably, 'Do stop talking like Daddy. "*All* Chelsea painters" . . . "*All* modern poets" . . . "*All* Russian novelists." I hate to hear people sneering at artists. Especially when they know nothing and care less about art.'

'I'm not concerned with his ruddy art. But when I see a hulking middle-aged swine, who presumably paints naked women, leering at my wife as if he were guessing what she'd look like without her clothes, I feel like punching his fat face.'

'Now you're merely being disgusting.' Furiously, she tried to march ahead of him but could not outdistance his long stride. He clutched her arm, though she tried violently to shake him off.

'I'm sorry. I just can't help it sometimes. I keep cursing myself and fighting like hell not to be jealous. But every now and then something just blows up inside me. Can't you make just a bit of allowance for me?'

Muttering 'Oh, I suppose so', she let her arm stay limply in his for the rest of the walk home.

When they got back to the house he fussed about remorsefully in the kitchen, making tea on the rusty gas-stove. Clara sat there without offering to help, her face sullen with the effort of trying to reason herself out of her irritation.

He said, with his rueful smile:

'God, I must bore you stiff sometimes. You ought to have married a poet or something.'

She made herself smile too.

'Poets probably prefer barmaids.'

'I'd do anything. Swat through books . . . go round cricking my neck in art galleries . . . if I thought it would be any use. But I'd only rile you more than if I kept off it altogether.'

Penitently, she put her arms round him.

'You will keep up this legend about my being intelligent. I daresay it was even true once. My mind's been going off steadily since I was fifteen. Look at me. I don't even *read* any more.'

He pushed back her hair and kissed her hot forehead.

'It's all there, still. You need people you can talk your kind of shop to.'

She said nothing. They sat down at the chipped kitchen table, drinking their tea black: the milk had, as usual, turned in the heat.

'Bet I'm right,' he went on. 'I know I can talk theatre shop for hours. I don't hang around with those boys *just* to get blind.'

Clara sighed.

'No, I'm sure. If you knew how I envy you, knowing exactly what you want to do.'

'Precious little hope of doing it. When you think of all the old pros who can't get a show. Why, even Jimmy's not had any work since the *Error* tour.'

'What ages ago that seems. I wonder what's happened to Maidie and all of them.'

'Heard some rumour that she was doing cabaret. Peter and Trev are booked for the *Aunt* again. Don't you ever hanker to go back, Clara? When we lost that chance, you seemed almost relieved.'

Clara sighed.

'I just don't feel capable of doing anything. Even if I had the chance of a marvellous part, I couldn't face an audition. Lost my nerve, I suppose.'

He said eagerly:

'That's the fatal moment to stop. They all say that. I met a chap the other day who's casting for a lot of really good tours. Put on your best bib and tucker and we'll go along together tomorrow. I haven't an earthly but maybe I could tag along as baggage man or something. If *you* could only get something decent . . .'

She interrupted in panic.

'No, Archie. Please. You don't understand. I can't do . . . anything at all.'

'Nonsense. Look at the marvellous job you're making of this play. Oh, I know it's donkey work for you and you should never have had to do it. But I almost thought you were getting a kind of kick out of it.'

'It's about all I'm fit for,' she said bitterly.

'What's made you suddenly so depressed again? Only this morning you were as cheery as possible.'

'Oh, don't use that loathsome word,' she exploded.

'Sorry, old thing. Every time I open my mouth, I seem to drop a brick. I'd better shut up.'

'I'm sorry, Archie,' she said wearily. 'I'd better get back to the grindstone.'

'Oh no, you don't. I've let you slave at that wretched thing till you're worn out. All my fault, like everything else.'

He looked so wretched that she said hastily:

'Let's blame the weather. I believe it's hotter than ever today.'

She stared through the dusty kitchen window at the little courtyard. The sun blazed on the flags and struck spots of light like the reflections of a burning-glass on the stiff shining leaves of the laurel.

'Some English summer!' said Archie. 'London's almost as hot as Santiago. That blue sky and that sun scorching on the stone makes me think of a rather decent house I lived in. About the only thing that *was* decent in that beastly job. White . . . with a *patio*. And an orange tree instead of that sooty old shrub.'

Clara fingered her damp forehead and nodded without answering. She was thinking how seldom she ever considered Archie's life except where it touched her own.

She said:

'I always meant to do something about that bed. But I put it off like everything else. Now it's too late.'

'Doubt if much would grow there. Soil's too sour. Might be fun to fix up a fountain like the one I had in Santiago. But the Woods might raise hell.'

Clara thought: 'Sour soil where nothing will grow. That's what I am!' Aloud she said:

'I suppose they'll throw us out if we can't pay the rent.'

'Something will turn up. It *must*. You'd really hate to leave here, wouldn't you?'

She asked suspiciously:

'Has Daddy been getting at you too?'

'You know the line he's always taken. But much as I love your Papa, I'd never let him talk me into doing anything you didn't want. What you say, goes. And *you* love the place.'

'It's Chelsea, more than the actual house. I can't think why now I've proved it's no earthly use.'

'Don't follow.'

'I had an idiotic idea that if I lived in Chelsea, I'd be able to write. All it's done is to show me up for an utter sham.'

Archie said after a moment:

'You've been in this black mood ever since you ran into that painter chap. Any connection?'

She felt herself flush and said quickly:

'I feel like that underneath all the time. Forget it. I'd better go and get on with the *Night*.'

'No. You're worn out with that wretched thing. Have another cup of tea.'

He took up the kettle to fill the teapot: it slipped in his grasp and sent a spurt of nearly-boiling water over his left hand. Clara cried out, but Archie merely swore and then grinned.

'Oh, my dear,' she said anxiously. 'What can we do? I'm sure there must be something one does . . .'

'No need,' he said. 'I'm tough. You know I'm always damaging myself.'

She had forgotten his extraordinary proneness to accidents. The first time she had met him he had been recovering from the effects of nearly blowing himself up with a hand grenade.

'It must hurt horribly.' The sight of the red swollen fingers afflicted her.

'Like hell for the moment. But pain can be almost a relief sometimes.'

She looked at him in surprise.

'Do you feel that too?'

'Yep.'

Clara said almost angrily:

'Why do I never know how other people feel? Why do I take it for granted I'm different from everyone else?'

'So you are. I thought that the first time I saw you. That's why I always felt I'd got to get you at any price. Like the chap in the parable about the pearl.'

'Oh, *don't*,' she implored. 'If you only knew what an absolute, utter sham you've got.'

'Rubbish,' he said sombrely. 'The pearl's genuine all right. Unfortunately it's cast itself before a swine.'

'Archie, please,' her voice was anguished. 'I can't bear it. I could *prove* to you that what you think a pearl is the cheapest, most rotten fake.'

'I'd like to see you try.'

She said hesitantly:

'I put down things in a notebook sometimes. About myself mostly. They show me up so that I can hardly bear to read them myself. I never thought I could bring myself to show them to anyone. But I think you should see that notebook. It's only fair.'

He shook his head.

'No, darling. I'm terribly touched that you'd trust me that much. But better not. You need some place where you can feel private.'

Clara felt rebuffed. Once again she perceived in Archie a fineness which made her ashamed. She said with a slightly false bitterness:

'The grave's a fine and private place.'

He muttered under his breath:

'But none I think do there embrace.'

She stared at him; then covered her surprise clumsily.

'I forgot. You love Marvell, don't you?'

'Dog on its hind legs,' he said with his rueful smile. There was a moment of difficult silence; then Archie fumbled unconvincingly in his pockets.

'Not a fag left,' he declared. 'Mind if I pop out and buy some?'

Suddenly solicitous she said:

'When you're out, *do* get something to put on your poor hand. It might be dangerous . . . such a bad scald.'

He seemed not to be listening. She babbled on urgently:

'You're always using your hands making those models. If the skin came off and you got some dirt in it, you might get a poisoned finger. You might even . . .' she broke off, suddenly aware that her voice sounded as high-pitched and ridiculous as when one realises one is addressing an empty room. Archie however was still there. He gave an odd laugh.

'Even have to have it cut off; is that it? Thanks for the jolly suggestion.'

Instead of kissing her as he usually did whenever he left the house, he went out abruptly, slamming the kitchen door.

10

Two or three nights later, Archie said:

'Feel like coming dancing tonight? There's a little club just opened off the King's Road. I know a chap who plays the sax there who could wangle us in.'

Clara's instant reaction was that they couldn't afford it but Archie assured her it was a cheap place and they need only drink beer. He added: 'Lots of Chelsea artists and models go there. Thought it might amuse you.'

'It's too hot to dance,' she began, but, seeing his disappointed face, said quickly: 'Let's go all the same.'

The small subterranean night club was hot and smoky. The floor was so crowded that they spent the first half-hour sitting at a rickety table, lit by a candle stuck in a Chianti flask, watching the other people. Archie had put on one of the tropical suits he had worn in Santiago and Clara, also for coolness, an old gauzy black evening frock. In the fashion of that year it was cut very low, leaving her arms and shoulders bare save for two narrow black velvet straps.

'I wore this in the last act of the *Error*,' she said, as Archie dealt clumsily with the straining hooks. 'I *can't* have got so much fatter in a few months.'

'Who cares? You look lovely tonight, anyway. What stunning

shoulders you have.' He kissed them when he had managed to fasten her into the dress saying, as judicially as if he were praising her handwriting, 'I'd be prepared to bet you have one of the softest skins in the world'.

Now as she looked round the room she seemed to be the only woman in an ordinary evening frock. There were women draped entirely in Spanish shawls; women in Augustus John frocks with tight square-cut bodices and long full skirts; women in crumpled cotton frocks that looked as if they were made out of curtains; one or two even in shirts and trousers. When at last they stepped on to the packed dance-floor, she felt self-conscious. Archie, with his loose shock of red hair and his creased shantung suit, looked far less out of place. She was glad when the dim lights were turned down and a cabaret was announced. People who could not find chairs sat huddled together on cushions at the edge of the dance-floor. A shaft of greenish limelight struck across the room: a young Jew dressed as a matador began to play the concertina. She turned her head away to study the groups. Here and there the harsh light picked out a striking head; a woman with smooth black hair coiled like a Russian dancer's; a crop-haired girl who looked like a sulky boy; a sad Indian face under a turban. Suddenly, leaning against the opposite wall, in the shadow, she saw Marcus Gundry. A tepid clapping announced the end of the concertina player. Then came a burst of louder claps. The band struck up 'Here comes Tootsie'. Archie gripped her shoulder and whispered:

'Would you believe it? Look who's here.'

For a moment she thought he meant Gundry. Then she saw that he was staring at the plumed and spangled dancer who had just appeared in the green shaft of limelight. He began to clap like a machine gun and she realised that the dancer was Maidie.

Forgetting all about Gundry, Clara clapped and called excitedly. As the slim, glittering figure spun and leapt and high-kicked with amazing speed and precision, she remembered that evening in Nuneaton and Maidie, in her pink chemise, scandalising the unhappy Munroe. She must have been working hard since then; there was no doubt now as to whether she could 'manage to get up on her points'. Maidie looked as neat and demure as ever. Not a hair strayed from the coiled flaxen plaits, the rosebud mouth was fixed in a conventional roguish smile. She must have caught sight of them for, as she whirled into her final curtsey, she managed to wink in their direction without disturbing another muscle of her dancer's expression.

'Let's go behind and dig her out,' said Archie when Maidie had vanished after loud applause. The dancers surged back to the floor, hemming them in. Before they could move, Maidie herself appeared through a dusty curtain and made straight for their table.

'Fancy finding you two dear old Wurzits,' she cried, flinging a slim, wet-whited arm round each of them. 'I'm breaking every rule of the house by coming out in my make-up but it's my last night, so who cares?'

'What'll you have, Maidie?'

'A Guinness for old times' sake, Starchy dear.'

While Archie was getting drinks at the small besieged bar, Maidie kept up an excited stream of chatter. After A *Clerical Error* she had been working hard at her dancing and taking cabaret jobs in obscure night clubs 'just to get warmed up'.

'But now,' she finished, 'I've got something ever so good coming off. I'll hold it till Starchy comes back.'

When he returned with the drinks, she said:

'Listen, you love-birds. This'll make you sit up. I've got a part in the West End.'

'You lucky little so-and-so. Here's to it!' said Archie.

'Well, you deserve it.' Clara drank too. 'What in?'

'Big new musical show. *My Girl Billie* at the Summer Palace. Half a dozen speaking lines, two speciality dances, and one singing bit in a sextet. Pray that I get over all right.'

'Of course you will. Knock 'em cold, won't she, Clara?' Archie drank to her again, then heaved a sigh.

'And how's life treating you two?' she asked, looking at them shrewdly. 'Did you sigh, Starchy, or was it the wind? I see Clara doesn't press your trousers for you.' She ran her hand through his untidy hair. 'Honestly, Starchy, I wouldn't be seen out with you if I were her.' She turned to Clara. 'Seeing you in that dress, I could almost fancy we were back in the dear old *Error*: Act III, Scene II. It always suited you, dear. But you've put on weight, haven't you? Now I come to look, you've got black circles under your eyes, too.' She pursed her pink mouth and began to count on her fingers. 'How long since the happy day? I only make it three months. You didn't waste much time.'

Clara said hastily:

'Three months and poor Archie still hasn't got a job. Did you hear about Lister and that club?'

'Heard rumours that something Jimmy and Archie were in had gone bust. I don't want to rub it in and say I told you so, old dears. Still stage-struck, Starchy?'

'Yep. Afraid so. But my hopes are getting pretty blighted. Run myself right on the rocks now. And Clara too.'

Maidie frowned.

'Seriously? As bad as that?'

He nodded.

'I wonder now. With that voice . . . Trouble is you've had no experience.' Maidie assumed the expression Clara remembered so well in crises over landladies' bills, damp beds and lost luggage. They both studied her face anxiously. Suddenly, it relaxed and she said: 'Chance in a thousand but it *might* work.'

'If it were one in a million, I'd take it,' said Archie eagerly.

'This show I start rehearsing on Monday. Nothing in it for Vere. She doesn't dance or sing and there are no straight parts. But . . .' she paused and frowned. 'No . . . it's so unlikely to come off. Might be cruel to raise your hopes, Starchy.'

'Go *on*,' he implored.

Clara could see his eyes shining in the dim light. He clutched her hand under the table.

'There's one tiny part not filled yet. A singing footman. He's got one quite good scene with Sherry Blane who's playing the comic lead. Of course all the chorus boys are after it. But they thought it would be funnier if they could get an awfully tall man. You know what a funny little knee-high Wurzit Sherry is. I bet Starchy could do it. Can you dance a bit, Starchy?'

'He dances beautifully,' Clara assured her.

'*You* wouldn't know,' said Maidie with her old asperity. 'But come to think of it, he can shake a hoof. Remember that adagio we guyed at your party at Coventry? It was after you'd gone off in high dudgeon for some reason, Vere.'

'D'you mean you might be able to get me an audition?' Archie was gripping Clara's hand so hard that her wedding ring was grinding into the flesh.

'I'll try. Come round on the off-chance. Ten o'clock at the Summer Palace. I'll meet you at the stage door. Bring a song with you. I'll spin them a yarn . . . say you were in Number 2 company of *The Maid of the Mountains* with me. There's no one from that lot in this show.'

Archie flung his arms round Maidie and kissed her heartily.

'Mind my feathers, old boy. This costume belongs to the management. I must go and change or Percy'll have kittens.'

As she stood up, she waved to someone on the far side of the room, pointed to her spangles, shook her head and beckoned.

'It's old Marcus Gundry,' she explained. 'Mind if I get him to come over? I daren't cross the floor in this outfit.'

'You know him?' said Clara, avoiding Archie's eye. 'How exciting.'

'I did a bit of modelling once for a chap he shared a studio with. *Not* what you think, Starchy. Ballet poses for illustrations complete with tights and *tutu*.'

The next minute Gundry's tall, heavy figure loomed beside their table.

'Mr Gundry, meet Miss Clara Batchelor,' Maidie giggled. 'Pardon me. Mrs Hughes-Follett I *should* say. This great gawk's her husband.'

Gundry bowed gravely.

'Mrs Hughes-Follett and I have quite literally bumped into each other before.' He turned to the scowling Archie. 'I'm afraid I interrupted your shopping. Sorry. I have to put on rather an act with Steen. Otherwise he mightn't let me have things on tick.'

'Clara's artistic,' said Maidie proudly. 'She writes tales. *And* gets 'em printed.'

Clara flinched. Gundry looked at her under half-closed lids and said non-committally: 'Indeed?'

'And he'll have his name in lights one of these days. Shut up, Starchy. You will.'

'And I paint a little. Oils and watercolours. All done by hand,' said Gundry solemnly.

When Maidie had skipped away to change, Gundry focussed all his attention on Archie. The one or two covert glances he darted at Clara were so swift as to be almost imperceptible. Archie was sullen at first but Gundry's manner was so easy and deprecating that they were soon laughing together. When Maidie returned, having exchanged her spangles for a school-girlish blue linen frock, she cried:

'What are you boys sniggering about? Swapping dirty ones, I'll bet. Time you broke it up. Come on, Tiny, let's dance.'

Left alone with Clara, Gundry's face assumed its mischievous, dimpled smile.

'Now we've been formally introduced, will you risk dancing with me? I'm heavy, but women tell me I don't actually trample on them.'

As he danced monotonously, but rhythmically, his face resumed the brooding Napoleonic look. At intervals, almost without moving his lips and gazing over her head, he spoke to her in a low abrupt voice.

'At least, dancing's an excuse for holding you in my arms. I've wanted to since the first day I saw you. At the window. You smiled. Remember?'

Clara fenced.

'I didn't really mean to.'

'Should be more careful, then. Grossly unfair to male sex. Raises hopes.'

'Actually,' Clara explained, 'I smiled at you because you were a painter.'

'Do you smile at all painters on principle? Bad habit in Chelsea.'

'Of course, if I'd known you were Marcus Gundry . . .' she began rashly.

He interrupted. 'Ever seen a picture of mine?'

She floundered.

'Well . . . I'm not actually quite sure. But I know . . .'

He said out loud and rather fiercely:

'You obviously *don't* know.'

'You'll think me awfully stupid . . .' she fumbled.

He held her closer.

'With shoulders like that, you can afford to be stupid.'

Clara felt humbled. She tried vainly to think of something intelligent to say. They danced for some moments in silence. Gundry muttered very low:

'Beautiful woman.'

Flattered but nervous, Clara said:

'Not *beautiful,* surely. No one's ever even suggested that.'

'I didn't mean your face. Women always assume one does, for some extraordinary reason. Don't look so deflated. I haven't really paid much attention to yours. Let's have a look.'

He stooped his head, examining her face with half-closed eyes.

'Nothing wrong with it. Rather a good phiz really.' He went on, with detached interest: 'Quite amusing to draw. I like the way the lower part pinches in to the chin just a fraction too late.' He removed his hand from her back to thumb a line in the air. '*So.* There's a woman in the National Gallery with that same pinched-in jaw. In pink. Cosima someone. But her forehead's too low. You've got the whale of a brow under those curls. Definite likeness though. But you're better looking.'

Clara listened greedily, her vanity more than appeased. No one had ever talked of her face in that way. She made a mental note to go and look at 'Cosima someone' as soon as possible.

'I'd quite like to do a drawing of it,' he went on. 'But I'd make you shove back those bangs or whatever they are. They mess up the shape. When could you come along to my place?'

The thought of being drawn by Marcus Gundry sent her off into an excited dream. She had visions of being admitted to the charmed circle that seemed so inaccessible. He must know other painters, perhaps musicians, even writers. The very idea of being allowed to watch and listen to these enchanted beings was so intoxicating that she forgot to answer his question.

'Well?' he pressed. 'Or don't you want to?'

'Oh, I *want* to,' she said ardently. 'But . . .'

'But what?'

She sighed: 'Perhaps I oughtn't to. Archie might be . . .' she was going to say 'angry' but substituted 'unreasonable'.

'Married long?'

'Only a few months.'

'You're not as much in love as he is, are you?'

'That's an unfair question.'

'Not a question. A statement.'

Again she could think of nothing to say.

Gundry laughed.

'He'd be perfectly justified, I suppose. But I imagine you usually get your own way. The point is, have you made up your mind?'

There was something about the man she could not help liking. She looked up into his face as if to reassure herself that he was not dangerous. Seeing her anxious face, he gave his rich laugh again. There was something so solid and genial about him that she had to laugh too.

'I must seem such an idiot. But things are rather complicated.'

He said kindly:

'You're very young, aren't you?'

'I suppose twenty-two is officially young. But I don't feel young any more.'

'Sure sign that you are. I'm nearly forty and I feel far younger than when I was your age. I was very earnest in those days.'

'Of course forty's not old,' said Clara reassuringly. Actually it seemed an immense age to her. It was a shock to realise that he practically belonged to her parents' generation.

'When you get to my age, you'll find life's much simpler than you supposed. You want something and you get it. Or you don't get it. Or you get it and lose it. Let's sit down, shall we?'

Clara was more at ease without his arms round her. Held close against that heavy, yet lithe body; feeling the hairy sleeve of his jacket against her bare back, it had been an effort not to relax unthinkingly into his embrace. Nevertheless, she was glad to see that Archie and Maidie were clapping for an encore of their dance.

'They're quite happy,' said Gundry with a chuckle. 'However did you come to know Maidie? You're not exactly each other's types.'

'We were on tour together. I got awfully fond of her in the end.'

'I adore Maidie myself. Quite dispassionately, though. I could be safely left on a desert island with her. At least till I'd made quite sure there wasn't some lovely brown-skinned Woman Friday about. What are you smiling at?'

'The thought of you and Maidie on a desert island. She'd keep you in order all right. I shared a room with her for five months.'

'Lucky Maidie.'

Clara said hastily:

'She is the most astonishing character, isn't she? I've enough material to do a whole book of Maidie's *obiter dicta*.'

'I see you're what she calls "bloody educated".'

'Do you get accused of that too?'

'I get accused of a great many things.' He glanced down at her bare shoulders and his face took on its heavy, brooding look. He said in a low, almost angry voice: 'Don't you *know* what a lovely body you have? Or what a marvellous texture of skin?'

'I'm getting fat. Maidie's just been warning me.'

'Rubbish. You're like one of those delicious Renoir girls – the early ones before the old man started blowing them up like air-cushions. Pneumatic bliss with a vengeance.' He smiled. 'I assure you, you could be twice as pneumatic as you are and still remain most disturbing. To me at any rate.'

Once again Clara could think of nothing to say.

'Don't look so alarmed. Surely you're used to being a disturbing influence.'

She said, without thinking:

'I can't imagine being an influence of any kind. You see I don't feel as if I existed at all. So when someone talks as if I did, my mind just goes blank.'

He stared at her.

'What an extraordinary statement from a creature like you. I can assure you that four of my five senses affirm that you do exist and in no uncertain manner. I admit I don't know exactly how you'd taste but I've a shrewd idea. You're talking nonsense, my dear.'

She said, frowning:

'I'm sure it sounds nonsense. But I do mean something by it. Someone on a desert island might feel like that when they got back to ordinary life, don't you think?'

He laughed.

'Maidie might, I grant you. But if you'd been marooned with me . . .' he began. Catching sight of her face, he broke off. 'Sorry. Forgive obvious joke. What is it, my dear? You look as if something were really worrying you.'

She smiled. 'I'm sorry. I'm being very heavy on the hand.'

He smiled too and gave her wrist a quick pressure.

'Not on this hand. I assure you it's strong enough to support the entire weight of a non-existent young woman.'

She said impulsively:

'I almost wish I didn't like you so much.'

He shook his head.

'I suppose there must be some connection between your various remarkable observations. I'm blest if I know what it is.'

She laughed. 'I'm blest if I do either.'

The band had stopped. Half-relieved, half-disappointed, Clara watched Archie and Maidie elbowing their way towards them. As he turned his face towards them, flashing an exaggerated smile of welcome, he said without looking at her:

'No need to pull the alarm cord. Here come the guard and the engine driver.' Turning off the smile, he added quickly: 'In case I don't get another chance – 100, Rosehill Gardens. Know it? Long dull street running up to Fulham Road. I'm in every day. Don't come till sevenish. I need all the decent light for painting.'

'If I come, will you let me see some of your pictures? Though I probably won't understand them.'

He answered in a gruff, almost hostile voice:

'Don't pretend to if you don't. I'll show you some if I feel like it. You needn't make remarks about 'em. I'll do the talking. If I think there's any point.'

He stayed only a short while after Archie and Maidie had returned to the table. During that time he conducted a fantastic dialogue with Maidie in alternate broad Lancashire and stage French. They were so absurd that the other two simply sat back and enjoyed the turn.

When Gundry had gone, barely acknowledging Clara in his goodbyes, Archie said:

'I must say he's damn funny, that man. I've seen far worse acts in quite good revues.'

'Old Marcus does a spot of acting now and then. Highbrow Sunday night shows. He's a great pal of that Russian producer – Kirillov. Lives in the same house, I believe.'

Clara's heart soared.

'Kirillov who did that wonderful production of *The Cherry Orchard* last year? I'd give anything to meet him.'

'You'd better get Marcus to introduce you. K. might give you some work. That sort of arty stuff's probably more in your line than the *Error* and suchlike.'

Clara shook her head.

'Oh, no. I'm not good enough even to walk on for Kirillov. I've practically given up all ideas of acting, anyhow.'

'In favour of domestic bliss? Congratulations, Starchy.'

Archie said:

'It's not my idea. I think it would do her good to act again. I'm sure she'd be jolly fine, given a chance.'

Clara sighed.

'I'd rather have written *The Cherry Orchard* than be Duse and Sarah Bernhardt combined.'

'Never heard of it,' said Maidie. 'Wait a minute though. It's not that awful thing about V.D. by Ibsen, is it? I know there was a line about cherries in that because it's the only line I remember.' She said to Archie in a pansy voice '"Mother, my brain is turning to cherry-coloured velvet." Cue for laugh, wouldn't you say? My dear, not a soul in the house even tittered but me.'

'If I'd been there, I'd have backed you up,' said Archie, when Clara had assured her that *The Cherry Orchard* was not the same play.

'Glad to hear it,' said Maidie severely. 'The other was ever so dirty. If something's dirty it's really a bit much if it's dull as ditch-water too. I'd have buzzed off after Act I only the boy who gave me the free pass was on in Act III.'

'That man Gundry,' said Archie. 'What sort of pictures does he paint?'

'Nothing spicy, if that's what you mean. At least *I* never saw anything in the *September Morn* or *Bath of Psyche* line. Ever so boring, I thought. Just old trees and things and he can't even get the colours right. Oh . . . and plates of fruit on the most shockingly crumpled serviettes. My dear, some of the apples were blue instead of red. I said "You're colour-blind, old boy." And he had the cheek to say "Perhaps you are, old girl." I ask you!'

'Clara says he's supposed to be famous.'

'Don't you believe it. He's never had one picture in the Academy. I know, because I asked him. And he's been at it for donkey's years. Tried to kid me he didn't want to. "Sour grapes, dear," I told him. "Sour pink grapes with orange knobs on to you."'

She glanced at the clock.

'Well, you dear old Wurzits, I must love you and leave you. Got to get all the way to Golders Green and it's Sunday tomorrow.'

'Have another Guinness,' Archie begged her.

'What, after midnight and break my fast? I'm shocked at you, Starchy.'

'You're wonderful,' said Clara. 'When I think we live right opposite a church. Archie and I never seem to get there before eleven.'

Maidie said severely:

'Then you both promise me to get up tomorrow, you bloody old slackers. Otherwise I'm damned if I'll even try and get that audition for you, Starchy. If you don't do the decent thing by God, you can't expect Him to do the decent thing by you. Now, come on, promise.'

Archie said sheepishly: 'All right, Maidie.'

'That's better. If you don't believe in answers to prayer, look at me. Two dozen candles, St Joseph's going to get the first night of My Girl Billie. If I do a prat-fall, I've warned him he'll only get one.'

'Monday . . . ten . . . Summer Palace?' said Archie anxiously.

'That's right. Cheerio. If you can't be good, be careful.'

'Oh, Maidie, you haven't changed a bit,' Clara laughed, as they kissed each other.

Maidie darted her a shrewd look.

'Hmm. More than one can say of some people. Still, it'll all come out in the wash, as the monkey said.'

'Dance, darling?' Archie said, when she had gone. They took

a few turns on the crowded floor. But tonight Clara could not follow his steps.

'What's up with you?' he asked. 'Tired, old thing?'

'I'm sorry. I'm dancing abominably. It must be worse than ever for you after dancing with Maidie.'

'Maidie's a pro. I'd a million times rather dance with you and you know it.'

'Not the way I'm dancing tonight.'

'You managed well enough with that great lout Gundry. I was watching you.'

'All right,' she sighed. 'Let's say I'm tired and leave it at that.'

'Like to give up?'

'Yes. I'm getting more out of step with you with every bar.'

11

On the Monday morning, Archie went off in high spirits to the Summer Palace. Even though the demand for the rent arrived just before he left the house, nothing could damp his optimism. Clara, watching his tall figure almost dancing away down the street, dreaded the thought of another disappointment more for him than for herself. Since that Saturday at the night-club, she had been aware of a sense of returning life which made it easy to share Archie's excitement. On the Sunday morning, for the first time since they had lived in Tithe Place, she found herself humming as she washed up the breakfast dishes. Later she had bought an armful of flowers from a coster's barrow and filled every vase and jug in the house. Archie had for once reproached her for extravagance.

'Mustn't count our chickens before they are hatched, darling. If I don't bring this off, our prospects are slightly grim.' She had answered, with most unusual lightheartedness:

'If we're going to be ruined, five shillings won't matter either way. Anyhow, I've got a feeling that our luck's going to change.'

As soon as he had left for the theatre, she slipped across into the church to pray for his success. It was a big, bare place, coldly lit with plain glass windows. There were no shadowy side-chapels; no stands of guttering candles. It did not even smell of incense but of damp stone and carbolic soap. The whole of the wall behind the altar was covered with a vast dull canvas of the Crucifixion. She had never known a Catholic church whose atmosphere was so chill and formal. This morning, coming in from the gay, sunny street and finding it empty but for herself, it seemed drearier than ever. However much she reminded herself that the atmosphere of a church was irrelevant, that all that mattered was the presence of the Blessed Sacrament, she could not help being depressed by it. It emphasised her growing sense of religion as something remote from her real preoccupations.

Staring at the huge painting with its three conventional lifeless figures and its pallid neutral colours, she felt such a longing for warmth, for mere human life however untidy and painful, that she could hardly remain on her knees. It seemed almost irreverent to pray for anything so worldly as Archie's getting a part in a musical comedy. Nevertheless she forced herself to stay for a few minutes with her face buried in her hands, adding rather guiltily to her petition 'Make me a better wife.'

It occurred to her that her sense of being chilled and rebuffed might be her own fault. What right had she to approach God like a confident child? She performed only the bare minimum of her religious duties and carelessly at that. Moreover, since Saturday night, her conscience was not altogether easy. The sun-shafts, pouring through the dusty greenish glass, were transformed into a cold glare like searchlights. They reminded her at once of the night-club and of the beam of a policeman's lantern searching for suspects. That sudden spurt of lightheartedness and hope – which had vanished the moment she entered the church – was certainly connected with Marcus Gundry.

Partly to appease her conscience, partly to prove to God that she was willing to make some sacrifice for Archie's success, she made a mental promise not to go to Gundry's studio; not, at any rate, during that week.

Back in the little house, she did some penitential tidying up in the effort to carry out her resolution of being a better wife. She was horrified to find how much mess and dirt had accumulated now that Mrs Pritchard no longer came to give the place even a sketchy cleaning. Untidy herself, Clara had long ago given up the effort to cope with Archie's quite astonishing capacity for reducing any room to chaos. Every carpet was littered with ash and cigarette butts; half-empty cups and glasses lurked behind chairs and even under the beds. His clothes were invariably thrown on the floor and, as he had a habit of wandering from room to room as he undressed, she would often find dirty collars, socks and underclothes strewn all over the house and even on the stairs. This morning, in his frantic search for a clean shirt, he had emptied the entire contents of a chest of drawers on the unmade bed. As she put them back, she noticed again how brutally he treated his clothes. Everything was torn, stained and frayed like a schoolboy's.

Finding that he had taken his last clean shirt, she rang up the laundry to know why their things had not been delivered for a fortnight. She received a curt answer that they would be delivered when the bill, now amounting to over five pounds, was paid.

Suddenly dispirited, she abandoned the hopeless task of trying to make the house presentable, went down to the kitchen and made herself some tea. Then, sitting at the chipped table, she tried to work out their financial situation. She found, to her horror, that it would take nearly a hundred pounds to clear the rent and the various small debts they had accumulated. Telephone, gas and light were threatening to be cut off; two crumpled bills she had never seen had fallen out of a jacket of Archie's when she hung it up: both for bottles of whisky. Till that moment she had believed that he drank only in bars.

She sat staring hopelessly at her accounts and gnawing her pencil. There was no way of knowing how much, if anything, she could put on the credit side. The most she could hope was that Archie had not yet spent the whole of this month's allowance. In her own purse she had exactly nine shillings and eightpence, the remains of the fifteen guineas the agents had paid for her last set of advertisements. Most of that Archie had borrowed in small loans, with ardent promises of repayment. Even if he were to get the part, it would be months before they would be able to save up enough to pay all they owed. Even saving up, in the unlikely event of their being able to save, would not solve the problem of the rent. The enormous sum of £61 8s. 6d. had somehow to be paid in a few days. The only faint hope was that Archie might sell his motorbike. She clutched her head, trying to think of some way out. Should she approach the advertising agents and ask them to give her a regular free-lance contract again as they had done before she went on tour? Their last letter had not been encouraging. They 'needed no more copy at the moment but would communicate with her in the event of their envisaging future plans involving her possible co-operation'. She knew that she had lost the light touch that had once made them so eager for her work. Should she grovel to them, offer to work at lower rates? Three years ago, they had offered her a good salary to join their permanent staff but her dreary year at the Ministry of Pensions had made her loathe the idea of working all day in an office.

Suddenly, on a desperate impulse, without thinking what she was going to say, she ran upstairs and 'phoned Rapson's number. She almost hoped to find it engaged, but by an extraordinary chance, she was put straight through to Rapson himself.

A rather irritated voice said:

'Rapson here. Who is that?'

She mumbled 'Miss Batch . . . I mean Mrs Hughes-Follett.'

'Speak up. Can't get the name. Is it something urgent? My secretary will be back in ten minutes.'

She managed to convey to him who she was and his voice became more genial.

'Yes . . . yes . . . of course. How's married life going, eh?'

Clara had meant to do no more than ask for an appointment. Instead, she lost her head completely. She began to babble nervously:

'Things are a little difficult at the moment. I was wondering whether . . . Do you remember you offered me a staff job some years ago? I wasn't willing to take it then but I've changed my mind.'

The geniality vanished from Rapson's voice.

'Steady on, dear lady. A lot of water's flowed under the bridge since then. I'm not contemplating making any additions to my staff at the moment.'

Clara was trembling all over. She could retrieve neither her self-control nor her commonsense. She went on in a high, almost hysterical voice:

'But it's rather different in my case surely. I mean I've free-lanced for you for years. You always said my copy was in a class by itself.'

'*Was*, my dear, certainly. You've done some very nice work for us, I admit. Incidentally, we've paid you more for it than we've paid any free-lance in my time. I don't want to hurt your feelings, but your stuff's deteriorated very considerably since you got married. Too busy looking after hubby to put your mind on it, I daresay.'

'I've been worried,' Clara babbled on insanely. 'I haven't been awfully well. My husband's lost his job. I'm sure, Mr Rapson, that if you'd give me a chance, I'd manage to . . .'

He cut in:

'Sorry, my dear. Nothing doing. I've built up this business as a business, not a charity institution. Sorry to hear you're not feeling fit. You'd better see a doctor. Excuse me if I ring off. Got a lot of work on. Drop in any time you're up our way and have a chat. Might have a few captions or suchlike you could have a bat at at home. Afraid I can't promise anything though. So long.'

Clara collected herself just enough to say coldly:

'Thank you. I'm sorry I bothered you. Goodbye,' before she hung up the receiver.

She knew that she had made an utter fool of herself; nevertheless she was as shaken as if Rapson had slapped her face. She remembered his effusiveness in the days when he had been only too anxious to have as much copy as she was willing to do for him. It was useless to tell herself that she hated the idea of working in Rapson's office, of being subject to that absurd little man with his patent-leather hair and his diamond tiepin in the shape of a fox's mask. The fact that he should have spoken to her like that was far more humiliating than a snub from someone she respected. She felt like an old actress, once a star, who has been refused a walking-on part. It seemed the measure of her utter failure that she could no longer succeed even at work she despised.

Catching sight of herself in the mirrors of the tiny room whose holland covers had long lost their freshness and whose carpet showed islands of stains in the merciless sunlight, she thought she looked as battered as the room. There were faint creases round her eyes and mouth and a dusty look about her face and hair. Words slipped into her mind . . . 'Abstinence sows sand all over the ruddy limbs and flaming hair.' She checked herself from finishing the verse. Against her crumpled blue dress, her arms still had the milky whiteness they showed in hot weather or when she was warm from sleep. She touched the inner side of her elbow, noticing the pure blue and violet of the veins and marvelling at the softness of this sheltered area of skin. Such softness, which meant nothing to herself, must surely be meant for some purpose, like the soft breast-feathers of a bird. All at once the memory of Gundry, overlaid since she had left the church, returned with violence. Forgetting her resolution, she would have set out then and there to find him, if she had not remembered his warning not to go before seven. With a pang of conscience, she brought her mind back to Archie. It was after noon. He had promised to telephone her the moment he had news. The fact that he had not done so yet might be a good sign. Though the house, tawdry and unkempt as an actress waking up with last night's make-up still on her face, oppressed her more every minute, she must stay in till he called up.

The paralysed lethargy she had managed to fend off for the last weeks began to creep over her. At all costs, the day which had begun so hopefully must not turn into one of those terrible ones when she wandered aimlessly about the house, stopping now and then to stare for long spells at an old newspaper whose meaning she could not take in, smoking cigarettes, mechanically combing her hair and eating, if she ate at all, with a strange compulsive greed; stuffing herself with anything she could find; sponge cakes, chocolates, old heels of bread and cheese, like a ravenous child. She must do something, anything, at once while she still had enough will to make herself act.

She went out into the glare of the courtyard feeling the flags hot through her shoes as she crossed it and went into the shed Archie now used as his workshop. There was no purpose in her mind beyond wanting to get out of the house and look at any objects which she did not know by heart in the effort to stave off inertia. The stone floor was littered with Archie's half-finished models for the play that she was sure would never be produced. Probably even the models would never be finished; Archie had only worked on them desultorily the last few days. She could not blame him. She had not finished her own part. Since that day when they had run into Marcus Gundry in the art shop, she had not been able to force herself to do another line of the wretched piece, though she was within twenty pages of the end.

Looking at Archie's sets, though the designs were banal and the colours crude, she had to admire the neatness of their construction. It was astonishing that anyone so clumsy in handling ordinary objects should be able to make such delicate adjustments of fine wires and tiny pieces of wood. She picked up one of the miniature stages with care, thinking what an enchanting toy it would make for a child. A child of hers and Archie's was something she could no longer even imagine. Staring out at the strip of parched earth at the edge of the courtyard, she thought again: 'Sour soil where nothing will grow'. Suppose things had been different between them, could her numbed body have produced a living creature any more than her numbed mind could produce even a fragment of living work?

Stooping to replace the model, she saw for the first time the cluster of empty whisky bottles it had screened. It was true, then, that he had been drinking secretly at home. She wondered how long it had been going on. All the bottles but one were thickly covered with dust. That one was almost clean and still had some whisky in it. She guessed he must have bought it the day he scalded his hand.

Standing there, holding the bottle, she thought how hopeless their situation was becoming. Was it her fault or his that they seemed to be slowly destroying each other? He had begun to drink long before their marriage; she could hardly be blamed for that. But was it her fault that it was becoming more and more of a habit? She wondered what compelled him to drink: was he, too, sometimes overwhelmed by that sense of being utterly cut off from life, gasping for air inside a bell-jar? If so, did drink lift the bell-jar? On an impulse, she uncorked the bottle and gulped a large mouthful of whisky. A fiery heat ran through her: she had the feeling that someone had switched on a light inside her skull. At that moment the telephone rang inside the house. The bell sounded insistent and accusing. She started guiltily, hastily corked the whisky bottle, and ran across the courtyard to answer it. It must be Archie. Anxiously she picked up the receiver, only to hear a stranger's voice asking for a quite different number.

The gulp of neat whisky on an empty stomach had made her head swim. Nevertheless, she felt better. The creeping paralysis was arrested. She could actually feel it move some steps away, as a circle of wolves is said to do when the menaced traveller throws a firebrand at them. Nothing, indeed, seemed to press on her quite so heavily any more. The unpaid bills, even her humiliating conversation with Rapson, retreated into a kind of fog where they became blurred and unreal.

Almost lighthearted again, she decided to finish the correcting of *A Night in Vienna*. As she worked, the play no longer seemed quite so idiotic. Perhaps it was not impossible after all that someone would want to produce it. Even if they could only sell the option outright for what Archie had given for it, two hundred pounds would clear all their debts and leave them a hundred in hand. And if Archie got this part . . . why shouldn't he get it after all? . . . one of their nagging worries at least would be removed. She finished Act III in a state of slightly drowsy exhilaration. By then, she was so sleepy that she went and lay down on her still unmade bed.

When she awoke, it was nearly four o'clock. The effects of the whisky had entirely worn off. The late afternoon sun poured through the window, hurting her eyes and pitilessly showing up every detail of the disordered bedroom. There was a sour taste in her dry mouth: the oppression had returned in full force. Each anxiety was like an actual weight on her diaphragm pinning her down on the rumpled bed: the bills, Archie's drinking, her own impotence to write, the impossibility of going either backwards or forwards in any direction. But more crushing than any of these was an overall sense of guilt, not localised, as if all these were a punishment for some mysterious sin she did not remember having committed.

The pink walls and blue check curtains mocked her with their arch brightness. They gave the untidy bedroom the air of a night nursery inhabited by two undisciplined children. Those pink distempered walls had the texture of sugar icing: she was reminded of the sugar house in which Hansel and Gretel were trapped. Archie and she were trapped too. But by whom? No wicked witch had lured them in to destroy them. Through the window, she could see part of the dark brick wall of the church where she had tried to pray that morning. Stern, heavy, uncompromising, it reminded her that, for her and Archie, there could be no escape.

Her mind wandered back to her wedding morning, to the Nuptial Mass and those tremendous petitions which seemed to have so little relevance for them. She remembered her father, fussing over his split glove and how his arm had trembled as he escorted her up the aisle. It was strange how little she thought of him nowadays when once her whole preoccupation had been to please him. Since her birthday, she had avoided Valetta Road. Suddenly his face came sharply into her mind, angry and disapproving as she had last seen it in the study. What would he say if he were to walk at this moment into the room and find her lying in broad daylight on the unmade bed? Her old fear of him, which she thought had been dispersed for ever except in dreams, rushed over her with new force. What would he think if he had overheard the things Marcus Gundry had said to her in the night-club? At that moment she heard a latchkey click in the lock downstairs. Such a thrill of terror went through her whole body that she hardly dared to breathe. She forgot where she was: she was convinced that it could be no one but her father coming to accuse her. She shut her eyes and clutched the sheet with both hands. Then her spinning head cleared. She let out her breath on a great sigh of relief. Before he had banged the door and called to her, she realised it could be no one but Archie.

She ran down to meet him. He was smiling triumphantly. Under his arm he carried a bulky parcel. For the moment, Clara was so dazed that she forgot to ask him what his news was. He pushed her into the front room, put down his heavy parcel, and clasped her in his arms.

'I've got it, darling,' he said. 'I've got it!' At first she could only stare at him. 'You look as if you didn't believe me. I can hardly believe it myself. But look – here's my contract.'

She collected herself enough to exclaim excitedly and ask for details.

'It's my lucky day,' he exulted. 'Maidie fixed an audition, bless her, and I did my stuff. And here I am with an actual part *and* an understudy and eight quid a week. What do you think of that?'

'Wonderful,' she said.

'You don't sound awfully excited.'

'Of course I am.' She had taken it in but her relief and pleasure were soured by an obscure resentment. 'Why didn't you ring me up? I've been waiting indoors all day for you to ring.'

'Sorry, darling. I wanted to give you a surprise. Besides, that's not all my news.'

She persisted, hating herself for taking the edge off his triumph.

'What time did you know about the part?'

'Round about two.'

'It's half past five now.'

'Late as that?'

She said meanly: 'No doubt you went straight to Mooney's to celebrate.'

'Right as usual. But don't look so peeved. I didn't go just to have a drink. Naturally I wanted to tell old Jimmy. I don't say we didn't have a round or two. But the real reason was that I'd arranged to meet that chap there. And he turned up all right.'

'Which particular chap?'

'The motorbike and sidecar one, of course. He's bought it. For cash.'

She asked anxiously: 'How much?'

'Sixty quid ... well fifty-five actually ... I had to give the chap who introduced me a rake-off.'

Penitent in her relief, she said:

'Poor Archie. I know you hated selling her. But it means we've nearly enough for the rent.'

His jaw dropped.

'Oh, damn. I forgot the bally old rent. But I'm sure we can wangle something. Hang it all ... £8 a week plus my rotten allowance ... that's not too bad? You're being a bit of a killjoy, aren't you, darling?'

'I'm sorry. It's all wonderful, of course. But we do owe quite a lot besides the rent. I've been going into our bills.'

'Forget 'em. Our luck's turned, that's the great thing.'

She only just checked herself from saying meanly: '*Yours* has turned' and asked instead 'Whatever have you got in that vast parcel?'

'Aha! I was waiting for you to ask that. It's something for you.'

'For me?'

'Yep. Belated birthday present.'

'Oh, Archie . . . you shouldn't have . . .'

'Rubbish. I've been planning it for ages but I couldn't raise the wind. But now I've sold the motorbike . . . Gosh, it was marvellous to have a bundle of fivers again . . . I couldn't wait to get it for you.'

She asked anxiously:

'Oh darling. It's not something terribly expensive?'

'Hang the expense. Anyway I've bought it now. Thought you'd be pleased. But you don't even seem to want to see what it is.'

He looked so hurt that she said quickly:

'I'm *longing* to see it. May I open it?'

He revived at once.

'No, you mayn't. You stay where you are and keep your eyes tight shut. Promise not to open them till I give the word.'

She shut her eyes and promised.

'I warn you, you may have to keep them shut quite a time. Rather go out of the room?'

'No . . . no . . . I'll stay. But *do* be quick.' She made her voice sound as eager and impatient as possible.

'Better put your fingers in your ears too. I want it to be a big surprise.'

She sat patiently, wondering whatever it could be, trying to identify certain strange noises which penetrated her stopped ears. It was like Archie to rush off and buy her an extravagant present the moment he had some money in his pocket. She thought, remorsefully, how churlish she had been. Whatever the present was, she must seem delighted. As she sat there for what seemed a very long time, with her eyes squeezed conscientiously tight, she realised that her prayer of the morning had been answered. Archie had got his job and she had not even had the grace to be thankful. She made a hasty mental equivalent of Maidie's 'Sorry, God'.

'Now!' said Archie, in a tone of immense satisfaction.

She opened her eyes. Spread out on the floor were two magnificent Bassett-Lowke model engines; a tail of coaches for each; stations, signal boxes and a glittering heap of rails. She could do nothing but stare, open-mouthed.

'Thought that would knock you flat,' said Archie, grinning with pleasure. Ignoring her silence, he went on:

'I'd planned to try and sneak into the workshop tonight when you were asleep and put it all up. It makes a grand big circuit – double track – when it's assembled. All electric. We'll have to start on an accumulator – there's a whacking big one being delivered tomorrow. Too heavy to bring home. But I'm sure I could fix a wire off the house and we could run it off the mains. I got two locomotives. No nonsense about one of them being mine. They're both yours. Only it's more fun with two. We can have races . . . crashes if you like. We've got the most marvellous points system you ever saw. Think it's too late to start fixing her up now? . . . You see . . . I've got to rehearse all day tomorrow and I'm dying to show you how it works so you can have fun with it on your own. I'll have to leave you alone such a lot till we open and you can amuse yourself for hours with it . . . Darling . . . whatever is the matter?'

For Clara had burst into a fit of uncontrollable sobs.

He held her close, questioning her anxiously.

'My pet . . . my little love . . . Are you ill? . . . Don't you like it?'

After some moments she managed to control herself to say that she wasn't ill and that it was the most wonderful model railway she had ever seen.

'It's not as big as the one at Crickleham . . . but it's a far better model. The latest and best. Remember my railway at Crickleham? I always connect it with you. We played with it the first time I ever set eyes on you. I believe I fell in love with you that moment.'

She remembered it as well as he. She remembered how he

staged a crash and a tiny engine fell down a bank which seemed as steep as a precipice. She wondered, as her tears dried leaving her exhausted and gentle, if he remembered the second time she had seen him with his model railway – two days after Charles's death. His face, as he looked up at her with a toy locomotive in each hand, had been blind with misery. It was then, simply to wipe away that hopeless look that matched her own sense of numb despair, she had, for the first time, said that she would marry him.

12

Some days later Clara received a patronising letter from Rapson offering her half a dozen pieces of copy at less than her usual rates. She sighed and said:

'I'd like to refuse. But I daren't.'

Archie looked up from the typewritten part he was studying.

'Refuse what, Clarita?'

She showed him the letter:

'Damn cheek. Send him a snorter. Turn him down flat.' He returned to his part and began to gabble another line under his breath.

'Archie . . . how can I? It means twelve guineas. Think of all our bills.'

'Let 'em wait. We can start sending them dollops once the show's running.'

'But they're urgent. They won't wait. We haven't even done anything about the rent yet.'

'I sent the Woods twenty quid. Absolutely all I could raise. That should keep them quiet.'

'You know it won't. We're supposed to pay a quarter in advance. That leaves £41 8s. 6d.'

'What a head for figures you have.'

'It's as well someone in this house has. And what are we going to do about the others? We haven't had clean sheets for a fort-night and the gas and 'phone are threatening to cut us off.'

'Let 'em. I'll send them postdated cheques. Stop fussing, old thing.'

'Postdated cheques on what? The date of the opening night isn't even fixed yet. You're only getting paid £2 a week for rehearsals. You don't seem to realise we've got to find something like sixty pounds as well as keeping going from day to day.'

'I realise I may lose this part if I'm not word-perfect at rehearsal this morning.'

'It's all very well for you,' she flared. 'You don't have to sit about here all day worrying about how to find money. You've got what you want. You don't care what happens to me.'

'Steady on, old thing. I daresay we are in a bit of a tight spot but there's no need to go off the deep end. Things will sort them-selves out somehow.'

'That's what you keep saying. You just won't face facts. About money or anything else.'

He turned rather white.

'I happen to care a good deal about what happens to you. Actually, I 'phoned Sybilla on the strength of having landed this part and tried to touch her for a hundred quid. But she was in one of her cheeseparing moods. So that was napoo.'

'Just as well. How could we ever have paid her back?'

'Sybilla could have afforded to wait. Hang it all, it's only just over a year till I come into my money.'

'A year! When you think of the mess we've got into in less than four months.'

'How about the old *Night*? Now you've smartened it up, I might take it along to the Summer Palace. Maidie's well in with the management.'

She almost screamed:

'Oh, stop, Archie. Of all the fantastic pipe-dreams! A child of six would have more sense. If someone gave you two pounds for that idiotic thing, lock, stock and barrel, you'd be lucky.'

'All right. I'll shut up then. Must be hell being married to a child of six.'

'I'm sorry, Archie. But you don't seem to grasp that something's got to be done here and now.'

He jumped to his feet, still angry, and thrust the script into his pocket.

'What I've got to do here and now is to get to rehearsal on time. So long.'

He strode out without kissing her and she heard him bang the front door.

She sat, staring down at the smeared plates and the cups full of dregs, with tears of irritation in her eyes. Archie had as usual spilt his tea, adding another spreading stain to the various brown blots on the cloth. Until they paid the laundry, they could not have a clean one. Untidy though she was, she hated dirty linen. Archie was no more perturbed than a schoolboy by wearing the same grimy shirt day after day but Clara loved the look and feel of fresh, clean clothes and felt demoralised without them. If the gas were cut off, they would not even be able to have baths.

She felt for some moments such a rage of resentment against Archie that she felt like walking out of the house and never returning. But where could she go except back to Valetta Road? That would be too humiliating. Anything was better than having to face her father's pained questions and her mother's triumphant sympathy. However exasperated she might be with Archie, she would rather be with him than with her family. The mere thought of having to live in Valetta Road again, having to appear punctually at boring meals, to listen to the bickering of her mother and her grandmother, to be asked where she was going and when she expected to be back, oppressed her more than their debts. The sugar house might be a prison but at least she and Archie were their own gaolers.

Still bitter against Archie, she pulled herself together. If he was utterly feckless, she must find some way out. She got up and washed the breakfast things with self-righteous indignation. Then, reflecting that in a day or two she might not even be able to boil a kettle, she went upstairs, turned on the geyser and washed clothes and table linen till her back ached and her hands were sore. For the rest of the day, she sat in the gloomy little dining-room, determined to earn her twelve guineas before nightfall. Anger sharpened her wits. With ironic enthusiasm, which developed almost into ironic conviction, she wrote six variations on the 'selling angle' of Glintex shampoo. 'Maybe you thought your hair was just "ordinary". Then you've never tried Glintex. You've never known what sunny glints, what hidden glories Glintex can reveal. Maybe you thought you were just "ordinary" too – that success, fulfilment, all that a woman hopes and dreams might never come your way. But Glintex affects your whole personality. New confidence . . . new charm . . . a subtle magnetism you suspected no more than that hidden radiance in your hair – that is what Glintex releases in you. In that little green packet is not "just another shampoo" but the key to a richer, more thrilling life. Let the rare, secret ingredients of Glintex reveal the rare, secret, dazzling *you*.'

The agents had enclosed a packet of Glintex shampoo. She washed her hair with it, assuring herself that this was merely a practical measure in case the gas was cut off. Nevertheless, as she rubbed it dry, she found herself hopefully watching for some astonishing change in its appearance. She even felt obscurely cheated when she combed it out and found it looked exactly the same as after any other shampoo.

Just as she had finished, the telephone rang. It was Archie, to say that he would not be home till late. Maidie had offered to coach him in his dance routine and he was going back to Golders Green with her after the rehearsal. He sounded brisk and cheerful; she could hear giggles and chattering going on in the background. Evidently he was 'phoning from the theatre. Suddenly the sense of isolation which she had managed to fight off all day came flooding over her. She felt as if even Archie had abandoned her. Fear and resentment put a cold edge on her voice. He appeared not to notice it.

'You'd better go and have a bite at the Three Cornered Hat. Do you good to get out of the house.'

She answered bitterly:

'No doubt. Only I happen to have exactly sevenpence halfpenny.'

'Oh well, that's napoo. But there are two eggs and a slice of cake in the larder.'

'So there are,' she said with savage brightness. 'And then I can have a nice game of trains.'

'That's the idea,' came Archie's heartiest voice. 'Mind the acid from the accumulator though. Cheerio.'

She hung up the receiver, furious and aggrieved. Here she was, having drudged away all day writing advertisements and washing clothes as a result of Archie's fecklessness, and he showed not the least sign of penitence or even concern. In justice, she had to admit that it was an excellent thing that Archie was making such efforts to succeed in his part. Nevertheless, she felt envious and neglected. Archie had got what he wanted: he was launched on something real. She saw herself desperately trying to scrape up money to patch up a life which was not really a life at all. As Archie became more and more absorbed in that intense private life of a theatre company, which she remembered from the *Error* days, she would grow lonelier and duller. Tonight would be merely a sample of the endless stretch of blank evenings which would begin when *My Girl Billie* opened in a few weeks' time. She thought bitterly how a real writer would have welcomed those uninterrupted hours. But she no longer had the confidence nor the will even to try any more. Even reading had become painful. It was weeks since she had so much as made an entry in the black notebook. The last time she had looked at it, one or two patches that seemed goodish, even to her jaundiced eye, had depressed her more than the morass of nonsense in which they were imbedded since they were a reminder of what she could never hope to do and yet obscurely longed to attempt. It would have been a relief to be able to tell herself that she had no aptitude whatever for the real thing and had better concentrate cynically on slick nonsense which might at least earn some money.

Money, she thought bitterly, that was the first necessity now. Well, with luck, she had made twelve guineas today but it was only a fraction of what they needed. It would take ten of her *London Mail* stories – and she hadn't the wits to concoct one of the wretched things – to make the thirty guineas still due on the rent. She seized a bunch of her newly washed hair in each hand, as if to tug some idea for raising money out of her skull by sheer force. Nothing occurred to her but the remote possibility of inducing Bassett-Lowke to take back the model railway. Until this moment, she would not have even considered it for fear of hurting Archie's feelings. Now she no longer cared; it even gave her a kind of pleasure to revenge herself on him.

She went out into the shed and stared at the shining, half-assembled network of rails and the two miniature trains still uncoupled to their engines. At first Archie had rushed to experiment with the railway the moment he came back from rehearsal and she had not had the heart to refuse to help him. But, in the last day or two, he had almost abandoned it: all his interest had been switched over on to studying his part. She picked up the two scale-model engines. They were so perfectly made that she could not resist a feeling of pleasure in them and even a pang of regret at the thought of parting with them. But, turning them over to examine their fine detail, she saw that already a great patch of the glossy paint on each boiler had peeled away, exposing the metal. Then she remembered that, the last time they had been running them, some of the acid from the accumulator had spilt on them. They were too spoilt for anyone to consider buying them now.

Her first reaction was to want to damage them still further. She stood with one in each hand, half-meaning to dash them down on the stone floor. Then she relented. Bending, she laid them down gently on a pile of shavings as if they must at all costs be preserved from even a single further scratch. For some reason, this gesture calmed her resentment. She stood up, with the oddest sense of having released herself from some pressing obligation. Even their debts no longer weighed on her so heavily; a space seemed to have cleared itself round her in which she was free to act on her own. Locking the shed door quietly and deliberately as if she had locked away some anxiety with it, she began to think how she should spend her evening. The first thought that occurred to her was to go and see Gundry. She had an odd sense of having somehow earned the right to do so. Nevertheless, her conscience was not quite at ease. Then she remembered Clive Heron, to whom she had not given a thought since the day he had avoided her in the King's Road. Now, the idea of seeing him seemed not only blameless but almost as pleasurable as going to Gundry's studio. She would just be in time to catch him at the Home Office if she rang him at once. As she asked for the number, she told herself that, even if he were not available, she would put off going to see Gundry at least till she could tell Archie that she intended to go.

A secretary informed her that Mr Heron had just gone abroad on three weeks' leave. It was not yet six o'clock. Without stopping to question herself further, Clara went upstairs, dressed herself with more care than she had done since the night they had danced at the club and, as seven o'clock struck, set out, trying to make herself walk slowly, in the direction of Rosehill Gardens.

13

It seemed to Clara, after she had been sitting in Gundry's room for two hours, that she had known it for years. Curled up on the broken-springed bed, she watched his tall, heavy figure moving with surprising deftness among stacks of frames and drawing boards as if it were as familiar a sight as her father sitting at his desk correcting Greek proses.

He had made two or three rough drawings of her head, some-times making jerky conversation, sometimes leaving her last remark unanswered while he worked for a spell with frowning concentration. Clara was not at all disconcerted by these inter-vals of silence. Provided she kept her head still, her eyes were free to wander round the room. It was not a studio but merely a large ground-floor room in a house which, from the outside, looked very much like the one in which her parents lived. It amused her to see how many features it had in common with the dining-room at Valetta Road; the marble mantelpiece, the Edwardian wallpaper, dingy serge curtains, a gas fire surrounded by hideous tiles. There, however, the resemblance ended. Except for one ancient armchair, a couple of battered chests of drawers, a deal table and the iron bed with its cheap Indian cotton bedspread, there was no ordinary furniture in the room. The paint-splashed boards were bare except for a rag rug. Everywhere, in a kind of orderly confusion, were Gundry's working materials: rolls of canvas, heavy palettes, a tin tea-tray full of tubes of colour, a zinc bucket holding a great bouquet of meticulously clean brushes. It gave her such extraordinary pleasure to look at these things that, at intervals, she would forget she was sitting to him, lose the pose and be barked at to keep still.

When he had finished his drawings, she was glad she had resisted the temptation to ask to see them.

'You're the first woman who hasn't rushed to the easel and said "Do I *really* look like that?" the moment I put down the charcoal.'

'Of course it's exactly what I'm longing to do,' she admitted, watching him as he sprayed the drawings to fix them. 'Only I'm too vain.'

'Are you? You strike me as rather a modest young woman.'

'Oh, this is mental vanity. Fear-of-giving-myself-away disease. I'd be sure to say the wrong thing. Have you forgotten how you warned me not to ask to look at your pictures?'

'No. But I'm flattered – and rather impressed – that you've remembered. Look if you like. You don't have to make any comment. They'll probably give you a shock.'

He passed the drawings to her one by one and she examined them in silence. They were done in free sweeping strokes; some almost as black and hard as the leading of stained glass; some mere indications, almost as delicate as pencil. He had simplified and slightly distorted her face, exaggerating the weight of her forehead and the fulness of her lips; minimising her eyes and treating her hair merely as a shape suggested by a few broken curves. It gave her a strange sensation to see herself presented in this brusque, unfamiliar way. When she had absorbed the shock to her vanity, she found the sensation exhilarating.

'Well?' Gundry asked at last. 'What's making you look so pleased all of a sudden, after knitting your brows for about five minutes? One would think you had just found the answer to a sum you'd given up as hopeless. Or have you thought of something intelligently non-committal to say?'

'I wish I had,' she laughed. 'No. I can't *think* at all at the moment. And what I'm feeling is so personal and vague that it would infuriate you if I tried to put it into words.'

'Risk it,' he said affably. 'I won't eat you.' Then he added, with his jolly monk's smile: 'Actually, there's nothing I would like better than to eat you. You're looking quite exceptionally appetising at this moment.' He advanced a step towards her and she instinctively stiffened. There had been some rather difficult moments before he settled down to draw her.

'All right,' he said. 'I'll retreat in good order. Go on. I'd be amused to hear these highly personal reactions.'

She summoned up her courage.

'Well . . . can you remember as a child tasting for the first time something grown up people like? Hock for example. Or olives. You don't immediately like the taste, even if you pretend you do out of pride. But if it's something you are really going to like one day, I believe you recognise it in advance.'

'Rather prettily put, if I may say so. Let's have some more of your subjective art criticism.'

Emboldened, she said:

'I can't judge your drawings as drawings. But I know you've drawn the lines you meant to draw. You can make that bit of charcoal do exactly what you want. That's always terribly exciting to me. Just the mere expert handling of anything, whether it's a man controlling a horse or a comedian timing a gag.' She added apologetically: 'I know it's nothing to do with art.'

'Nonsense. Obviously it's not the whole story. But one's got to have technique. One's got to have it all there . . . and yet be able to forget it. One can get so damned expert that it turns to tricks. Goes off and turns its private somersaults just for the sake of showing off. Doesn't wait on the eye or the mind . . . or, to use a word I loathe but I can't think of another . . . on one's vision.'

'Yes, of course,' she said excitedly. 'But that's what I want to know . . . which comes first . . . the hen or the egg. The vision or the technique. How does one know that one is . . . I hate that word too . . . an artist? I suppose everyone at some time wants to be one . . . not necessarily a painter of course – or even imagines one may be. But how does one know that one has the *right?*'

'That's a rum question. You talk as if it were a case of conscience.'

'Perhaps I think of most things like that. I expect it's the result of my convent education.'

He gave her a shrewd, considering glance.

'Oh . . . you went to a convent school, did you? That explains a lot. Still believe it all?'

'Certainly.'

He smiled.

'It doesn't explain everything. I've known a great many women who went to convent schools and who would have been extremely offended if one had suggested they weren't *croyantes* and even *pratiquantes*. But they weren't as difficult as you are. Or are Catholics more puritanical in England?'

'I've no idea. Anyhow I'm not going to follow your red herring. I want to know how people . . . you yourself for example . . . *know* that they are artists.'

'What a formidable creature you are. When you stick your chin out like that, you look like a little bulldog. Don't do it. It ruins that nice pinched-in line.'

'I won't . . . if you'll tell me.'

He sat down in the battered armchair which creaked under his weight and placed a hand on each of his knees.

'I've never really considered it. Obviously I was always what's called "good at drawing". Rather too good in fact. There wasn't a style I couldn't imitate like a monkey. Scholarships. The white-headed boy of the Art Class. When I was in my twenties, I made over a thousand a year copying Old Masters. Absolutely indistinguishable. Like a Chinese tailor who reproduces even the patches and the frayed buttonholes on a coat. I was a wow at getting the famous patina without stopping to think it was only dirty varnish. When I painted pictures myself, they looked so like Old Masters – patina and all – that everyone foresaw a highly successful future for me. Provincial art galleries and collectors bought Gundrys as a safe bet. One year I even made two thousand. I'd like to get hold of every one of the beastly things and burn 'em.'

'What happened to change everything?'

'I suppose it all started with seeing a Cézanne. He knocked me flat. Hated it at first. Colours, drawing, everything seemed to me all wrong. Heretical, as you'd say. But the beastly thing haunted me. I even tried copying it to get it out of my system. Oh yes, I imitated it all right, down to the last brush-stroke. All the time, I kept asking myself why the hell does he do this or that? Hasn't he ever heard of perspective? Why treat the sky like a solid? What's that damn white spot where he hasn't even covered the canvas? Then I came to love that wretched picture as much as I'd hated it. Call it a religious conversion. I saw every Cézanne I could. I was excited by Pissarro and Monet too, but it was always that old boy I came back to. I painted a lot of sham Cézannes, trying to work out from the outside what his game was: such and such a palette, such and such relations of forms. I even fancied I'd worked out an underlying theory of his proportions – a mathematical rule of thumb. So I became a promising "modern" painter. I didn't make so much money but I sold my pictures. Now I looked a safe bet to the cautious *avant garde* collector.'

'And then?' asked Clara, leaning forward with clasped hands and gazing reverently at his averted head.

'Don't quite know,' he said slowly. 'I suppose I gradually began to look at things. Really look at them off my own bat. Cézanne and some of the others had shown me that they really saw what they saw. My eye had got all cluttered up with other people's images of things and I had this damn facility for reproducing those in any style, ancient or modern. So I started right off from the very beginning, merely trying to see. I even did silly things like drawing with my left hand so that I wouldn't go off into tricks.'

'How wonderful,' Clara breathed ardently.

He turned and glanced at her.

'You odd creature. Anyone would think all this desperately concerned you.'

'Oh, forget about me. Please go on.'

'Not much more to tell. Still experimenting. Half the things I do, I don't finish. Half the ones I finish, I destroy. I paint things that people find uninteresting or even ugly. I don't paint what people call beautiful objects or scenery because I don't *think* they're beautiful. I do. But I'm trying to clear away all the accumulated mass of associations and expectations they arouse. I want to keep my eye clear . . . look at a thing with detachment . . . for itself . . . not because of any feelings I've got about it. At the moment I'm deliberately painting things which don't in themselves excite me. Exercises, really, in simple *seeing* with all the concentration I'm capable of. Now the critics wonder what the hell's happened to me; the collectors fight shy and I'm lucky if I sell two pictures a year for a quarter of what I got for muck.'

Clara said softly:

'If thy eye be single, thy whole body shall be full of light.'

'That's good,' he said. 'Blake?'

'It's in the Gospel. Christ says it somewhere.'

'Does he indeed? Good for Jesus Christ. But he'd be scandalised at having it applied to painting, though.'

'I wonder,' said Clara. 'It's one of the things that's always nagging me . . . the connection between art and religion.'

'No connection at all, if you ask me. Old Cézanne was a pious Catholic. He also had a beard. One's as irrelevant as the other. He'd have been just as great a painter if he'd been an atheist. If I believed in the devil, he could have my soul tonight for the price of five good pictures before I die. That shocks you, doesn't it?'

'I don't know. I suppose it would if you *did* believe in the devil. Anyway no one could call you worldly.' She looked round at the uncarpeted room, furnished with only the barest necessities besides his painter's equipment. 'I wonder how many people would give up as much for their religion as you have for your work. I'm sure plenty of monks and nuns who've made a vow of holy poverty live in far more comfort than this.'

He laughed.

'I don't think there's any virtue in poverty. It's a damn nuisance. I assure you I have no scruples about getting money by any other means, however frowned-on. Often I haven't got the money to buy paints and canvases. I go round to different art shops that knew me in palmier days getting stuff on tick and trusting to be able to pay some day.'

'Oh . . . if only I had some money,' Clara said earnestly. 'I'd be so awfully happy and proud to help you.'

'What a nice creature you are. I warn you I'd have no hesitation in taking it if you could afford it.'

She burst out:

'Oh . . . I feel so ashamed of myself. It's true we haven't any money at the moment: we're up to our ears in debt. But it's all my fault . . . if I hadn't wanted to live in that absurd, pretentious doll's house.' Twisting her hands, almost in tears, hardly caring whether he listened or not, she poured out an incoherent stream of self-accusation. 'And not only now,' she ended. 'To think I used to make quite a lot before I married and spend it on idiotic things like clothes and taking people out to restaurants and here were you . . . *needing* even tubes of paint . . . and I could have bought them for you. I'll never, never be able to do anything myself but I could have helped someone who can.'

She was aware of Gundry staring at her with a strange expression almost as if he were angry. When at last she stopped, he said nothing. They sat for some moments in silence while she stared miserably at the rag rug, not daring to look at him. Then he stood up, padded over the bare boards and, sitting beside her on the bed, took her very gently in his arms, saying gruffly:

'You absurd creature. You quite preposterously absurd creature.'

She said with relief:

'Laugh at me, if you like. I thought you were furious.'

'Silly one. I'm only laughing in self-defence. Otherwise I might cry.'

'What nonsense.'

'Nonsense, indeed. Look at me!'

She turned her head in the crook of his arm and looked up at his face. It had relaxed again into his mischievous, dimpled smile but his eyes were wet. He put up his forefinger to them and solemnly showed her a glistening streak.

'There, doubting Thomas. Have you got a tear-bottle handy? These authentic specimens are rare.'

She said, imitating his smile rather shakily:

'If I let myself go now, I'd never stop. I'd fill buckets. I don't know what's come over me. I just want to howl and bellow. And I've no idea why.'

'Howl and bellow by all means. But for God's sake don't sniff. Here . . .' He offered her an enormous handkerchief. 'I've wiped my brushes on it but there's a clean space in the middle.'

She blew her nose obediently.

'Well, what do you want us to do now?' he asked. 'Have a good weep over our overdrafts? I daresay I could pump up another tear or two to keep you company.'

Suddenly, for no reason at all, she felt so violently happy that she had to laugh. She said, trying to get her breath between the gusts . . .

> 'Two walking baths, two weeping motions
> Portable and com . . . compendious oceans.'

He laughed too. Then suddenly the laugh broke off; his face

made its sudden switch to the brooding mask. He clutched her close against him and muttered:

'There's something much better for us to do than crying. Isn't there, my sweet, my lovely one?'

He put his mouth against hers, gently at first, then as she half-willingly yielded, with a fiercer and fiercer pressure as if he were trying to suck the blood from her lips. Crushed against his great body, she was aware only of a blank darkness in her mind and a sense of suffocation. He shifted her weight expertly, holding her tight in the hollow of one arm, while his free hand caught her under her knees and lifted her so that she lay on the bed. Still with his lips fastened on hers so that she could hardly breathe, he leant over her and began, gently but urgently to pull her dress off one shoulder. Under the weight of his body, she could not move. She had lost all sense of his identity or her own; she was only aware of a desperate need to get her breath. When at last he raised his head and buried his face in the hollow of her bare shoulder, the relief was so great that she could not think connectedly enough to protest. She lay for a moment with closed eyes, gasping between her stiff, swollen lips, feeling the unexpected softness of the hair on the hard round head under her chin. Then, as suddenly as he had closed on her, he let her go, walked across to the window and drew the curtains. The room, already dusky, became completely dark.

She sat up, pulled her dress straight and groped along the wall.

'Marcus . . . please . . . put the light on . . . I can't find the switch.'

He did not answer. She heard him stepping carefully over the bare boards. Then he struck a match and lit some candles stuck in saucers on the mantelpiece. The room immediately took on a mysterious beauty, full of monumental shapes and wavering shadows. Some crumpled brown paper, torn and showing patches of the white canvas it covered, became a pile of rocks with rifts of snow; a naked mirror propped against the wall, reflecting tubes and brushes at an odd angle, became an aquarium with silver fish and spiky plants glimmering through dusky water.

Gundry's face, too, as he stood at the mantelpiece, putting a taper to the candles with the slow, careful movements of an acolyte, had changed its aspect in the soft, transforming glow. His profile was grave and intent; modelled in clear light and shadow, the broad, simple planes of cheek and brow, the full jaw, the small straight nose reminded her no longer of Napoleon or a jolly monk, but of a Buddha.

Now, removed from her and condensed once more into a human being, she could hardly connect him with that blind force, impersonal as an avalanche, which a few moments ago had threatened to crush her. The silence during which she watched him methodically light and foster each little tongue of flame, cupping it from the draught with his large, sure hand, seemed to spin out for ever. Somewhere at the back of her mind was a nagging sense that there was something she ought to say or do, but she could only sit there on the edge of the bed, intent as an animal on his every movement.

Suddenly he crouched down and lit the gas fire; the small explosion shattered the silence which had become so intense that it was like a third presence in the room. The air, which she could have fancied congealing in solid layers under its pressure, moved again. She shook herself out of her almost hypnotic state and said uncertainly:

'Marcus . . .'

He turned at once and came towards her. The next moment his arms were wrapped round her again, this time gently.

'What is it? Why do you look so frightened? You like me, don't you?'

'Oh I do . . . I do . . .'

'Well then,' he laughed softly. 'What's all the trouble about?' He held her closer, still gently, but as she tried to recoil, more insistently. He put his mouth against her ear, saying in jerky whispers: 'I've wanted you for so long. I want you so terribly. No one ever wanted you more.'

She turned her head away, trying to loosen the hand that was once more busy with her dress, saying miserably:

'Oh . . . please let me go . . . It's all my fault . . . I feel such a cheat . . . I should never have come here . . .'

He raised his face which he had buried in the hollow of her neck, gripped her by the shoulders and looked at her under his heavy lids.

'You don't want me? Is that it?'

'Even if I did . . . oh, how can I make you understand . . . I can't . . . I mustn't . . .'

'What is it? . . . scruples of conscience? . . . This infernal religion of yours? You're not a fool. You can't seriously believe that there's anything wrong in something so natural. Do you think it wrong to eat when you're hungry and drink when you're thirsty?'

She hedged:

'Do remember that I'm married.' She realised, as she said it, that it was she who had forgotten.

'Of course you're married,' he said impatiently. 'I'm not a barbarian. I don't seduce virgins. If you find me repulsive, that's another matter. But I don't believe you do.' He caught her in his arms again; kissing her neck, her ears, her eyelids, very gently and murmuring: 'You silly, adorable creature. There's nothing to be afraid of. Just forget everything and let's be happy.'

In spite of herself, Clara could not help yielding to the comfort of his warm, solid embrace. Her strained nerves relaxed, her mind grew numb and drowsy. She nestled against him, feeling small as a child in his powerful arms. Without thinking she began to return his gentle, reassuring kisses. But, as his became more urgent and his heavy body pressed closer against her, she tautened again and tried to push him away.

'No . . . no, my girl. Enough of that,' he said between his clenched teeth, leaning down over her so that she could hardly move.

Suddenly, he let her go and started to his feet. She caught a glimpse of his face set in a strange, blind look; lips parted and forehead damp with sweat, before he turned away, tore off his jacket and began to drag at his shirt.

'Take your clothes off,' he said abruptly. 'I can't make love to you like that.'

Her mind went blank. She could only utter an incoherent sound. He turned about and faced her with his shirt hanging out; half his heavy torso, smooth and padded as a wrestler's, bare; the flesh almost golden in the candlelight. Even in her dismay, she was struck by something at once ludicrous and impressive in his appearance. He said more gently, with a twitch of his old mischievous smile that made his face recognisable through the mask of desire:

'Don't be shy, my sweet. There's not a line of your body I don't know by heart already. I'll put the candles out if you insist. Anything you want. Oh . . . for God's sake, woman, what is it now?'

For Clara had burst into hysterical tears. She crouched on the edge of the bed, her face clutched in both hands, giving great gulping sobs as uncontrollable as hiccups. She could hear him moving about the room, muttering under his breath; then came the noise of a door opening and shutting. When at last she raised her head, she found herself alone.

She had pulled herself together enough to get up and begin to grope for her coat among a jumble of objects, in the deep shadows beyond the range of the candles, when Gundry returned. He had put on his jacket again; his face was still pale and glistening but composed in a distant, almost severe expression. For a moment she thought he did not see her where she stood in the dark patch behind his easel. He opened a cupboard, took out a saucepan, a tin and two chipped enamel mugs.

'I'll make some coffee,' he said over his shoulder.

'No. Please. I must go.'

'Sit down. In the chair.'

As she still hesitated, he said irritably:

'You needn't be alarmed. I can take a broad hint.'

She obeyed meekly.

'Shove the chair back, can't you? I want to get at the gas ring.' She watched him as he crouched at her feet, heating up his saucepan and putting on his kettle. He seemed so absorbed as to be quite unaware of her. Once again she could not help admiring the deft way he handled objects. His mood had changed so completely that she felt rebuffed. She wanted to restore the intimacy she had felt with him before that violent interruption. It was as if she would lose something precious, hardly acquired yet already indispensable, if she did not at once make some effort to retain it. Tentatively she put out her hand and touched the silky dark hair at the nape of his neck. He started as if she had burnt him and swore.

'None of that. Or this time you'll bloody well take the consequences my girl. Here . . .' He swung round and thrust a saucepan into her still outstretched hand . . . 'Put that damned little paw to some practical use.'

As he turned, he glanced at her face and his severe expression relaxed into a grin. He snatched the saucepan back.

'No . . . better use it to comb your hair. There's a bit of looking glass on the mantelpiece.'

In the glimmer of the now guttering candles, she saw that her face was blotched and swollen beyond recognition under her wildly disordered hair. She set to work almost savagely with comb and powder puff.

He sat back on his heels, mocking her.

'What is this fetish women have about plastering their faces? I believe even you would rather be seen naked than with your nose unpowdered. There . . . stop dabbing. Come and drink your coffee.'

He thrust one chipped mug at her and retired on to the bed with the other.

She sipped the sweet strong coffee in silence, feeling herself revive with every sip. He drank his without looking at her, in three long gulps, put the mug down with his usual care and lit a cigarette.

234

'Well,' he said at last. 'That was rather a violent reaction, wasn't it? One might almost have supposed no one had ever attempted to make love to you before. Or do you find me as repulsive as all that?'

'Oh, not you . . . Not you yourself.'

'Then what? I can't believe that outburst was entirely due to moral indignation. It was a little too primitive.'

She said nothing. He looked at her questioningly.

'You've got a very odd expression on your face. As if there were something you wanted to say and couldn't quite bring out.'

'Yes . . . perhaps,' she said slowly.

He gave his reassuring smile.

'Come now. We've both given ourselves away pretty thoroughly tonight, haven't we? I think it's your turn.'

She shook her head.

'If it were only myself, I would gladly. But this involves someone else.'

He stared at her for a moment; then said abruptly:

'Look here . . . Something quite fantastic has just occurred to me.' He broke off, frowning. 'No. It's inconceivable.'

'Is it so fantastic? I've no means of knowing. Perhaps it's quite usual.'

'Quite usual?' he said fiercely. 'You can sit there calmly and talk about "quite usual" . . . Why, it's the most monstrous, unnatural thing I ever heard. A woman like you. No . . . I can't believe it.'

'It's true. But I wish I hadn't told you.'

'You've told me nothing. But, my dear girl, this is serious. I've got to get this clear . . . for your sake as well as mine.'

Seeing his face almost angry with concern, she could only tell him the truth. He did not look at her as she spoke. When she had said the little there was to say, he continued to smoke for some moments in silence. Then he threw away his cigarette, crushed it out with his heel and asked shortly:

'Well, what are you going to do about it?'

'Do? What can I do?'

'You're not seriously proposing to go on with this farce of a marriage?'

She stared at him.

'But I have to go on. We're both Catholics. We have to go on whatever happens. Even if I were ever to leave Archie, there's no question of divorce for either of us.'

'I'm not talking of divorce. Even that hidebound institution, your Church, recognises one or two basic facts of human nature. If things are as you say . . . Yes, yes, I believe you now . . . then you've got a clear, foolproof case. The sooner you start consulting your priests and lawyers the better.'

It was Clara's turn to be incredulous.

'But are you sure?'

'Of course I'm sure,' he said impatiently. 'I knew someone else in that situation. Hers was more complicated because she'd had a lover before she married this man. I take it you haven't.'

She shook her head.

'Then it's simple. Mere matter of routine. I believe it takes the hell of a time though. You ought to get going at once.'

She said in sudden panic:

'Oh . . . no. It's such a huge decision. I'd have to think it over. I still can't take it in properly.'

He said grimly:

'You'd better start thinking quickly. You're very young, presumably normal, and uncomfortably desirable. Have you thought of the alternatives? Sooner or later, you'll land yourself in an intolerable position. If you take a lover, you'll be overcome with guilt and incidentally block your way of escape. If you don't you'll do yourself incalculable harm, physically and mentally. Either way, that young man will suffer less in the end if you make the break now.'

Her mind was in such confusion that he seemed to be remorselessly attacking her.

She pleaded wildly:

'Oh please. Don't be so cruel. Give me time to take it in.'

He said more gently:

'You really mean you hadn't the least idea?'

'No . . . Not the remotest . . . I never even dared imagine . . .' She could not go on. Her throat had gone dry and her head was swimming. The shadows in the dim room suddenly thickened and seemed to have swallowed up the last glimmer of the candles. She became conscious for the first time of the heat and smell of the gas fire and the rasping wheeze of a broken jet. The smell of the gas, the growing darkness seemed to mix together in her head, blowing it up like a balloon. From very far away she heard a minute, authoritative voice, which she could just recognise as Gundry's, saying:

'Put your head down . . . No . . . right down between your knees.'

She tried to obey but the balloon head seemed to be floating up to the ceiling. Before she could establish any connection with it a heavy weight fell on the back of her neck. Gradually the balloon descended, and shrank back into a normal head again and now she found it was nearly touching the floor and that someone's hand was forcing it down. She had just grasped the fact that the hand was Gundry's when his voice muttered close in her ear: 'All right now?'

When at last she raised her head, she found he was sitting on the arm of the chair. He threw one hand across the back and, with the other, gently pulled her back so that she lay in the crook of his arm.

'Lie quiet,' he said, almost in a whisper. 'Keep your eyes shut. Don't be afraid. We've given each other enough shocks for one night.'

She lay back obediently, exhausted and relaxed. Gradually, an extraordinary sense of contentment crept over her. When at last she forced herself to open her drowsy eyes, she glanced up and saw him sitting above her solid as a statue, his face in profile. She watched him for a moment, thinking that he looked older and sadder than she had seen him yet. The glow of the gas fire caught his jaw, showing the just-slackening line of the chin, the creases by his mouth and in front of his ear. She felt such a wave of warmth towards him that she wanted to speak, but dared not, for fear of breaking the spell. Lying there in quiet bliss, she let the warmth flow out of her to embrace everything in the room, from the candles burning low and crooked in their wax-clotted saucers to the gigantic shadow of the bunch of paintbrushes which half covered the ceiling. She said at last, on a long sigh: 'I could stay like this for ever.'

At once he started, and, turning his face to her, switched on his jolly monk's smile and said:

'I couldn't. I've got pins and needles in my left arm.'

She sat bolt upright.

'Oh . . . I'm so sorry . . . I never thought . . .'

'Don't apologise.' He flexed his stiff arm, heaved himself off the chair and pulled her to her feet.

'You'd better go now, my dear, if you're feeling up to it. Want me to see you home?'

'No, of course not.'

She felt extraordinarily forlorn as she watched him pick up her coat, shake off a paint rag that had clung to it, and hold it up for her to put on.

As she slipped her arms into the sleeves, he kept his hands on her shoulders and turned her to face him.

'Well, young woman, I hope you're grateful to me.'

'Oh I am . . . I am . . . You'll never know how much.'

'There's a charming irony about my situation, you must admit,' he said drily. 'That I of all people should be the one to point the way out of yours. And in doing so, effectively spike my own guns.'

She said fervently:

'Marcus . . . dear Marcus . . . it's not just that. You don't know what it's meant to me. Being here with you . . . watching you work . . . hearing you talk . . . It's been like coming to life after being dead for months . . .'

He caught her chin in one hand and turned her face into the light.

'What's come over you?' he asked. 'You look entirely different.' Suddenly he slapped her cheek lightly and pushed her away. 'Out with you. That face gives me ideas I've been sternly repressing. It's how I imagined you'd look if . . .'

'If?'

'If I hadn't behaved so bloody well. Now be off with you, you baggage.'

'All right. I'm going.' But she still lingered, looking round the room. 'I suppose I'll never see this place again.'

'Not in these circumstances you won't, my good girl. You can't have your cake and eat it too.'

'Goodbye then, Marcus.'

She made a step towards him and he put his arms round her. He kissed her eyes and said with his reassuring laugh:

'Portable and compendious oceans.'

'Don't,' she said, managing to smile. 'I'll begin again if you're not careful.'

'Heaven defend,' he said, loosening his hold. 'I, at least, have the sense to come in out of the rain.' He gave her one mocking kiss and marched her firmly to the door.

14

The air struck chilly after the heat of Gundry's room. She had no idea what the time was but she suspected it must be very late. The long lamp-lit street was empty but for two cats, alternately crouching motionless in the gutter, then darting across the road in pursuit of each other. She stood, for some moments, watching them while the damp wind played on her face. At last, she began to walk very slowly in the direction of the King's Road.

So many new and confusing ideas were fighting in her head that she hardly knew which to try and follow up. Like the cats, now one, now another would start up and chase the rest away: then her mind would freeze again and she would be aware only of the sound of her own footsteps. It seemed so long since she had set out from Tithe Place that it was difficult to remember the chain of small events that had led to her going to Gundry's room. When she did manage to reconstruct them, they seemed to belong to another time; almost to another dimension from the one in which she had been living for the last hours. It was as if she had undergone an operation and were trying to force herself back to normal consciousness.

Gradually, as her mind cleared enough to focus it on Archie, she had to make an effort to remember how he looked and spoke. Having recovered his image, she was seized with such terror that she stopped dead in the street. If what Gundry had said were true, how could she ever bring herself to suggest that possibility to Archie? Almost she wished that she had never heard of it. The more she concealed it, the more false and constrained she would become with him. If she told him, even with no idea of taking action, he would always be conscious of a threat.

Either way, their old freedom and frankness had gone for good.

She walked on again, this time as fast as possible, treading with deliberate noisiness in the effort to drown any attempt at thought by the clatter of her heels on the pavement. As she turned into the King's Road, the sound of passing cars and of other footsteps muffled her own. The sounds and the brighter lights brought her back to the immediate. She realised it could not be as late as she supposed. A headlight lit up the clock on the town hall. It was only a few minutes after midnight.

She crossed the road and almost ran down the turnings that led to Tithe Place. If she hurried, she might get back in time to be in bed, with the light off, before Archie returned from Maidie's. When he did come in, she would pretend to be asleep. There was only one thought in her mind now. At all costs she must avoid any conversation with Archie tonight.

As she turned the corner by the dark bulk of the church, her latchkey already in her hand to save even a moment's delay, she saw there was a light in their sitting-room.

He came out into the passage as she opened the door, saying fervently and without a tinge of reproach:

'Thank God, you're back. I had a fright when I got in just now.'

He put his arm round her, kissing her so affectionately that she felt as much remorse as if she had betrayed him. She could not quite bring herself to return his kiss.

He drew her into the sitting-room, still keeping his arm round her. After the dark streets and the hours in the dim, candle-lit studio, her eyes hurt, as if suddenly exposed to limelight. The tiny room was like a brightly lit box; wherever she turned her head to avoid the glare, Archie's face and her own confronted her from the ruthless mirrors.

'Still fed up with me, old thing?' he asked. 'Sorry I was snooty at breakfast. I didn't mean to be.'

She frowned, trying to take in the fact that he was apologising to her when she expected questions, even accusations.

'Ah, come on, Clarita,' he pleaded. 'Can't you forgive a chap? Hang it all, you've punished me enough, haven't you? I rang up from Maidie's just to say "Hullo". I thought you sounded peeved when I said I wasn't coming straight back after rehearsal. No answer. Then I tried Valetta Road. Napoo too. Of course I didn't really think it was likely you'd be there. Nothing matters except that you're here now.'

Freeing herself gently from his arm, Clara sat down, shading her dazzled eyes.

She said in a stifled voice:

'I'm the one who ought to say I'm sorry. Of course your part's the most important thing at the moment. How was Maidie?'

'Oh, in terrific form,' he said heartily.

'Have you got the hang of your dance now?'

He nodded.

'Maidie's some teacher. Ruthless but damned efficient. Could do it in my sleep now.'

'Did she take you through your song, too?'

'Rather. Played my accompaniment by ear and sang all Sherry's part. Word perfect too.'

'And you've got your own lines right at last?' Feeling they could go on like this indefinitely, she removed the shading hand from her eyes and looked at him for the first time. His face was radiant. Was it a trifle too consciously radiant as her questions were too consciously eager?

Over his shoulder she caught the reflection of her own, looking so extraordinary that she was amazed he seemed to notice nothing. For a moment she forgot his presence; the face in the glass bore such a startling resemblance to the drawing Gundry had made of her that it was as if her features had imitated it. Her hair, blown back by the wind, revealed the broad, high forehead that was normally hidden by a fringe; her lips were still swollen and her eyes almost invisible from that violent burst of tears; the high collar of the dark coat emphasised, almost to caricature, the pinched-in line of the jaw. Suddenly, she realised that the woman who had been in Marcus's studio and the woman who sat in this doll's house room were the same person. This came as such a shock that, though she could hear Archie talking excitedly, she did not take in a word of what he said.

Focussing sharply on him again, she heard him say:

'. . . and they've asked us to do a stunt for this first-night party. Jolly decent of Maidie to let me do a turn with her . . . she could have asked practically anyone in the cast. I'm not risking a dance, you bet. Just pantomime stuff. But the song's an absolute ringer for our two voices. Maidie's got a friend in the new show *Sally* that's just gone into rehearsal and she's bagged a top-hole number from her. No one's heard it in London yet.'

Clara asked, with the attentive stare of one whose mind is on something else:

'Won't this other management mind?'

'No. It's O.K. We've got permission because it'll be a private audience, not a public one. You see this party's being kept absolutely to the members of the *Billie* company. I won't even be able to wangle you in, old thing. I swear I did my best. But they're not even letting Sherry's wife come though she's raising hell. Understand?'

'Of course,' she said brightly. 'Anyway, one feels out of a first-night party if one isn't in the cast.'

'Don't mind my going?'

'No, no. Of course not.'

'You're a sport. I'd back out like a shot only it would be letting Maidie down after she's been so decent. You see she thinks it'll be a chance for me to show off the old voice. My little bit of nonsense with Sherry is really only burlesque. He keeps interrupting and guying me every bar or two. But I can really let the old vocal chords rip in this number.' He began to hum. 'Can't get the words of the verse right yet – but this is the refrain. Don't look so frightened . . . I'll do it pianissimo so as not to wake the neighbourhood. Pity you can't sing the girl's part: you need the harmonies to get the real effect. Listen.'

He stood up and, eyeing an imaginary partner, sang softly:

> 'Dear little, dear little church round the corner
> Where so many lives have begun
> Where folks without money
> See nothing that's funny
> In two living cheaper than one.'

He broke off looking slightly offended.

'What's the matter?'

'Nothing – why?'

'You put on such an odd expression.'

'Did I?'

Suddenly he smiled. 'I've got it. Why, it's just like us. I never noticed that.'

'Do go on.'

He picked it up again.

> 'She's a girl, so it's no use to warn her . . .
> He's busted, but what does he care . . .
> "I'll be dressed all in white" . . .

that's Maidie's solo line of course –

> "I'll be dying of fright" . . .

yours truly's solo.' He took a few prancing steps, holding one arm out to his invisible girl.

'We go into a little routine here but this damn room's too

small to demonstrate; then both together, all out, rather showy harmony . . .

"At that church round the corner
It's just round the *corner*
The *corner* of Mad-i-son Square."

There! Catchy don't you think?'

Clara had pulled out her handkerchief and was holding it to her lips. She nodded violently.

Archie broke off a dance step he was tentatively trying and stared at her.

'I say . . . you're not crying are you?'

She shook her head.

'N—no,' she said unsteadily through the handkerchief. 'Laughing.'

'It's not meant to be a really comic number,' he said doubtfully. 'The way Maidie and I work it, it's more like "The Only Girl".'

She removed the handkerchief and twisted it in her fingers. Seeing there was a spot of blood on it, she tried to hide it and hastily licked her lower lip where she had bitten it.

'I say, what's the matter?' he asked, staring at her. 'You've hurt your lip or something. Clarita, darling, whatever is it?'

'Nothing. Nothing at all. I'm sure it'll be a great success. You'll both do it beautifully. So sorry I can't see it,' she gabbled.

In one stride he was kneeling beside her and had clutched both her hands.

'What's upset you so? You're shaking all over.'

'Nothing. Really nothing,' she repeated feverishly, looking wildly round the room to avoid his troubled eyes.

'You know, Clarita, I'm worried about you. You're getting a bundle of nerves, old thing. You don't look like yourself tonight. Anything wrong?'

She said nothing. He went on after a moment, in a hesitant, rather strained voice:

'Maidie said she was quite worried about you that Saturday at the night-club. She said you looked queer. As if you'd been ill or were going to be.'

'Well, I'm not ill, am I?'

He frowned.

'N—no. I hope not. I don't think she meant just ordinary ill-ness.'

Clara said, with the sharpness of one who has something to hide:

'Maidie's usually pretty explicit. She's said something you don't want to tell me.'

He stared down at the arty raffia rug and nodded. There was a dull flush all over his face, extending even to the back of his neck.

'So you and she have been discussing us?'

He said wretchedly:

'I didn't mean to. But Maidie started pitching into me a bit. Somehow I blurted out a lot more than I meant to. It seemed quite natural at the time. Maidie being a pal of yours and so on. But on the way back I felt absolutely hellish. And when I got home and found you gone, I felt it bloody well served me right.'

She said gently:

'You shouldn't have felt hellish. Perhaps there comes a point where one *has* to talk.'

'There's something I haven't told you,' he said, still with his eyes fixed on the rug. 'Maybe I ought to. But there's also some-thing I haven't asked you. Perhaps that evens things out.'

It was Clara's turn to stare at the floor. She longed to be able to tell him the truth but dared not. If she so much as mentioned Gundry, she was terrified that she would say everything that was on her mind. She sat there, feeling so mean and treacherous that she could hardly endure to be silent any longer, when Archie said abruptly:

'After all, you've had to put up with pretty good hell one way and another, Clarita.'

She passed a hand over his untidy red hair.

'So have you.'

He turned his face up to her sharply.

'Maybe. But *you* weren't to blame.'

She frowned, staring out through the uncurtained window at the lamp on the opposite corner of the street. He sat there at her feet, leaning his head against her knee and staring out of the window too, for what seemed a long time. The cone of misty light cut across a section of the unadorned brick wall of the church. She said at last, as slowly as if she were making out words written on that wall:

'I haven't told you where I went tonight.'

He gave her hand a convulsive clutch.

'You don't have to tell me. I know.'

'You mean you knew when I came in?' she asked, startled.

He shook his untidy head.

'I wasn't quite sure. Only in these last few minutes.' After another pause he said: 'It had to come sooner or later, I suppose.' He added with bitterness: 'I wish it had been anyone but that man.'

She told him, very quietly, only enough to reassure him. He listened without comment, only removing his head from where it rested against her knee and dropping it forward on his chest. Suddenly he straightened his body and turned towards her a face so stricken and distorted that she thought for a second he had not understood.

'My God,' he said savagely. 'I almost wish it had happened. Then at least you could never marry anyone else.' His body collapsed as suddenly as it had stiffened. He buried his face in his hands and his shoulders heaved once or twice. When he spoke again, his voice was low and almost steady.

'Clarita,' he said, pulling one of her hands forward over his shoulder and pressing it against his cheek, as he sat there with his head averted and his face lifted towards the window. 'There's something I've known quite a long time but hadn't the guts to tell you. I kept hoping . . . no, never mind.'

247

'Yes?' she said softly.

'Well . . . I thought by some miracle things might come right. Or . . . even if they didn't . . . perhaps it wouldn't matter so much. That we two . . . forgive me, dear . . . might be alike in some queer way. Not wanting exactly what everyone else wants. Oh, I know you've had the rawest possible deal with me. No money. And my going off and getting tight like a hog.'

'Only because you were miserable,' she urged, feeling a desperate need to comfort him. 'Now that you've got your job . . .'

He interrupted: 'Yep. I kidded myself like that. It's even true up to a point. Theresa Cressett thought that, if we got married, everything would come right. But there are some things even Theresa doesn't understand about people.'

Clara said despondently:

'If I'd been what Theresa thought I might be . . . something that, when I'm with her, I almost fool myself I could be . . .'

'Rubbish. You're all right, Clarita. Or could be. Only not with me . . . see? I suppose I never could admit it till tonight.'

'What was it you said you'd known a long time?'

He hesitated.

'You've heard me speak of Sammy Sissons?'

'The Jesuit you liked so much at Beaumont?'

'Yes. Well . . . oh, long ago now . . . it was in the days when I was around with Lister and Bell and Co. I ran into him in a pub and I went back with him to Farm Street. And we talked about this and that.'

'Yes?' she pressed him, feeling a weight begin to lift from her heart.

He muttered: 'Well . . . he said that if things went on like this . . . naturally he kept saying "give yourselves a chance" . . . that you'd got a way out.'

She gave a sigh of relief. He asked sharply:

'Did you know about this? Lots of Catholics don't.'

'I knew vaguely that some people . . . Nothing definite.'

248

'I know I should have told you. Maidie went for me about that and I knew she was right. But I'd made all sorts of excuses. How beastly it would all be for you. It *is* beastly. Father Sammy admitted that. Told myself that if you could hold on till I came into my money, I could give you everything you wanted. No worries. A decent house anywhere you fancied. Travel. Time to concentrate on your writing. We could have adopted some children. Only if you'd wanted them too, of course.'

She interrupted:

'Oh, don't, don't. All the time it's you who've been thinking of me. What I might feel. What I might want . . .'

He said simply:

'Well, I loved you, didn't I? It was up to me.'

'But when did I think what *you* wanted? I've been nothing but a beastly spoilt child.' She looked round the bright room, smirking still in its shabbiness. '*You* never wanted this house. Now I hate it every bit as much as you do.'

'This house?' he said wonderingly. 'You were so keen on it. I admit I wasn't so keen myself. Not that I really care much where I live. Still, this is a bit like living in a box of sweets. Bit of a strain for a great clumsy gawk like me. I admit it looks pretty. Or did before I started messing it up. Everything in it's so damn flimsy that it breaks off in your hand like barley sugar.'

'Exactly. A sugar house. Hansel and Gretel's sugar house.'

Suddenly he stood up and pulled her to her feet facing him.

'My darling old thing,' he said. His eyes were haggard and bloodshot. Every touch of warmth and tenderness and gratitude she had ever felt for him came flooding over her and with it a terror of the unknown. She flung herself into his arms seeing, in a wild jumble of images, herself returning to Valetta Road alone; an endless, featureless stretch of living again with her parents; interviews with priests and lawyers; prying questions; gloating pity; humiliation of every kind. She said wildly:

'Archie . . . I can't. I *can't* face it . . . Let's go on as we are.'

'No, Clarita.' His voice was quiet, almost stern.

She began to plead with him, trying to force him back into the Archie she could dominate.

'We don't have to decide at once. Let's wait at least till after your first night. That's the only thing that matters here and now. Only a few minutes ago you were thinking of nothing else. Let's forget all this for the moment.'

He said, his voice sounding angry with pain:

'Now it's come up, do you suppose we could forget? It'd be hanging over us like a knife. I'd rather it came down short and sharp.'

In panic she went on appealing to him, saying disjointedly anything that came into her head, in a desperate attempt to gain time. She chattered on feverishly, her voice rising shriller and shriller till it broke on a cry of 'Archie' that was almost a scream. He remained absolutely still and silent. Frantic at her impotence to reach him by words, she began to claw at his coat.

He said roughly:

'Stop it. I'm not made of iron.'

Suddenly all his firmness crumbled. His shoulders drooped, he moved his head slowly from side to side with a gesture of such exhaustion that she thought he was going to fall. She stepped close to him, and felt him lean almost his whole weight against her as she put her arms round him.

'I've gone as far as I can. It's up to you now, Clara.'

They clung together, feeling each other's cheeks wet yet hardly conscious that they were crying. Archie jerked his head up at last and said, with a caricature of his old smile:

'The bloody silly things one remembers.'

She sobbed: 'Oh, don't Archie . . . don't. Isn't there anything else we can do?'

He said gently:

'We'd better face it, old thing. The sooner, the better.'

She swallowed hard and said, as steadily as she could manage:

'Is there anything . . . anything at all I could do to make it easier for you?'

He nodded.

'Let me go off now, at once. Before I lose my nerve.'

'But where?'

'Doesn't matter. I'll find somewhere. Can't face coming back here again and finding you gone.' He was making absurd grimaces in the effort to control himself.

She had to call up every drop of her strength to gasp:

'Yes.'

'That's bloody good of you. Goodbye, my darling dear.'

She said incoherently:

'Not in here . . . don't let's say goodbye in here. Not in this house.'

Hand in hand they went out into the empty street. In the patch of darkness by the locked railings of the church they held each other close and long without a word. When their arms dropped at last, he moved away quickly, without looking back. For a moment his tall figure stood out under the street-lamp at the corner as clearly as if he had stepped into a spotlight; the next he was gone. She stood clutching the railings to stop herself from running after him until the sound of his footsteps died away. Letting go her hold, she turned towards the church, too exhausted to offer any prayer, only some wordless cry for pity for him and courage for herself. Then, very quickly, she crossed the road and let herself in to spend her last night in the sugar house.

www.virago.co.uk

Virago

To find out more about Antonia White and
other Virago authors, visit:
www.virago.co.uk

Visit the Virago website for:

- Exclusive features and interviews with authors,
  including Margaret Atwood, Maya Angelou,
  Sarah Waters and Nina Bawden

- News of author events and forthcoming titles

- Competitions

- Exclusive signed copies

- Discounts on new publications

- Book-group guides

- Free extracts from a wide range of titles

PLUS: subscribe to our free monthly newsletter